POSSUM

Running FERAL

ERIN RUSSELL

By Erin Russell

Copyright © 2024 by Erin Russell
Cover and formatting by Erin Russell
Cover Image by Cadwallader Photography, LLC

All rights reserved.

No part of this book may be reproduced or transmitted in any form or by any means, electronic or mechanical, including photocopying, recording or by an information storage and retrieval system—except by a reviewer who may quote brief passages in a review to be printed in a magazine or newspaper—without permission in writing from the publisher. No portion of this book may be reproduced in any form without written permission from the publisher or author, except as permitted by U.S. copyright law.

This book is sold subject to the condition that it shall not, by way of trade or otherwise, be lent, resold, hired out, or otherwise circulated without the publisher's prior consent in any form of binding or cover other than that in which it is published and without a similar condition including this condition being imposed on the subsequent purchaser.

The text and artwork of this book were entirely created by humans. No generative AI was used.

Any references to historical events, real people, or real places are used fictitiously. Names, characters, and places are products of the author's imagination.

ISBN 979-8-9899256-7-4

Running FERAL

ERIN RUSSELL

Contents

	A Note on Content	VII
1.	Chapter One	1
2.	Chapter Two	10
3.	Chapter Three	18
4.	Chapter Four	29
5.	Chapter Five	41
6.	Chapter Six	50
7.	Chapter Seven	59
8.	Chapter Eight	70
9.	Chapter Nine	83
10.	Chapter Ten	93
11.	Chapter Eleven	102
12.	Chapter Twelve	112
13.	Chapter Thirteen	124
14.	Chapter Fourteen	136

15.	Chapter Fifteen	146
16.	Chapter Sixteen	155
17.	Chapter Seventeen	163
18.	Chapter Eighteen	171
19.	Chapter Nineteen	178
20.	Chapter Twenty	187
21.	Chapter Twenty-One	195
22.	Chapter Twenty-Two	208
23.	Chapter Twenty-Three	221
24.	Chapter Twenty-Four	229
25.	Chapter Twenty-Five	240
26.	Chapter Twenty-Six	251
27.	Chapter Twenty-Seven	264
Epilogue		280
Up Next		286
Acknowledgements		288
About the Author		289

A Note on Content

Possum Hollow is a fictional small town in rural Missouri. All the roads and surrounding towns mentioned are also fictional, so don't look for them on a map. The world was inspired by real places where I spent some of my childhood.

The backdrop for the series is one of rural poverty. Across the series, you'll find common themes of drug & alcohol abuse, family violence, parental neglect, toxic masculinity & violence, cultural homophobia and untreated mental illness.

This book deals with the sensitive topic of Intimate Partner Violence. It's something I consider important to handle appropriately, and write from an informed perspective. I've done my best to treat the subject with the care and respect that it deserves, especially in the context of a queer relationship.

Everyone should go into the book informed, though, so you can be sure it's right for you.

The IPV in this book is emotional, physical and sexual. It is **not** between the MCs, and is never glorified, romanticized, or portrayed in a positive light. There is no redemption plot for the abuser.

I've kept the majority of the violence and sexual assault off-page, referenced, or fade to black. There are no graphic descriptions of rape. However, many of the after-effects of IPV/DV—such as PTSD, hypervigilance, negative self-image or self-blame, catastrophizing, negative treatment or blame by third parties, difficulty with consensual sexual encounters, hypersexuality or inappropriate sexual behavior as a coping mechanism, etc., are played out in detail. For many survivors of IPV/DV, this alone could be triggering.

This is the story. It's not reflective of every individual's experience, but I believe it reflects the spirit of the issue, including many of the things survivors struggle with that are often overlooked in fiction, because the creator is too concentrated on a revenge arc instead of the long, sometimes tedious process of escape and recovery. Just because Hollywood doesn't think the truth of people's experience is cinematic enough, doesn't mean they don't deserve representation, in my opinion.

The dismissal that men face in this situation—both externally and internally—due to societal pressures and views on masculinity, is something I felt obligated to discuss. The difficulty being taken seriously trying to escape a queer/non-conforming relationship within a legal and healthcare system designed for a heteronormative society should also never be underestimated.

I guess this is my way of saying I felt there was too much here to talk about, and it was all too important to shy away from or gloss over. So this book is a little heavier and a teeny bit less spicy than the previous ones. But for me, it was a story that needed to be told. And there is still plenty of spice, and humor, and happy endings to go around.

Please go into it with your eyes open.

✗

For support or more information on domestic and intimate partner violence:

USA: *https://www.thehotline.org/ / https://rainn.org/*
UK: *https://www.nationaldahelpline.org.uk/ / https://mensadviceline.org.uk/*
Australia: *https://1800respect.org.au/*

✗

For a comprehensive list of triggers that includes spoilers for the story, please visit my website:

www.erinrussellauthor.com

Chapter One

TOBIAS

I don't have a drinking problem. Seriously.

I never get drunk. Or at least I never used to. I may only be about 40% Asian—my dad is Polish, while my mom's family is from the Philippines with a little Colombian thrown in for flavor—but I was unlucky enough to catch the gene that makes my face fucking burn whenever I have more than a couple of drinks. It's not debilitating, but it is embarrassing, which is one of the many reasons I normally avoid alcohol.

Another reason is that my deadbeat sperm donor definitely did have a drinking problem. Not that he was around for me to witness it, but I've heard stories. And so did his dad, according to my lola, who's carried a flaming torch of hatred for both of them since her daughter got knocked up and abandoned over two decades ago.

The last reason is that alcohol slows your reflexes. I've made my peace with the fact that I'm a prey animal in this life. It sucks, but it's my destiny. Still... It means I need my reflexes to always be sharp if I want to survive.

You never know when the predators are going to show up.

Today I threw all my reasoning out of the window. My lack of practice keeps my tolerance low, so once I committed to the concept, it didn't take long for me to get shit-faced.

It's not like I have anything to be sober for. Most of the time, I need to be at least functional enough to help Lola around the house and make sure she takes her insulin on time. I moved back here to take care of her as her diabetes got worse, because my mom couldn't. And because my mom had enough mouths to feed without me loitering and taking up space. But Lola has been in and out of the hospital so much lately, it feels like the trailer is empty more often than not. Being there fills me with a deep sense of dread.

Work only happens when they call me, and there's no way to know when that'll be. Inevitably, at the worst possible time. Until then, I'd rather be here than alone.

The Feral Possum is kind of an anomaly around here. It's cute and clean and makes a big deal about being inclusive. And while a lot of the bars in this area have a certain libertarian give-a-fuck attitude, it's not quite the same as actively billing yourself as a safe space.

No space is really safe, of course. I know that. It's nice to pretend, though.

"Are you planning on propping up the bar all night?"

Gunnar doesn't look at me when he speaks. For a friendly bartender, he almost never looks directly at me. He rarely looks me in the eye, and he's always careful to keep the bar between me and him. Those are the two main things I've noticed. I don't mind, though. I'm assuming he knows enough about the crowd I run with to keep his distance.

It doesn't help that Eamon likes to bring me here and parade me around like a prize. As soon as I moved back here and figured out petty gang crime was my only real option in life, Eamon claimed me as his. I think he likes to show me off to make people see how untouchable he is. Not only does he get to take whatever he wants from the younger guys in the Banna organization, but he's so hardcore, he manages to openly fuck men in a notoriously homophobic world of gangsters and mafiosos.

At least, that's what he thinks. I think he'll push someone's buttons too hard one day and finally get what's coming to him. Until then, he's got me on a short leash. And I can't get rid of Eamon without leaving the Banna, which is my only source of income.

Illegal or not, I need the money. Insulin's expensive.

"Give me somewhere else to go, and I'll go," I reply to Gunnar when my brain catches up. "Unless you have a better idea, this is what I've got."

At that, his eyes do flick up to meet my gaze for a second. I can see the same expression he almost always wears; like he wants to say something, but he's biting his tongue.

He doesn't need to say it. I know it all already. Crime is bad. Being a walking punching bag for a lowlife criminal is bad. There are other options.

Except there aren't. Not for me.

"At least drink some water." He slides a glass in front of me, next to my beer, then gestures to his own face in a way that lets me know my cheeks are probably flaming right now, because I didn't have the foresight to take an antihistamine before I started my mini bender. Except my face is permanently stuck in late teenage-hood, making people always think I'm younger than I am, while Gunnar has a well-manicured salt-and-pepper beard and the kind of sharp cheekbones which scream *not old, but mature*. I'm sure everyone in his life treats him like an adult. I'm sure it helps that he dresses like a fucking GQ model, even out here in buttfuck nowhere.

"Whatever," I grumble, making a point of reaching for the beer instead.

I sound like a petulant child, but I don't care. I don't need another person in my life deciding to boss me around.

Gunnar already watches me like a hawk. I've been coming here for nearly a year, because they haven't been open much longer, and ever since day one, he's watched me.

I should find it more irritating than I do. Probably. But part of me finds it nice to know if I wind up being disappeared one day, at least someone I'm not blood related to will notice. There's a comfort in that, even if it's meaningless. It's not going to stop me from eventually being aggressively disappeared. It's becoming more obvious every day that's what the future holds for me.

At least someone will care, though. And until it happens, I don't have to think about it. I wall the idea off behind the fortress in my mind that holds all of my unthinkable thoughts. It's been steadily getting bigger and bigger, the walls weaker and weaker, and it feels like every day I spend around Eamon chips away at them a little more. But they're still holding for now.

As long as I can keep Lola alive, I can keep my other shit at bay.

"Can I get you some food?" he asks in that eternally patient voice of his. The one that always rubs me the wrong way when I'm too far down the self-pity trap to listen to reason.

"I don't understand why you even give a shit," I say, giving him a hard look and forcing him to hold eye contact with me as I gesture to myself. The fading bruises that I know he knows how I got. The snake tattoo on my neck that tells everyone the Banna has me for life. "What part of all this says anything other than 'lost fucking cause'?"

There's a disproportionate amount of vitriol to my words, but I can't stop myself. I'm thrumming with misplaced adrenaline, and I have been for days. I haven't heard from Eamon in too long. It's suspicious. I feel like he's going to pop up from around a corner any second now, and my heart has been keeping a steady staccato the entire time, holding me in suspense. I wish he would get it over with, so I can take a full breath and stop feeling like the edges of my world are on the verge of graying out with my anticipatory panic.

None of this is Gunnar's fault. But I've been on high-alert so long my logic-brain can't scream loud enough to get through to the rest of me anymore.

Gunnar sighs, but more like he's being patient than pissed. When he puts both hands on the bar and orients himself toward me, the movement makes him seem larger than usual and I can't stop myself flinching away just a bit.

He notices—like always—but doesn't say anything.

"I can almost guarantee that more people care about you than you think."

His expression is so earnest as he says it, I almost melt right on the spot. But I can't afford to get soft and mushy in public. Especially not when there's no one around to scrape me up afterward. So, I focus on hardening myself instead.

"Sorry. That was rude," I say to Gunnar, because I'm in emotional freefall all the time, but I'm not trying to be a total asshole.

Gunnar shrugs, leaning back a bit.

"Do you have a ride home?"

Now it's my turn to shrug.

Another sigh before Gunnar bites his lip and narrows his eyes at me.

"If you stay until it gets late, I can drive you home while Kasia closes. Just don't drive, okay? I've seen that ragged little motorcycle you ride, and it's a death trap even when you're sober."

Honestly, the offer makes me flinch more than it did when he loomed over me before. Gunnar's always been kind, but he's also noticeably careful to keep his distance. This feels like some kind of line that can't be uncrossed.

Not that I'm going to cross it. It's not safe to let him do me favors. If word got out, it would put him straight in Eamon's crosshairs, and then who knows what the fuck would happen.

I'm not that selfish.

"Sure," I lie. It seems like enough to satisfy him, so he only nods and doesn't press the issue before turning away to help another customer.

I resolutely do not let myself stare at his ass once his back is turned to me. It's the same game I play every time I'm in here. Sometimes I just can't help myself.

The man may be a little older than me, but he's one of those guys that seems to ripen like fruit on the vine as he gets older. He has olive skin, darker than mine, even though I think he's 100% white, and it's still smooth. His beard and hair are thick in the way that makes your fingers ache to touch them, and his body also has a thickness to it—a solidity—that I'm constantly stopping myself from reaching out to touch. Or lean into. He's so tall and firm I feel like I could collapse into him and he'd just... absorb me. Wrap me up in those strong arms and long-fingered, capable hands.

These are the mental tangents I'm *not* supposed to go on, though. Because if Eamon would be pissed that Gunnar gave my drunk ass a ride home, hell knows what he would do if he knew how often I'd sat here drooling over him like a schoolboy with a crush. So, I consciously snap myself out of it and tear my eyes away from an ass that looks round and fucking impeccable in the fancy suit pants he's always wearing for no real reason.

Of course, as soon as I look elsewhere, I meet Kasia's eyes. Kasia is the opposite of her boss in a lot of ways. For one, she embraced the nineties grunge aesthetic as a child and never let go. Right now, she's wearing Doc Martens; fishnets under ripped stonewashed jeans; some kind of shirt that's really a corset; and a bunch of dark makeup that's gorgeous, but clearly meant to scare off men more than entice them. Another way she and Gunnar differ is that she also watches me, but it's with a constant level of distrust. Or distaste. Dis-something.

She fucking hates me, basically. And I get it. I fucking hate myself half the time. But I've never known what specifically turned her down this road, and she's always careful to be polite enough to my face not to cause waves.

"What?"

I'm too over it to play games today.

"Nothing. You looked like maybe you were *thirsty* or something." The smirk on her face gives the sentence all the subtext it needs to, though.

Busted.

Well, fuck her. I can look, can't I? It's not like I'm going to do anything about it.

"Can I get the check?" It's time for me to abandon ship before this day gets any worse.

She nods, starting to reach for the computer, but then she hesitates, and I see the smirk fall off her face with a hard twist.

My heart rate seems to triple in an instant and the rest of my body locks up. In the question of *fight or flight*, it seems to go for *freeze* more and more these days. Like it's all too much and I've turned into the human equivalent of a record scratch.

Thankfully, the panic is already dulling my reactions and letting my mind sink into the heavy, drowsy place, which lets me stay numb to most things. So, when a hand lands roughly on my shoulder, I don't react. More flinching would not help my case here.

I'm not normally this bad. This thing between me and Eamon has highs and lows. But ever since the last time... I can't seem to snap out of panic-mode.

"I thought I might find you here, pet."

His voice is too close to my ear, his breath hot and moist on my skin, but I don't let it penetrate my awareness. Instead, I focus on putting a smile on my face that isn't too wooden.

"Hey," I say as I turn to look at him. Blue eyes. Blond hair. Nice features. It's all a very pretty package covering up how terrifying he can be underneath. He's young enough that he still looks a little boyish, like me—or at least he would without all the gang tattoos—and it's completely incongruent with everything I know about his personality. "You should have called if you needed me. I wasn't doing anything important."

Eamon must smell the alcohol on my breath, because his eyebrows climb a fraction. Then his eyes scan the rest of my face, taking in what must be flushed cheeks and possibly a throbbing pulse in my throat.

"I wasn't expecting you to be day drinking by yourself. What if something happened to you? How were you going to get home? What if work needed us?

You know I don't like you being out in the world unprotected. Especially in a place like this. You could end up getting molested in the bathroom."

The comment leaves a sour taste in my mouth, but I'm careful not to show it. Never mind that *he's* more queer than most of the people in this bar; and also loves to hang out here. And if anyone's going to "molest" me...

No. Don't think negatively. Just make peace. Before anything has the chance to escalate.

"I'm sorry," I say with a pout that I know is adorable. "I knew you were working, and I didn't want to bother you. But I missed you. Thank you for coming to find me."

I glance around to make sure we're not the focus of anyone's attention, then I quickly peck him on the lips. He's not big on public displays of affection. Or private ones, for that matter. He prefers displays of ownership. But anything I can do to mollify him is worth the risk.

It must do the trick, because his face softens a little. I hop off the bench, swaying slightly as the alcohol hits me in a wave and parlaying that into an excuse to lean on him. Instead of waiting for Kasia and getting more of her dirty looks, I throw too much cash on the bar and turn Eamon toward the door.

We're almost out of there unscathed. It's only at the last possible second that I turn without thinking and catch a glimpse of Gunnar in my peripheral vision.

He's watching me. Watching *us*. With a face more furious than I've ever seen.

He's almost always placid, like the surface of a lake, but I think I'm getting an unexpected glimpse into the churning water underneath. It's only for a second before he slips his mask back into place, but it's enough. I saw the real him, watching me like I'm someone worth watching.

Maybe I'm not the only person who hates Eamon. For whatever reason, just like the idea that Gunnar might miss me when I die, that thought buoys me enough to keep myself together as Eamon grabs my hand, dragging me out the door and toward his car.

I'll remember that face through whatever else happens tonight. It's not a lot, but it's something to think about other than whatever this is I've let my life become.

Thanks, Gunnar.

Chapter Two

GUNNAR

Well, I've worked hard to stop being a man who *hates* constantly. It wasn't easy, but I think with plenty of time and honest introspection, I've been relatively successful.

But I fucking hate everything that just happened.

Bearing witness to Tobias's slow but steady implosion over the last year has been one of the most unpleasant, impotent experiences of my life. Every time I see him, I'm hit by a Mack truck-sized urge to do something—*anything*—to help him escape the pit he's fallen into, and every time I'm immediately reminded that I'm utterly powerless in this situation.

I can't help him unless he wants help. Until then, I can only watch. And try to be supportive in whatever ways a casual acquaintance can be.

"Who pissed in your cornflakes?"

A deep voice interrupts my spinning thoughts, and I snap my attention away from the door Tobias disappeared through several minutes ago. Sav, my new barback, is staring at me, not bothering to hide the concern in his eyes, even if he is smiling at his own joke at the same time.

"I'll give you three guesses, but you're only going to need one. Your BFF was here again."

All traces of humor fall from Sav's face. If there's anyone here who hates Eamon more than me, it's him. I don't know why, but I'm sure he has his reasons. All of which fall under the general umbrella of Eamon being a selfish, arrogant, abusive piece of shit.

"Was he looking for me?"

"Not this time. He came for the kid."

I try not to say Tobias's name out loud too often. I know it's irrational, but I worry that something about the way I say it or some expression I make might give away how overly involved I am with this one.

I have plenty of people in my life who I helped get out of shitty situations they didn't deserve to be in. Not because I'm some sort of hero; it's just my thing. It's the only thing that lets me sleep at night, if I'm being honest. I have enough to redeem myself for. But I'm known for collecting strays.

Kasia was one; when I first moved back here, and she was escaping from her own shitty, abusive relationship. Sav is another, although he's still pretty new and I don't know the details of what he's got going on. All I know is he's got the same Banna snake tattoo as Eamon and Tobias, which means he's gang-affiliated, but he's also got a lot more tattoos that scream *extremely-fucking-affiliated*, and he came in here one day, begging for someone to give him a break on a normal job. A normal life. So, if he's not free from it already, he must be trying.

Sav only grunts in response to my answer, looking as pissed as I feel as he picks up a rack of dirty glasses and starts carting them away to wash.

I can't stop myself from interrupting him.

"Hey," I say, making him turn around a little to look at me. "Do you think there's anything else I—we—could do for the kid that we're not doing already?"

Sav sighs and shakes his head. He doesn't even give me any words. He just shakes his head, holding my gaze for a minute, before continuing his march to the kitchen.

"You need to let go of your fixation with this guy. You're already way too involved. You're totally powerless to help him and if you try, you could get hurt. The people he runs around with do not fuck around, and you know that."

Kasia is staring at me from the other side of the bar. Thankfully, it's still early on a weekday, so no one is close enough to overhear her, but still. I don't appreciate her pointing out the obvious flaws in my plan when I'm already aware of them.

"He's just a kid, Kasia. He doesn't deserve this."

She moves closer, still holding a cocktail shaker in one hand that she uses to point at me.

"A) Of course, he doesn't deserve this, but that doesn't change the fact that he's mixed up with dangerous people who will fuck you up if you try to take him away from them. And B) He's not a fucking kid. He's an adult who ended up in a terrible situation. Just like me. Just like the walking wall of muscle you hired, because we didn't have enough homophobes floating around here already."

"Sav's not a homophobe," I interrupt. "I think he's been through a lot. I can tell. He needs to be around people who aren't going to make him feel like he has to stay in whatever toxic criminal box he's spent his life in. His brother's gay. He's coming around, I swear. We're good for him."

"Yeah, well, that doesn't change the fact that he still gapes at any same-sex couple who shows affection in here. Or nervously averts his eyes. Which are both equally bad. It's embarrassing."

"That's not—" I start, but Kasia continues before I can really figure out what I'm trying to say.

"And like I said, the *kid*, as you keep calling him, is not a kid. You don't look at him like he's a kid. You look at him like you're a *Looney Toons* character and he's a cartoon steak. You can't even keep your eyeballs in your head and treating him like a child isn't fooling anybody. Including yourself. So, stop—" she waves her fingers in a circle in my general direction with a humorless grin, "—doing all of this. You're not fooling anybody. Leave that man alone unless you need to call the cops for him."

I huff. "Because they're so helpful in these situations."

"They're helpful in not letting you get yourself killed over someone who probably wouldn't appreciate the effort right now. He has to *want* to get out, or it's all a waste of energy."

"Fine."

I don't have anything else to say to her right now. She's right, but I don't want to admit it. It's already annoying enough to know that I haven't been hiding my stupid, problematic infatuation as well as I thought.

It's not like I would ever, *ever* get involved with him. Not only is he too young for me—even if he is an adult, like she said, twenty-two years old is still a big screaming leap away from my thirty-six—but I don't get involved with people who I help. It's too murky, ethically, and the consequences are potentially too severe if things go wrong.

I learned that the hard way.

"Do you want to close tonight, or do you need to head home?"

It's an obvious attempt to change the subject, but I don't care.

"I'm fine. Magdalena doesn't work until late tonight. She's leaving her kids with me, and I'll take over all the child-minding when I get home."

"I guess that's a system."

"Yeah, well, you gotta do what you gotta do. I would rather have a sister I actually see, but at least the kids can hang out with their cousins every day, and no one has to pay for childcare they can't afford."

"Fair. If you ever need help, let me know, though. I'm still here for you, even though you've pulled your life together on your own."

She rolls her eyes at me fondly.

"Yes, *daddy*." Her tone is facetious, but it still makes me cringe. "You're first in line to be my personal savior. I'll never forget."

"You know that's not—" I rub at the bridge of my nose, where the pressure of a headache is swiftly forming. Today has been weird and unpleasant. I'm already ready for it to be over. "You know it's not like that."

"I know." The smile she gives me is softer this time. "But I like teasing you, anyway."

"Yeah, yeah, yeah. You're hilarious. Go do some work instead of trying to put me in an early grave, maybe."

Kasia shrugs and turns away from me. I want to breathe out a sigh of relief, but I can't find it. There's too much pressure. In my head, on my chest, in my general state of existence. No matter how hard I try to focus, I can't stop thinking about what Eamon and Tobias are doing right now. If this is going to be the day that Tobias never comes back again, and I'm left spending the rest of my life with nothing but *what ifs* for company.

Soon, more customers filter in, and at least I have something immediate to distract myself with. For whatever that's worth.

Whenever I visit my mother, I go after work. Because it's late, and it's kind of a drive, which gives me an excuse to cut the visit short if she starts to rub my nerve endings raw.

The deliberateness of this makes me feel like a horrible person. But I have to do something to protect my sanity if I don't want to end up abandoning her altogether.

"Do you want some tea?"

"I'll get it, you sit down," I say, seizing the opportunity to escape the initial bustling around me she does when I walk in the door. I'm never quite sure what she's fussing over, but it always feels artificial, almost performative, in a way that makes me deeply uncomfortable.

I return to the sitting room a few minutes later with two glasses of iced tea in my hands and place one in front of her before I install myself on the well-worn couch.

"How are you doing? Do you need anything?"

Mama blows out a breath, already in the eye-rolling stage of our conversation, obviously.

"I'm fine, Gunnar. I can take care of myself. I'm a grown woman, after all." She peers at me over the lip of her glass for a minute, and I feel like I'm about to be peeled apart and placed under a microscope. "What about you? You seem more high-strung than usual. Do *you* need something?"

"No," I answer on instinct. There's a pause while I huff out a breath and run a hand down my face, trying to collect my frazzled thoughts. But those images from before of Tobias—where he might be right now and what he might be suffering at Eamon's hands—are still screaming front and center in my mind, distracting me from reality. "I'm just tired. It's been busy at work recently."

Mama shakes her head in that way she always does, and it makes the tiny muscles in my neck tense up. If I stay here too long, I'm going to develop a migraine. I can feel it in my bones.

"I still can't believe you moved home to open a gay bar. In these parts, after you made such a fuss about wanting to get out of Missouri. You could have stayed in Chicago if you wanted to do that."

Now it's my turn to roll my eyes, which feels immature but is also unstoppable.

"It's not a gay bar, Mama. It's inclusive. If everyone who cares about being progressive moves to the city, then there's no one left to support the people they left behind. Believe it or not, but queer people in the countryside also want to have safe spaces to exist."

"I suppose," she says, taking a large sip of tea.

There's a mountain of unsaid words there, but I mentally breeze past them. My mother's not a homophobe. She's just... I don't know. I can't even think of the word.

Because the only one that comes to mind is 'hateful' and that's the kind of thing you're not supposed to think. Maybe 'bitter' is a nicer shade of the same concept.

Yep, that's definitely a migraine I feel brewing. All the muscles in the back of my neck are tightening bit by bit, like ropes slowly being ratcheted to their full tautness, and the skin around my hairline is beginning to feel like it's pressing inwards into my skull.

I need to flee before lights start doing that glittery, overwhelming thing they sometimes do, and driving becomes a crapshoot.

"It's not too late to buy your father's shop back. Have something to show for his hard work. Help people instead of selling them liquor."

I manage not to scoff. Only Mama could do the mental gymnastics required to consider a pawn shop proprietor some kind of pillar of the community. She acts like my dad was out there running soup kitchens instead of barely legal grifts. Ever since he died, it's like she's trying to canonize him in her memory. There's a faint sneer at the end of her words, though, and it combines with my burgeoning headache to make this situation seem suddenly intolerable.

A thought flashes through my mind—*you can't sit in the same room with your mother being snide for twenty minutes, but you'll stand by and wring your hands while Tobias suffers god-knows-what.* But I don't have time to pull it apart right now.

"Look, if it's going to be one of those conversations, I'm going to go home. I'm tired, it's been a long day, and I have a headache. I'll come back in a couple of days to see how you're doing, okay?"

Mama sighs and looks away from me, clearly dedicated to being in a huff.

I get up and put my glass in the kitchen sink before coming back and leaning down to kiss her on the cheek. She softens a little, looking me in the eye.

"Do you want some aspirin before you go?"

"No, thank you Mama. I have some meds in the car. I'll see you in a few days. Call me if you need anything."

She rolls her eyes again, but the tension has leached out of the atmosphere at least.

"You too."

That's all I need to slip out of the door. I couldn't have picked a better moment; my forehead is starting to throb, and the streetlights are bright, sparkling little points on the horizon that are disorienting for no particular reason.

It's time to go home and bury all my thoughts in sleep.

Chapter Three

TOBIAS

My entire body is dry. So dry, it feels like a desiccated husk that my shriveled organs are rattling around inside, while my brain is nothing more than a condensed lump of tissue that only knows how to quiver in response to basic, instinctive stimuli.

Everything hurts. The world is still sliding to the side whenever I lose focus on keeping it still, and my ass is pulsing with the painful reminder of whatever I did with Eamon last night, even if my mind has successfully blacked that part out.

After we got back to his place, he offered me another drink. Despite all his posturing about being concerned about how drunk I was, I know he likes me that way. Pliable. As long as I'm not so far gone that I'm messy. Then he also offered me a few lines of something, which he's never deigned to identify for me. Not coke. Something more synthetic, that's more sedating than stimulating. Ketamine, maybe. Whatever it is, it always fucks me up beyond measure.

It makes it a lot easier to lie back and take the kind of brutal, relentless poundings that he's so fond of delivering. Not that I wouldn't, anyway; I don't exactly have a choice. But the ketamine gives me that little lift I need to peel back my skull, pull out my brain and deposit it on the bedside table as a patient observer, instead of a participant. Which doesn't hurt.

I would love to be in my own bed right now, encouraging my brain to continue sinking into the oblivion of my Swiss cheese memory. Unfortunately, I can't. I'm out in the world, and even though we're headed toward winter, so it's not that warm, it's still bright as fuck. It's that cool, brittle kind of brightness that lights up every surface and somehow smells like frost.

My shitty dollar-store sunglasses are on, but they're not helping. I quickly changed into clothes that didn't have cum and blood on them after I picked up my Ninja—which I've had since I was seventeen and has also seen much better days—from the bar and drove to the trailer. Now I'm headed to the hospital in Lola's 1996 Ford Lazer that inexplicably still runs, because she's finally coming home.

She's been in Critical Care for four days and then Med/Surg—which I guess is hospital speak for gen pop—for another six, and I'm over it. I hate seeing her in there, but I can't not visit and leave her all alone. It'll be good to have her home. I just have to concentrate on not letting her notice the limp I picked up at some point last night. And hopefully the bruises from last week are faded enough that she won't see.

It takes a long time waiting in her hospital room before all the discharge paperwork is sorted out, but she seems in good spirits. She's also happy to see me in that genuine, undemanding way that only she manages. Eventually, we get everything sorted out, and then I'm able to take her to the exit in a wheelchair before we pile into the car.

"You seem tired, Apo," she says once we're on the road.

There's no accusation in it, but it makes me tense up, all the same.

"I am. I've been busy. I'm glad you're coming home, though." My voice is wooden as I speak, but at least we've slipped into the conversational space where we've both tacitly agree not to get into details.

I'm under no illusions that she isn't aware I'm doing illegal shit. But we need the money too much to fight about it. Her social security only covers so much.

"You still need to take care of yourself. Have you been eating?"

I shrug, because it's easier than saying 'no'.

She makes an unhappy sound and fusses with her purse.

"I'll cook once we're home, and then we can both have a quiet, restful evening. How does that sound?"

Honestly, like fucking heaven. But I won't be able to stay for long, because I know Eamon has a job for me tonight. Maybe I can get away with pretending to go to bed and then sneaking out, so she's not twisted up worrying about me for once.

"Sure thing, Lola. Sounds good."

By 10pm, I'm feeling relaxed for the first time in weeks. I have a full stomach, because Lola insisted on cooking, even though I tried to stop her. Eating an actual hot meal made from (mostly) fresh vegetables is a real change of pace and comforts me somewhere deep in my core.

She made something she calls 'Ozarks sinigang', which is an adapted version of a recipe from her childhood that accommodates not being able to find most of the same fruits and vegetables here. It's not authentic, and a bunch of the ingredients are powdered or frozen, but I've only grown up eating this version of the dish, so it tastes like home to me.

We're both settled in front of the TV, watching some mindless cooking/travel show that she likes, while I slowly sink into the couch when my phone vibrates. I was so cozy, I'd almost let myself forget that this was coming.

Immediately, my body goes on high alert. He's not here, but my nervous system acts like he is. I curse myself for getting so comfortable, because it makes the switch I've done a million times before too abrupt; like jumping into an ice bath.

I don't move a muscle, because part of that frame of mind is being like a rabbit under the scrutiny of a hawk. Still and silent, hoping you'll be passed over, but every muscle strung tight and ready to sprint if you need to. Lola notices regardless.

"What's wrong?" she asks, already frowning like she knows I'm going to lie to her.

It doesn't stop me.

"Nothing. I think it might be time for bed. I'm tired, like you said."

There's a long, tremulous silence while I can practically feel her weighing whether now is the time to speak or not.

"I'm tired, too." She pauses again, and I'm very concerned about what's about to come out of her mouth. "Tomorrow, we're going to sit down and talk about all this. Because I've been silent for too long, and I'm sick of seeing you look like this. Now go to bed. To *sleep*."

I wither a little under her hard stare, but nod and agree politely. I'm looking forward to that conversation almost less than I'm looking forward to tonight, because I don't have any idea what's going to come of it, but that's tomorrow's problem.

If she decides she's had enough and this is the last straw with me, I guess I can deal with that. It's not like it'll be my first time being abandoned by someone who's supposed to love me. I should be used to it by now.

It takes another hour, almost, before the dishes are cleaned up and we're both 'in bed', so I can sneak away. Then it's just a quick shimmy out the bathroom window and a short drop to the empty lot behind the trailer. I half-walk, half-jog until I make it to the main road, well out of her sight, and pretty soon I see those familiar headlights, bearing down on me like an alien spacecraft about to beam me up.

"You took your sweet time."

He didn't speak for the first ten minutes we were driving, and these are the only words that have come out of his mouth since. I could tell him about picking up my grandmother from the hospital, because that's a rational excuse, even for career criminals. But I try very hard not to remind him that she exists and could hypothetically be used as leverage against me.

"I'm sorry, Eamon," are the only words that come out of my mouth, because making some half-assed excuse would be inviting a fight that I'll lose.

Even if he didn't hold all the power here, I'd lose anyway. I've never met anyone so capable of twisting everything I say, until he somehow convinces me that I'm the asshole here. Or just crazy. Or both.

He's a murderer and a gangster—and looks the part, despite his youth—yet somehow, he can talk anyone into believing him about anything. A mask of congeniality and over-the-top rationality comes down. As if everything he's saying is so sensible that it's a foregone conclusion he's right.

No one should ever talk to him. It's the quickest way to question your own sanity.

He doesn't say anything, and the tension continues to mount as I imagine what could be coming next. It's bad enough that when he reaches toward the dash to adjust the air, I flinch on instinct. I'm normally good at controlling it, but I feel like my nerve endings are all dancing on razor wire right now. I'm still brittle from my hangover, and I've had too little sleep in the past week. I wouldn't be surprised if pieces of me started peeling away and fluttering off in the wind like dead leaves.

Eamon just laughs. A deep belly laugh, like my flinch was completely absurd. Then he looks at me from the corner of his eyes in a way that might almost be called fond, if I didn't see the simmering, predatory anger beneath it.

The urge to act like the child he considers me to be and sink into my seat is overwhelming. I make a concession by pulling the sleeves of my hoodie over my hands. It's not a lot, but it's the best I can do without showing him how fragile I feel right now.

I still don't know where we're going, but I know better than to ask. I just continue to bite my tongue and do my best to remain still and invisible. Eamon mostly stays quiet, thank god, only occasionally bitching about whatever Banna drama is up his ass lately. I try to tune it out. When I was initially recruited into the organization, I knew it was shitty and unethical, but it seemed like the only way to potentially make a decent amount of money, given my history.

There were a few grandiose thoughts of rising through the ranks and becoming powerful and respected, which was clearly dumb as fuck. As if my obvious queerness and my obvious non-whiteness weren't already hamstringing me, whether they acknowledged it or not. Instead, I was still just a baby recruit when Eamon laid eyes on me and declared me his property. He promised his attention would come with all kinds of extra boosts up the chain of command, but instead, it made me a barely tolerated pariah.

Everyone immediately shifted from seeing me as a kid with potential to either a victim or a whore. Neither of which work in this kind of setting. These are old-school guys who respect strength and independence. They take Eamon and his quirks and queerness because he's obviously in charge. But me... I'm one step up from a barracks bunny.

Or maybe one step below. I don't know anymore. Who the fuck cares? It's not like I can do anything about it now.

I'm shaken out of this train of thought—with an indecent amount of relief—when Eamon pulls onto a side road. We're at the edge of town, but still close enough that it's lit up and not completely deserted. I don't know what he's planning, but I already have a bad feeling about it.

Eamon starts to talk quickly and quietly as he pulls over by some trees and kills the headlights.

"At the end of this road is that little feed store that keeps refusing our services. I need you to sneak in and roll the place. Make as much mess as you can, take whatever valuable shit you can grab. Take some spray paint and leave some bullshit race-hate graffiti, so they think the Aryan Nation assholes did it. Whatever you can to convince them to come to me begging for protection. They think they can rely on the rent-a-cops that pass for law enforcement around here, and we're about to prove just how dumb that is. Got it?"

As the words sink in, dread hits my gut like lead. But I'm already reaching around for the things I'll need, all in his car, exactly where they always are. Spray paint. Lock pick kit, because I'm better at finessing things than brute forcing them if I'm by myself. Gaiter to cover my face, just in case, even though Eamon always gets these ones with skull patterns that I think are so childish I would almost rather be arrested than caught wearing it. Cell jammer and Wi-Fi jammer, to bypass their alarm systems.

Once it's all shoved in the pockets of the tactical pants I'm wearing for exactly this reason, I pause.

"Are you sure this is a good idea?"

The words are out of my mouth before I can stop them, and I reflexively cringe away as soon as they're out in the world. Questioning his orders has never ended well for me.

But he seems to still be coasting on whatever endorphins he siphoned out of me yesterday, because I get a raised eyebrow instead of anything more violent.

"Why wouldn't it be?"

I don't want to tell him, but I feel like I've already dug my own grave here, so there's nothing more to lose.

"Well, we did the same thing at Ford's garage. And it was kind of a disaster. All we did was piss him off and cause a bunch of drama, plus we almost got caught. Lucky stabbed Silas, and his boyfriend choked me out when he found out I was involved. If he'd died, we would have been fucked."

Eamon snorts, like that's the dumbest thing I've ever said. It's a noise he makes a lot when I open my mouth, so I've accepted that I must say a lot of dumb shit.

When he responds, it's with barely concealed disdain.

"If he'd died, the world would have been short one more redneck." He sneers as he says it, like he's not from the exact same place as Silas. "The cops wouldn't have done anything about it. They never do. And I think that whole situation worked out pretty well; I may not have gotten a protection contract out of it, but I did get myself a pet paramedic. Ford's smarmy butt-buddy being indebted to us has already paid off more than I expected. Although maybe it wouldn't if you people weren't dumb enough to constantly be tripping over your own feet until you need medical care."

This time, he looks me right in the eye as he says it. It immediately feels like I've been shoved back in time a few weeks, to when my face was so busted open, I considered crawling to Tristan begging for his off-books patch-up job. Not that there was anything I could do. It was more the fact that he's nice, even though he knows I'm an asshole who robbed his boyfriend's auto shop. He would have treated me like a real person, and right then, I was gasping for it.

All those thoughts get shoved deep into my mental lock box, because they're not helping right now. And the wary look that Eamon's giving me is just daring me to start something that I can't finish. When I lower my eyes and soften my posture, he can clearly see he's won.

Again. Was there ever a question?

"Good. Now go do the job I fucking pay you to do. We both know that independent thinking isn't your strong suit, so you could stand to run your mouth a little less. Unless this is your way of asking me to stick something in it that'll shut you up."

As he says it, he rubs one hand over his crotch in a way that's meant to be seductive, but lands firmly on menacing. It doesn't help that he then drags his hand over to the gun tucked in his waistband and strokes the barrel with the same languorous, sensual motion.

I practically tuck and roll getting out of the car before he has the chance to test out whatever he's thinking, despite the fact that we're stationary. All the shit I need is in my pockets, and right now, getting out of that car seems way more important than whatever danger I might be walking into.

The lock is easy.

The security camera system is fucking antiquated, and my jammers take care of it, no problem. No motion sensors. A feed store is probably not really expecting to get robbed, in the grand scheme of things.

When I pull out the spray paint and try to hype myself up to get destructive, I'm weighed down by an exhaustion that is gripping onto me by my bone marrow. Deeper in me than any other emotion I'm capable of containing. But it's not like there's an alternative.

Then I hear the voice, and all hell breaks loose. Both inside and outside of me.

With adrenaline rushing through my veins, I duck to the side before whoever the voice belongs to can see me.

It's an old man. Not super old, but old enough to be slow. Bent over a little and choosing his way in the dark more carefully than a young person might.

"Who's there?" he calls out, sounding not nearly as afraid as I would like him to.

Fuck.

I need to get out of here, but I haven't even started working yet and I know Eamon's going to be pissed.

For just a second, I finger the small knife that's strapped onto my belt. The one for emergencies. Without a doubt, Eamon would want me to at least do something threatening to terrify the man if I can't manage any actual damage to the store.

I know I won't. It makes me a shitty criminal, but this is probably someone's grandfather. The thought of scaring the shit out of him for the sake of one of Eamon's pointless power plays makes me feel sick.

I have to run.

Instead of moving toward the man, I sidestep as nimbly as I can while crouched, moving down the big, echoey aisle in the direction of the far wall. A rustle tells me he might be able to hear me, but I know I'm faster, even in this position.

In less than a minute, I've made it to the wall and then hustled to the exit, still too low for him to see me clearly. As soon as my feet hit the dry, packed dirt outside, I'm sprinting. The cameras are still down, and I need to be fast enough to get out of sight, because he almost definitely has a gun tucked away somewhere.

I'm completely out of breath by the time I pile into Eamon's car. His eyes widen, obviously not expecting me back this soon and also not expecting me to be running. On instinct, he cranks the engine and takes off back to the main road so we can melt into whatever passes for traffic here at this time of night.

It takes a long time for me to catch my breath. Especially because as soon as the adrenaline of running begins to filter out of me, I get a new batch of something worse. Something that's less like normal fight or flight and more like terror. Because now that my mind is clear, I'm acutely aware of how pissed Eamon is going to be when he figures out what I did.

"What happened?"

His voice makes my focus sharpen, but I repress the urge to shiver.

"There was someone in there. He came out and saw me, so I had to run for it."

"Before or after you trashed the place?"

I want to lie, but I know it'll only make things worse in the long run.

"Before," I say in a shallow whisper.

"What? Speak up."

"Before."

A glimmer of pride shows up somewhere deep in my chest, and I raise my head to meet his eyes. They're stormy, and I can only imagine what's going through his mind.

Tobias is a fuckup.

Tobias never does his job.

Tobias jeopardizes my reputation and can't be trusted.

I'd be better off if he were dead.

Something along those lines, I'm sure.

When I'm met with endless, simmering silence, I know things are going to be worse than whatever I'm imagining. It's only reinforced when we pass the turn to my lola's place and keep going toward his.

Maybe this really is the night that I'm not going to come back from. Once I realize this, a kind of fragile calm spreads through me. Just like last night, Gunnar's face flashes in my mind. The one that was so angry when he saw Eamon come to get me from the bar.

I do hope he notices when I'm gone. I know that's cruel, and he'd be better off not being sad about something so inevitable. But the small part of myself that still insists on being selfish is going to hope for it.

Chapter Four

GUNNAR

Being a night owl is part of the bar-owner territory. There isn't space downstairs for an office, but the upstairs was already zoned for residential space when I leased the building, and it didn't take much to turn it into a functional little apartment. It also doesn't have space for an office, but there's an open-concept living room that is split into a TV-and-couch area, plus a desk-and-computer area.

It's enough. I've been sitting here for hours trying to get caught up on boring shit like inventory and payroll, but no matter how hard I try, my mind keeps wandering. At least yesterday's migraine isn't making a repeat appearance. The petulant, unloved child in me wants to blame Mama for it, but I quash the thought every time it slips into my mind.

What's the point? Old grudges are better left to wither away, unfed by your current anger.

I'm staring at the screen, letting my eyes unfocus and the lines blur, when I hear something weird downstairs. At first, it sounds like an animal. There's an entrance to the apartment from inside the bar, which I normally use, but there's also a door and some stairs at the back of the whole building that no one ever comes to, because it's difficult to spot. It is closer to the dumpster and the tree line edges right up onto it, so it's not unusual to get raccoons or possums digging around back there after dark.

And it's well after dark. It's only when the noise makes me snap out of my daze that I realize it's past 3am, and I should probably give up for the night. I look longingly toward the bedroom at the same time as I stall at the thought of how much work it's going to be to get there, until I'm interrupted by another, louder noise.

This one sounds like something *hitting* the door. Maybe on purpose, maybe not. There's another thud—even louder—so I finally get up and tread carefully to the back.

The staircase is outside the building, and the door is at the top. Normally, wildlife doesn't venture up here. All the trash and bar scraps are down on the ground. But I can definitely hear something moving just on the other side of this piece of plywood, which suddenly feels much thinner and more friable than it usually does.

Then there's a noise that makes me jump, because it's unmistakably a rapping sound. Made by human knuckles. Whatever fears I have coming from late night paranoia get shoved to the back of my brain, because this is most likely Sav or Kasia or someone else I know in an emergency.

All my hesitance disappears as I throw open the door to darkness. It's dark in here, too, lit only by the glow of my computer screen, so it takes me a second to see who's there. Before I get the chance, though, the figure collapses through the open doorway like they were leaning against it, and I have to scramble to catch them before they hit the floor.

It's too small to be Sav and too male to be Kasia. I'm not sure who else would come to me like this, but I pull down the dark hoodie covering their head to look. This elicits a groan, even though they keep their entire weight slumped into my arms while I do it.

"Jesus Christ, Tobias. What the hell happened?"

Even as I say the words, I put two and two together and know exactly what happened. Because what else could it be?

He doesn't say anything, which is good because I already feel like an idiot for asking. He's trembling through his whole body, too weak to hold himself up, and what I can see of his face is a swollen mess of cuts and bruises.

It only takes a few attempts to help guide him over to the couch to give up. He's completely failing in any attempt to walk. It's like the second I opened the door, whatever adrenaline or hope had powered him here evaporated. Instead, I lean down and scoop one arm under his legs to pick him up bridal style, desperately hoping this isn't too invasive.

Normally, I would ask permission, but he hasn't said a word yet or even been able to focus his eyes on me. I need to get him lying down before he completely collapses.

The swift movement upwards makes him gasp. Something in his lower body must be hurting, because he lets out a painful groan. I try to get through it as quickly as possible. As soon as I kick the door shut, I cross over to the couch with long strides before leaning over it to lay him down as gently as I can.

When I pull back, I feel resistance I wasn't expecting. It only takes a second to realize that he's holding onto me; trembling hands digging into the soft fabric of my sweater and refusing to let go. Some piece of my heart breaks off and floats away right there and then, and I know I'll never really get it back.

I've seen some of the truly horrible shit that people can do to each other. But for whatever reason, this is hitting me harder than most of it.

Instead of standing back up, I fold up my body and slowly slide to the floor in front of the couch, keeping myself close enough to him that he can hold on to me. It makes me loom over his prone form awkwardly, but it's what he seems to want, so I'm not going to deny him.

He was breathing normally through all of this, although a little fast, like you would expect from someone in pain. But as soon as we're both settled in our final positions, his chest begins to heave. Big, body-shaking breaths that come quickly and with too much force.

"Hey, hey," I say softly. "It's okay. You're okay. You're safe now."

I don't know what else to say, and his eyes are wild enough that I'm not sure if he's really hearing me, even though he's not trying to get up and still clinging to my sweater. Instead, I put one hand flat on his chest. Gently, with no real pressure, but enough so he can feel it.

"It's okay, Tobias. You're okay. Take some slower breaths for me. In and out, one at a time."

I can feel his chest rising and falling under my hand. The rest of his body is ramrod tight, so stiff his back is bowed, but his breathing is still so labored. I hold his gaze for a minute and take a deep, slow breath, trying to get him to copy me.

He does his best, and we repeat it. In and out, one after the other, until his body finally catches on and slows down.

Unfortunately, it seems like that energy still has to go somewhere. Instead of breathing like someone on the verge of a panic attack, his body seems to settle on taking all that trembling and dialing the notch up to eleven. The tremor becomes a shake, and then the shaking becomes so violent, racking his entire body, that for a second I'm scared he's having a seizure.

But he's still looking at me. Still holding onto me. It's just the rest of himself he can't seem to control.

I'm at a loss for what to do, but the urge to try to fix it is too powerful to ignore. I make yet another risky decision without waiting for permission, which I can feel guilty about later. Once he's not shaking so hard, I'm scared he's going to fall off the couch, while looking at me like I'm the only person in the world who can help him.

I lean closer to him, put my hands behind his shoulders, and lift him up a little. His body is pretty slight; not just his frame, but also like someone who maybe skips too many meals. It's easy to lever him up and then slip myself underneath him.

It takes a little maneuvering, but I'm able to settle him in between my legs, both of us looking up at the ceiling and my knees bent on either side of his hips, so he can't roll off the couch. I have to twist his hands out of the fabric they're clutching, but I quickly thread his fingers through mine before wrapping both our sets of arms around his chest to hold him against mine. His head rolls back to rest on my right shoulder, his face turned into my neck as he maybe tries to hide the way his teeth are chattering with stress or fear or *something*, but then I have him completely contained.

Our bodies move in sync, chests rising and falling together as he mirrors my rhythm. Little by little, the shaking calms down until he's barely moving.

The whole process seems to take forever. In reality, it probably only takes minutes. But I'm so relieved when it's done, I take the first calm breath of my own since he fell through my open front door.

I don't push him to talk at first, because I want to cement this new state of comfort that we've achieved. Eventually, he seems to drift a little. Not truly sleeping, but dazed, and finally out of the *panic-flee-fight* mode that he was in before. Once we've been there for a while, though, I let out the question that I've been holding in all this time.

"How badly are you hurt?"

Tobias doesn't answer. He stays still, as if he hadn't heard me, continuing to mirror my slow, careful breaths.

"I didn't know you wore glasses," is what he says when he eventually opens his mouth. His voice is raspy, like he's been crying a lot or shouting. But there's a teasing lilt to it that makes me feel optimistic that the Tobias I know is still in there, buried under all this hurt.

I let myself do a little half-smile/exhale combo, because that's all the mirth I can muster.

"I wear contacts when I'm working. This is after-hours Gunnar. Lots of old-man cardigans, glasses and complaining about how tired I am."

Now it's Tobias's turn to snort.

"You're not old. I like the glasses. They're very distinguished."

"See, I feel like 'distinguished' is just a fancy, polite synonym for 'old'."

He doesn't reply, but he tugs on my arms until I'm holding him a little tighter. How we've ended up like this—when we've never even touched before and less than a day ago, I said I was going to leave him alone—is surreal. I'm trying not to make myself crack that nut open until I have to.

"You didn't answer my question." I jostle him a little, so I know he's paying attention.

"It's not that bad."

The words are a whisper, and I know without a doubt they're not true.

"I don't know you very well, Tobias. But I think I know you well enough to know that's probably code for 'I'm basically dying'. Will you let me take you to the hospital to get checked out? We don't have to tell them anything."

Tobias tries to sit up, but immediately cringes and gasps in pain, so I hold him against my chest and don't let him move too much.

"No! As soon as he realizes I'm gone, that's the first place he'll look. He could already be there, for all I know."

It's telling that neither of us pretends I need an explanation of who 'he' is or what happened. Tobias is fighting against me a little as he speaks, but at the same time pressing his face against my neck, like he's seeking comfort there. It's the weirdest dichotomy, but I refuse to do anything that might limit his ability to take what he needs from me.

I know I should suggest he goes to the police, but what's the point? He would definitely refuse, and he'd probably be right to do so. Police have a hard time protecting women from their abuser when it's just some schlub. But two men, which already throws most people through a loop? When the abuser in question is a violent, intelligent criminal, living in a network of criminals?

No. The cops won't protect Tobias, and making waves will put him in even more danger than he already is.

I sigh, not bothering to hide it from him. I know his face is a mess, but I can also feel wetness on his clothes that I'm hoping isn't blood. Although hope isn't going to get me far in this situation. He needs more care than I can provide.

"Maybe I could—" he hesitates. "Would it be alright if I took a bath? I think I'm dirty and shaken up more than anything. If you help me into it, I can get myself cleaned up and then it won't look so bad."

"Okay." I manage not to sigh again.

I peel myself out from under him, even though we both seem reluctant to let go, and pad over to the bathroom to turn on the water. While the tub is filling, I grab whatever soft clothes I have that might not be too insanely big on him and lay them on the lid of the toilet before finally turning the water off. It's warm, but not so hot it'll be a shock to him when he's already shaky.

My mind is cranking in the background, trying to figure out any options I have for getting someone to look at him that he won't immediately refuse. But I guess I can focus on this first, and maybe get a better evaluation of how bad his injuries really are.

This time, when I help him up from the couch, he's able to walk. He still leans heavily into me, but together we get him limping over to the bathroom. For once, I'm grateful my apartment is so small. Once we're standing next to the tub, I help him slip out of his worn sneakers that don't have socks underneath and then his pants. He's got worn black boxer-briefs on, and I leave them on so he can remove them himself once I'm gone.

I try not to stare at his skin where it's revealed, but it's hard. I can already see that he's at least sprained one ankle, because it's twice the size of the other, and there's bruising coming up everywhere.

Tobias moves to step into the tub, even though his hoodie is still on, and lets me brace him on my arm. He's shaky, but he makes it. As soon as he's standing in the water, he turns to look at me.

"I think I'm good. Thank you. I won't be long."

Part of me is terrified to leave, like he's going to fall or drown or pass out or anything else. But I'm also hyper aware that his boundaries have probably been shredded beyond belief, and the last thing he needs is me—practically a stranger—pushing them.

More than I already have.

"Okay. I'm going to close the door, but don't lock it, just in case you need help. I'll be in the living room, so just shout if you need me. There are clothes here and a towel. Take your time."

He nods, giving me a look of gratitude that would be hard to express in words. I slide out of the room, shutting the door behind me before I have the chance to second guess myself.

While I wait for him, time seems to slow down to a glacial pace. I'm spending so much energy telling myself to calm down and not be an overbearing asshole that I lose all sense of how much time is actually passing, because everything seems surreal to me right now.

Then I notice a slight shift in the tone of darkness streaming in through the windows. Not like dawn, but the first hint of it. The kind of thing you become attuned to when you spend more of your life awake at night than during the day.

I look at my watch then and realize I'm not being crazy. He really has been in there too long.

In a heartbeat, I'm over there and knocking on the door. I call out to ask if he's okay a couple of times, but there's no response. My heart feels like it's wrapped in barbed wire, slowly tightening with every passing second, so as soon as I'm sure he's not responding to me, I don't hesitate to throw open the door.

"Aw, hell."

The words are muttered under my breath while I lunge for Tobias and pull him higher out of the water. His face wasn't in it, and he's still breathing, but it looks like a close call. He's so deeply asleep, I think 'passed out' would be a much more accurate term.

Tobias's eyes flutter open once I shake him, although he looks disoriented and a little afraid.

"It's okay. Tobias, wake up. It's only me. You fell asleep in the water."

I try to keep the frenzy that I'm feeling out of my voice, but I don't know how successful I am.

The water is ice cold and more than a little pink. He's bleeding from somewhere, I can say for sure, now. And it seems like it's still going. There's more bruising than I saw before, including a huge, mottled one covering half his ribcage. I hate it. And now that his face is a little cleaner, I can see clearly that his lip is split open and already scabbing over.

He seems to almost choke on air as his consciousness settles back into his body. He's shivering again, and I want to get him out of the water as soon as possible. Grabbing the towel I put out for him, I somehow manage to half drag him out of the water while wrapping it around him, so he's not totally exposed. There's another towel hanging on the rack, so I grab that as well, even though it's not clean.

Who fucking cares? I throw it around his shoulders and then pick him up again like before, because the water seems to have drained what little fortitude he got back from resting before. It doesn't take long to return him to the couch, then snag those clothes and swap the towels out for them, one by one, keeping his modesty more or less intact. There's a soft knitted blanket on the back of the couch that I cover him with as well.

Once we're both settled, this time with him lying on his back and me sitting on the other end of the couch with his legs draped gently across my lap, I don't let him avoid the subject any longer.

"I get why you don't want to go to a hospital, but you have to do something. You are hurt, Tobias. You could be bleeding internally. I'm not going to watch you die slowly on this couch and do nothing about it."

His head is thrown to the side. I don't like it when he won't look at me directly, even though I've been the one to avoid eye contact most of the time we've known each other. As if he'd be able to sense how fixated I've always been with him.

The dampness from the bath means his hair is a little curlier than usual, falling in his eyes in dark ringlets. His eyes are just as dark, staring at something only he can see, and his skin has lost its cool undertone, looking pallid and drained instead.

"What's the point?" he mutters, still not turning to look at me.

Yep. There goes another chunk of my heart, cracking and falling into the ocean like a fractured iceberg.

The urge to gather him to me and hold him is almost overwhelming, but his body language is much more prickly and insular than when he was grabbing at me before.

I settle for taking his hand, slowly and carefully, and holding it gently enough that he could easily pull away. It gives me another swell of hope when he holds me back, though, squeezing my fingers a fraction as he continues to stare at the faded gray fabric of the couch.

"I know you're not going to like this, but if you refuse to go to the hospital, I'm calling Sav."

His eyes go wide as his gaze snaps up to meet mine.

"Wha—"

I cut him off before he can panic anymore. "I know he's part of the Banna. But I also know some shit you might not. He's getting out. Really. You can't tell anyone, but I know he is. And he hates Eamon more than anyone in this world. I can't tell you why, but I know your location will be safe with him, without a doubt. His brother's an ER nurse. I've met Micah a few times, and he seems sweet. I think he would be happy to help. These are your options, Tobias. I call them or we go to a hospital. We can go to one out of town. Hell, out of the state if you want to go to Arkansas. But I'm not letting you bleed to death and I'm not letting you leave until you're safe. Got it?"

I'm breathing a little hard after my rant, and Tobias is still staring at me, wide-eyed.

For a second, I think he's going to argue with me. I almost want him to, because it would show me that he's still got some fire in him. But then his shoulders sag and his gaze drops, and he looks so fucking exhausted I want to gather him into my arms and never let go.

"Fine," he mumbles. "Call them. It doesn't matter. It's not like he's not going to find me and kill me eventually, anyway. Why not speed the process along? But I don't want to go anywhere."

The resignation in his voice is heart-wrenching, and I would normally want to fight with him over his myopic take on the situation, but I know this isn't the time. He's tired, he's coming down from what must be a colossal adrenaline crash, and he's probably in more pain than I can imagine.

Instead, I suppress my natural urge to lecture and focus on him. My hand travels across the space between us of its own volition, and before I know it, I'm smoothing back all that damp hair that's fallen into his face. I keep my touch gentle, because he's bruised everywhere, but he sinks into it all the same and seems to luxuriate in letting me pet him like a cat.

Time stretches out and then folds in, distorting itself. I lose my focus watching him relax, bit by bit, until I'm jarred out of my weird moment of serenity by remembering I'm supposed to be calling someone right now. Waking them up, most likely.

I'll owe Sav some overtime or something. This is worth a few IOUs.

Before I call, I make one last imploring pitch to Tobias.

"Can you just trust me for a few hours? You came here because you needed help, right? Let me help you."

The words come out in a pleading tone that I'm also not proud of, but I can't stop myself. The only thought worse than him not letting me get him medical attention is him getting up and leaving, possibly to go back to that piece of shit.

There's a moment where I think he's going to fight. A certain kind of tension sitting around his mouth. But then he shrugs again and looks at me with a world-weary 'what does it matter' expression that doesn't belong on the face of someone so young.

"Just trust me," I repeat, grabbing his knee with my free hand before reaching for my phone. "For a little while. Please. Everything's going to be okay."

I don't get a response, but it's still better than him running away, so I'll take it.

Chapter Five

TOBIAS

I only catch snippets of the conversation Gunnar has on the phone, but I'm trying not to focus on it, anyway.

Whatever's going to happen will happen. I can't control it any more than I've been able to control the rest of my life. Right now, I'm letting the exhaustion wash over me as I sink deeper and deeper into Gunnar's plush old couch and work on burying all my memories from tonight in the deepest recesses of my mind.

Eamon's face. His touch. Everything he did. I thought I knew what he was capable of before, but this was so much more than just violence. There was a darkness to it all that I never expected.

I suppress a shudder and wish that Gunnar would come back to the couch. Of course, I don't say it out loud. But I think it as fiercely as I can, as if the universe will maybe hear me.

The one good thing about how tired I am is that it's insulating me from feeling embarrassment over how I've behaved so far tonight. Not only did I show up on his doorstep in the middle of the night begging for help when he barely knows me, but to cling to him like a little child...

It's pathetic. But I feel pretty pathetic right now, so I'm giving myself a pass. Hopefully, he understands and isn't too disgusted with me.

I couldn't get a job that didn't make me a garbage human. I've been lying to my grandmother, the only person who genuinely cares about me, for longer than I care to admit. And I have never been able to stand up to the redneck asshole who takes his personality disorder out on my ass.

Ugh. I deliberately let my brain soften, kind of like when you make your eyes unfocus for a minute. I can reconcile all these things later. Right now, I just need to breathe and exist.

I must drift off, because it feels like crawling out of the deepest part of the ocean when someone eventually shakes my shoulder. I know it's Gunnar before I even open my eyes, because he always smells expensive. Like a real grownup. Some kind of cologne that doesn't come from the drugstore and probably lists its scent as something hyper-masculine, like 'leather' or 'whiskey' or something.

Knowing it's him doesn't stop my skin from humming with fear for a second, but I take a lungful of that cologne as I open my eyes, and it helps my body catch up to my mind and settle itself.

"I'm glad you called," someone says. I don't recognize the voice, and it's barely a whisper in the dark room.

As soon as my eyes focus, I pick out the figures in the blackness. Gunnar is kneeling next to the couch, one hand still on my shoulder, looking at me with the same grimly compassionate expression he seems to pull off so well. Standing a few feet away is Sav, whose face is tight and carefully neutral. Like he's trying to control his anger.

For my sake, I'm hoping he's angry *for* me, not at me, because the man is even more jacked than Eamon and has enough tattoos to tell me he's higher ranking, as well. The gang cumdump doesn't get invited to a lot of inner circle meetings, but I know enough about *Savage*—mostly from Eamon bitching about him—to know that him showing up here was important for the Banna. If he's really getting out, like Gunnar said, it's going to be a very big fucking deal.

Next to him is a man I don't recognize. He's almost as tall as Sav but more lithe than muscular, and he has the kind of delicate, boyish features that make it hard to guess his age. Older than me, but probably not by that much. He's pretty. And he's looking at me with practiced, detached compassion that would scream *nurse* even if Gunnar hadn't told me already. He has a little bag that looks like a portable first aid kit slung over one shoulder.

"Hi," he says as soon as I look at him. "My name is Micah. Gunnar asked me to take a look at you, if you're okay with that?"

I'm still a little groggy, so the words don't come out as quickly as they're supposed to, and Gunnar fills the silence.

"Micah is Sav's brother, remember? You can trust him."

"Stepbrother," they both correct in unison. Probably with more energy than is really required.

"Former stepbrother," Micah continues. "It was a long time ago. It doesn't matter." He walks away from Sav's side so he can crouch down in front of me beside Gunnar, leaving Sav flexing his fingers in the air next to him and looking uncharacteristically awkward before he decides to back up to the wall and stand there like a gargoyle with his arms crossed.

Once Micah is on eye level with me, he looks at Gunnar briefly before tossing his head. Gunnar takes the hint and also steps back, although he seems even more reluctant than Savage.

When Micah speaks to me again, it's in a quiet voice. Just between us, even though I'm sure the others can hear.

"Look, I'm sure you just want to sleep right now and the last thing you want is some stranger poking around your space. I'm not going to force you to do anything or say anything, even if Gunnar asks me to. But you do look really roughed up, and we can just take it slow. This is my job. I work in an ER, and I'm also certified as a Sexual Assault Nurse Examiner. Which means I've seen people who've gone through pretty much the worst shit imaginable. I promise not to hurt you or force you to do anything."

The words are meaningless. But there's something about the lulling, calm sincerity in his tone that is getting to me. An upswell of emotion threatens to hit me square in the chest, and I hate the thought of looking even more pathetic in front of these people, so I push it down.

"Whatever, it's fine." I choke the words out through a throat that feels like it's swelling shut, my voice more croaky and rough than I expected. "Can we just... Not do this here?"

Micah nods, giving me a faint smile. "Sure. We'll go into the bedroom. Do you want anyone else in there to sit with you, or just us?"

"Just you. This is humiliating enough."

Micah makes the same face I've seen Gunnar make a lot tonight, like he's holding in the urge to lecture me. As long as he keeps holding it in, we're fine. Normally I try to control my tendency to be morbid and self-deprecating, but if there's any day I get a pass, it's today.

What part of this situation would scream 'I've got my life together and should be proud of myself,' to them, anyway?

"Gotcha."

Nobody says anything else. I feel Gunnar and Savage tracking us with their eyes as Micah helps me up from the couch very slowly and carefully, before helping me limp my way over to the bedroom. He sits me down on the bed and thankfully turns on the bedside lamp instead of the overhead light before closing the door behind us with a *snick*.

I thought I was okay. I thought I could power through this. But as soon as we're trapped in here together, it feels so much more exposing than I expected. Like his eyes are on me and he can already see everything, even though my clothes are still on. I see him move a little and immediately flinch, even though he's nowhere near me.

"Sorry," I mumble, avoiding eye contact. I blow out a breath and then shake my head, like I can shake out this weird, pulsating anxiety that I suddenly contain. Even though the shaking makes the throbbing in my head that much worse. "I don't know why I'm acting like this. I'm fine. It's not a big deal."

Micah looks at me for a moment, and I feel like a puzzle or something that he's trying to crack. When he speaks, his words are slow and careful. His voice is soft, but he's not giving me the hangdog pitying look I'm already sick of from Gunnar, which I appreciate.

"When humans go through something traumatic, it often takes a long time for our brains and our bodies to catch up and be in sync again. They're operating from completely different information sets. Your body is reacting to all the immediate stuff: what just happened, how hurt you are, how much cortisol is tearing through you, etc. As well as the long-term effects of dealing with abuse on a regular basis, which takes a toll.

"But while your body has been chipped away a little at a time, your brain can get used to it. So, your brain is telling you that everything is normal, that you know how to deal with this, that how you feel in your body is clearly an overreaction. But those thoughts can be partially a product of your brain trying to protect you from how bad things have gotten, and partially whatever conditioning the world around you has given to reinforce why you should just take what's happening. Man up, or whatever. It's all bullshit.

"Your mind and your body are trying to alert you to how bad it is and insulate you from it at the same time. They're doing their best. The more you can try to listen to yourself and be honest about how you feel, even if how you feel doesn't seem like how you think you *should* feel, the easier it'll be for you. I promise."

I only manage to absorb about half of what he's saying, but it helps a little. I feel steadier. Or maybe it's just how steady he is while he's saying it. Like he's completely unperturbed by me writhing out of my skin over here. It lets me dial back the static in my brain a little and I nod, so we can get on with the next part.

He explains a little about what he's about to do. We go through the song and dance about the hospital one more time, with him assuring me that if I want to go and have an actual exam with evidence collection, nothing will be reported to the police unless I want it to be. But when I still refuse, it's clear by his expression that he gets it.

Then he asks permission, and once I nod, he starts to touch me. He pulls gloves out of somewhere that I don't see, so it's all very clinical. It's also all very gentle, with constant stopping and starting to make sure I'm okay and explaining what he's looking at while he looks. He goes over all my cuts and bruises, listens to a bunch of seemingly random spots with a stethoscope—the works. Each little wound gets cleaned as we go: bandages applied, an ice pack put on my ankle, some painkillers handed to me. And I spend it all in a state of suspended panic and shame.

Then we get to the part I was hoping he wasn't going to ask about. His questions regarding 'sexual trauma' make me freeze up so hard, I can hardly push the words through my lips.

I don't want to talk about it.

It's fine.

It's no worse than anything I've had before.

Which is a lie and we both know it, but I'm not telling him the truth. Not him, not anyone. Ever.

"I know this sucks, but it would help if I could take a quick look. To make sure there's no severe damage. I won't touch you if that would help."

Eventually, I nod. It takes us a minute to get adjusted, using the blanket on Gunnar's bed like a drape over my body for the illusion of privacy. Then he asks me to take off my pants, roll onto my side, and bring my knees up to my chest. Micah looks, but he doesn't say anything like he normally does, and the pattern of his breathing changes in a way that spikes my heart rate.

"What?" I straighten my legs.

Micah sighs. "What happened?"

Silence hangs between us, veiled and heavy.

"It's fine. I don't want to talk about it."

"Tobias—"

"It's fine!" I cut him off, because we are done with this conversation. I flail around until I find the sweatpants Gunnar lent me, tugging them back on under the blanket and dislodging the ice pack in the process. "Are we done? Can we be done? I'm not dying, right?"

Micah blows out a steady breath. "Okay. But I want you to keep an eye on things and let me know if anything gets worse." He stands up and takes a big step back, so he's not crowding over me, before saying, "I swear to god, no joke. If you start shitting and/or vomiting blood, you call me. Or go to the hospital. It is not *fuck-around-and-find-out* time anymore if that happens. Y'hear?"

Until now, he's been soft spoken, with a mild accent and an unmistakably 'gay' lilt to the way he talks. Pronounced, like he leans into it. But as soon as he gets a little heated, it's like I can see the redneck coming out of him and it's almost a little intimidating.

Like always, I try my best to hide the flashes of real fear that are running through me. Fear that I might genuinely be fucked up, and fear that Micah isn't as nice as he seems and will run straight to Eamon after this to hand me over.

"Yes, ma'am."

Micah rolls his eyes, but doesn't seem offended. "Don't be a bitch just because I'm fabulous. Try saying 'thank you, Micah,' instead."

He's gathering his stuff up, not waiting for a response. It almost catches him by surprise when the words "thank you" actually do slip out of my mouth.

Then I'm back to huddling into my oversized borrowed clothes and praying for this day to come to an end. Finally.

I try to get up when he opens the door, but he turns around to *tut* at me.

"No. You stay. Be a good boy and ice your ankle. I'll send Gunnar in to continue his *Prince Charming* shtick while I see myself out. Oh, and be prepared,

I'm ordering you an at-home STD panel, and this one is not optional. I'll put it under someone else's name. Don't worry."

My mouth is hanging open, but I don't have the chance to say anything before he disappears through the doorway.

I hear him murmur a few words to Gunnar, but not nearly long enough for him to be giving a rundown on everything he just saw. Thank fuck.

Eventually, the murmuring disappears and Gunnar peeks into the bedroom.

"You should sleep in here," he says, hovering in the doorway. "I can take the couch. It's late. Well, early now. Do you need anything else?"

There's a ping-pong battle in my brain for a minute because I do need something, but asking and getting a 'no' might be that final humiliation that makes me crumble away into dust. When I think about it, though, he's been falling over himself to help me ever since I got here. More generous than I expected, so maybe this whole vibe I've been feeling between us isn't just a delusional fantasy, like I suspected.

"Will you…" I hesitate, almost stuttering at the words, which is embarrassing in and of itself. "Will you sleep with me?"

There it is. Out in the open, waiting to be snatched up or slapped to the floor.

Gunnar's eyebrows climb up his forehead and his breath catches. His lips begin to form a word, and for a second I think he's going to say yes. I need him to say yes, because while normally being by myself is my most form, there's something about the bulk and warmth and smell of him that sets me at ease even more.

"I, um. I don't think that would be a good idea," he says, at last. Something churns in my gut, but I try to keep the feeling from making itself known on my face. "You're hurt, and this is all confusing. I don't want to do anything that might blur boundaries. I'll be right outside this door, though. You can keep the door open if you want. Just yell if you need something."

He starts to move toward me, and I think it might be to stroke my hair back like he did before. But I don't want him to touch me right now. I feel too twisted.

I pull his blanket over me and curl up, making myself into a tight, uninviting parcel as quickly as I can.

Gunnar seems to take the hint and stops moving. After too long of a pause, he steps back through the doorway and slowly moves into the living room.

"Like I said. I'm here if you need me."

Chapter Six

GUNNAR

I don't think either of us sleeps for what little remains of the night. I doze, but I'm too focused on keeping alert in case Tobias needs something. And I hear him rustling blankets constantly in a way no sleeping person would. Although, of course, he never asks me for anything.

It makes sense that he wouldn't, considering the one thing he did ask me for, I refused to give him. But Lord help me, I'm trying to have some boundaries. I'm already forcing myself to admit I have had an infatuation with him that's all bound up with how much I want to help him. None of that sounds fucking healthy. Add that to the fact that he's here and has nowhere else to go. Crawling into bed and holding him exactly like I want to is dangerous territory that I can't let myself enter.

Just because I caved at the start, when holding him seemed like the only thing between Tobias and totally falling apart, doesn't mean it can become a habit.

So, instead of sleeping, I lay on the couch and stew in my guilt. When it gets to late morning, around the time I might normally get up, I slip into the kitchen to brew some coffee. I have a headache in my left temple, accompanied by the kind of tightness that's threatening to become a migraine, but hasn't committed yet. Caffeine might head it off at the pass.

"Hey."

The sound of Tobias's voice is quiet and raspy, but I'm lost in my thoughts that it still makes me jump.

Turning around, I see him leaning heavily against the wall before making his way over to the table. He looks like an extra from a zombie movie that's on the verge of fraying apart, so on instinct, I duck toward him to help. Which is a stupid move, because it's sudden and aggressive and makes him flinch away, hurting him enough in the process to make him gasp.

We're both breathing hard after barely a few seconds of uncomfortable interaction, and he's still struggling to stand. Slowly and carefully, I reach for him again. He lets me take hold of his arm, even though he stiffens under my touch, and I help him get to one of the chairs I have around my little table that passes for a dining area.

"Jesus, you scared me. Why didn't you shout? I would have helped you up."

Tobias huffs but doesn't make eye contact with me.

"It's fine. You don't need to make such a big deal about it. I'm sore and bruised up. I don't need to bother you for every little thing when I'm already trampling all over your place."

I give the words a second to settle before I answer, busying myself with pouring coffee for both of us, then placing the mugs on the table, along with some cheap creamer I find in the back of my fridge that he might want. I'm about to sit down, but as an afterthought I catch myself, pulling sugar out of a cabinet first.

He probably hasn't eaten in a long time. That should happen soon.

Mentally planning out the rest of the day is taking up so much of my attention, I almost forget to reply entirely. Then I notice that Tobias is finally looking at me and snap my attention back to the real world.

"It's not a burden to have you here. I'm glad you came somewhere you could be safe. I worry about you. I know I don't really know you, but still."

There's a hint of an eye roll in Tobias's expression, but it's so endearing I can't bring myself to be annoyed. I'm grateful anytime he shows an emotion other than self-hatred, self-pity or abject *blankness*.

"I'm fine." There's a pause, then some sincerity creeps into his voice, although he's not looking me in the eye anymore as he blows on his coffee, which he didn't end up putting anything into. "Thank you, Gunnar."

"Of course. You're welcome to stay here as long as you want. What did Micah say? Is there anything you need me to get for you?"

Tobias shakes his head, still looking down. He still looks pallid, blue bruising spread over too-pale skin, but it's a little better than last night. My eyes drift and get caught on the tiny smattering of freckles over the bridge of his nose. They're faint—normally almost blending in with the sand-colored blush of his skin—but so perfectly placed they almost look fake. You have to look so closely to notice, but whenever I do, I can't look away.

"He said I'm fine." Tobias holds the mug in front of his face, the sleeves of my giant hoodie covering his fingers, and squirming a little. "I'll heal."

I don't say anything, and then he finally looks up at me and sighs again, a little more dramatically this time.

"No one's dying, Gunnar. You can take a breath."

There's a hint of a smile behind his sass, and it makes me smile back. A real smile, for the first time since he got here, and I threw all my energy into worrying about him.

This time, when I take a deep breath in before letting it out, I swear half the tension in my body goes with it. I stand up from the table, letting myself graze my hand along his shoulders for a second. Hopefully, there are no hard feelings about last night.

"I'm going to get you some food. What do you want?"

He looks up at me, a little confused this time.

"You don't need to do that. I'm fine. Thank you."

I can't stop myself from raising an eyebrow at him, but he doesn't relent. "I have plenty of food and you haven't eaten. If you don't pick, I'm picking for you, but you're eating something one way or the other."

Tobias chews on his bottom lip for a second and then shrugs. "Whatever you want."

Close enough to a 'yes'. I hum for a second but decide not to fight him on it. Instead, I focus on pulling things out of the pantry and the ancient fridge. I have enough to make something that passes for a real meal—eggs, sausage, tomatoes, toast. It'll do. Living on my own for so long has made me lazy, and I hardly ever cook anything more complicated than an egg or something I can reheat. Especially when I eat down at the bar half the time, anyway. Not that it's doing my health any favors. But he needs to eat real food right now.

While I start frying and toasting things, Tobias's gaze follows me. His expression is carefully neutral, but he watches all my actions intently. I'm not sure why, but it doesn't bother me, so I don't point it out. Maybe if he gets relaxed enough, I can get some more information out of him.

"Do you live with him?" I ask, treading lightly.

It's childish, but I don't even want to let the man's name pass my lips.

Tobias doesn't get upset, though. He does snort.

"No. Hell, no. Even if I wanted to, which I never would, I don't think his creepy boss would allow it. Blue-collar crime organizations are not exactly known for flying the rainbow flag and accepting *alternative lifestyles*," he says, using air quotes and wearing a disdainful expression.

"Okay, so where do you live?"

He gets quiet for a second. Eventually, he answers me. "With my lola. My grandmother."

The food is ready, because it was all pretty quick to cook, so I messily dish it onto two plates and drop one in front of him before returning to my own seat with mine. He picks up the fork and looks at it, but doesn't seem eager to eat.

"Got it. And you didn't want to go home because…?"

Tobias looks at me, but it's enough to make his point. I assume going home looking like that would have forced him to confront a lot of things he doesn't want to, and probably would have ended in a non-optional trip to the hospital and potentially the police station. The way a normal, loving grandmother would respond.

"Do you want to at least tell her you're safe?"

I don't think he had his phone with him when he showed up. He barely had clothes. I can make an educated guess that he climbed out a window or something as soon as he had an opening, and he's not offering up any details yet.

"Yeah, maybe." His attention turns inward for a second. "Actually, yes. Can I use your phone, please?"

"Sure." I pull it out, unlock it and hand it to him, then leave my plate for a minute to give him some privacy.

I pretend to be doing something important on the computer for the five minutes he talks on the phone. He keeps his voice low, so I can't really hear what he's saying, and a few times I don't think he's speaking in English. But his tone is unmistakable.

Ashamed. Stressed. Apologetic. Frightened.

I can tell when he hangs up, but I give him a minute because there's still a heavy sense of shame lingering around him. Once he's had time to take a breath, I go back toward the kitchen.

"Are you okay?"

As soon as I speak, Tobias wipes all traces of emotion from his face and gives me a blank expression. It's not quite quick enough, though. I can see that he's hurting, even if I don't know which specific thing is causing it right now. There's a lot to choose from.

"It's fine. She's sick, so I hate not being able to check on her, but she can't see me like this. Plus, he'll be watching her place, I'm sure."

I frown, because that hadn't occurred to me before, but it definitely should have. Maybe I'll ask Sav later if there's anything we can do about it. Tobias's grandmother getting caught in the crosshairs of that lunatic is the last thing anyone needs. I know if I ask him about it right now, it won't help his anxiety, though.

"How much help does she need? Can anyone else take care of her for a while, if you say you had to go away for work, or something? Do you have a mom or dad?"

It's the only way I'll ever phrase that question, instead of 'where's your mom?', because it's neutral enough that someone can say 'no' and we leave it at that. I'm not forcing their hand at revealing whatever tragic story they have hidden inside them, because most of us have one.

I hope I'm not forcing them, at least. That's my intention.

Tobias scrunches up his face in a way that would be cute if it weren't in such agonizing context. He lets out a sigh, and I'm already preparing to drop it when he answers the question with more than the 'yes' or 'no' I was expecting.

"My mom lives in Oklahoma on a rez. She married this guy who's Chickasaw a long time ago and had three more kids with him. But one of my sisters has asthma and the easiest way for her to get healthcare is if they live there, so when Lola started to need help, it didn't make sense for her to drag everyone back here and make all of us spend even more on medical bills. I was a lot older and getting in everybody's way, anyway; it made sense for me to leave. Mom can't leave the kids just to come up here and take care of my mess. I wouldn't ask her to do that."

Well, we don't have time to unpack all that right now. But suppressing the urge to is really freaking difficult.

Tobias is still standing up, shifting awkwardly on his feet and chewing on the skin around his thumb in a way that belies his anxiety. He keeps swaying until I suddenly remember something.

"Shit, Tobias, your ankle. Why are you standing up? Come sit on the couch."

I reach out to grab his elbow to help him balance, and for the fiftieth time since he showed up, I'm careless about it. My movement is sudden, and he flinches away. Which makes me jerk my hand back, and then we're staring at each other.

Again.

The blank expression from before has been slowly chipped away, and I can see the churn of multiple conflicting emotions. All with a toxic coating of fear over the top. I want to reach for him again, but I already feel like I'm making the same mistakes again and again, so I don't.

Tobias's mouth is hanging open, and there's a sudden rush of color to his face. I can see it like it's happening in slow-motion—his cheeks flush, his jaw sets tight like he's trying to control himself, and then his eyes are glossy.

I don't know if it's because I just scared him or because a bunch of other things just hit him at once, but it doesn't matter.

"Oh, honey." The endearment slips past my lips of its own volition.

I'm holding myself back from a lot of things right now, but that's the small fight that I lost.

Tobias takes one rough breath. No tears are falling, but his eyes are shining and bloodshot, getting worse by the second. He keeps looking at my face before darting his gaze away, like he's grappling with something inside himself as well.

Then he takes a step toward me, and I see the moment his resolve breaks. I reach for him again, but this time he doesn't flinch. He curls into me, letting me wrap my arms around him and hold him close as he starts to shake. Not as bad as last night, but still bad.

His body sags in my grip, even though he's still not crying. He's clinging to me, but it's weak and formless, and between that and his ankle, I'm worried he's about to be taken by exhaustion and slide right down to the floor.

Without stopping to second-guess myself, I lean down a little to get a better grip on him and then hoist him up my body. It's awkward, because he's still a full-grown man, even if he's smaller than me, but he unfolds into the hold immediately. His legs wrap around my hips and his arms are slung around my neck, as we press together from chest to hip so I can walk him over to the couch.

At least I go to the couch, not the bedroom. There. That's a boundary.

Sort of.

He holds the same position, even once we're sitting, and he feels like an anchor in my lap. Not in a bad way. Like something steadying that I want to orbit around forever.

Gunnar, you must *stop this.*

This is pathetic. I'm an adult, and not only am I attracted to someone much younger than me and vulnerable, it's apparently progressed to shitty high-school level poetic mooning.

But none of that knowledge stops me from stroking his hair while he breathes deeply and leans his weight into mine. He deserves at least that much.

I'm not sure how long we sit together for. Tobias doesn't say anything, but I guess he rarely does. It's long enough that my thoughts wander, and at some point, I remember that I'm supposed to be downstairs helping Sav open.

Shit.

I pull back as much as I can to get a look at Tobias's face, which isn't easy, considering I'm pinned between him and the couch.

"Hey," I whisper. "How are you?"

He doesn't answer. He's looking at me, at least.

"I need to go downstairs soon—"

"I'm fine."

He cuts me off, his voice cold and dispassionate. As soon as the words are out of his mouth, he pulls back from me. Tobias swipes at his face with the back of his hand, even though he never actually cried, and stares over my shoulder for a few seconds before attempting to clamber off my lap. His ankle almost gives out on him when he tries to stand, but he grits his teeth and catches himself, even though it's not necessary.

"I told you, you don't have to babysit me. You can go do your job."

"Do you want to come with me? You can hang out behind the bar and keep me company." I want to reach for him again, but we're clearly in the *cold* part of his hot and cold reactions. Not that I blame him for it, after what he's been through.

He exhales, giving me a world-weary expression that doesn't fit his delicate features. The ones that make him look even younger than he is sometimes, if he didn't always look so fucking exhausted.

"Where Eamon will be waiting for me? No, thank you."

"You don't know that. He probably has no idea where you are."

Tobias shrugs, flicking his gaze around so he's looking anywhere but at me.

"Can I take a shower?" he asks.

"Of course." At least there's less chance of him falling asleep in a shower like he did in the tub. "Help yourself to anything you need."

"Thanks." He looks at me one last time before heading for the bathroom. "I'll see you when you get back from work."

Once again, I'm left with a knot of discomfort from the interaction. I keep feeling like he's drifting away from me, but the closer I try to keep him to me, the harder he seems to fight.

There's nothing I can do about it now. Work first, Tobias after.

Anxiety about it all the way through, I'm sure.

Chapter Seven

TOBIAS

I thought once Gunnar left, I would feel less uneasy. It seemed like a logical assumption.

It's uncomfortable to invade someone's space. I don't really know him. I feel guilty about taking advantage of his kindness.

Not to mention having to navigate the way I'm ping-ponging between wanting to run as far away from him as I can or wanting to grab him and kiss him and lay out all my suffering at his feet. It's exhausting. And he never asked for any of this.

Guilt pulses through me at a low, steady voltage while I take a shower. I don't know why I decided to do this. I didn't need a shower. I just needed to get away from Gunnar so I could clear my head and escape his forlorn, pitying looks. But now I'm wet, cold and half-washed, while my ankle is throbbing so much, I feel a genuine urge to cry.

No. This situation is already embarrassing enough. If I spend all my time weeping about it now that I'm safe and lucked into someone taking care of me a lot more than I deserve, I'll never forgive myself.

Instead, I focus on rinsing off as quickly as possible, then half-hopping, half-collapsing out of the tub. I sit on the toilet while I towel off, which is sweet fucking relief, and then give myself a breather before facing the monumental task of getting dressed again.

It's when I'm finally sitting still that I hear a noise. Nothing much, just a faint scratching from somewhere out in the apartment.

My blood buzzes in my veins, and I can already feel my sense of self disconnecting from my body. Like I'm preparing for whatever's coming. Like I know that it has to be more than just a noise.

He found me. It's the only explanation.

I have thirty seconds of sluggish inner debate between trying to quickly dress and prepare myself or just sitting here, resigned to my fate. Ultimately, I settle on something in between.

With leaden movements, I pull on my borrowed sweats and the hoodie I slept in. It still smells a little like Gunnar, and that hint of his warm scent grounds me back in reality. Possibly more than I would like, right now. If what I think is about to happen is, in fact, happening.

I allow myself a sigh before slowly pushing open the bathroom door. My footsteps are whisper-soft because of muscle memory, even with my fucked-up ankle. I hate that my body continues to thrum with fear through it all, although I don't show it externally. It feels like I should be acclimated to this by now.

Once I'm out of the bathroom, I look around for wherever *he* is. Lurking in the shadows maybe, ready to scare the shit out of me for his own amusement. Or standing in the middle of the apartment like he owns the place, and it's a done deal that I'll be leaving with him. No questions asked.

But there's no one here.

I explore further, moving slowly and silently, pain throbbing higher and higher up my leg with every careful step. There's no one in the kitchen. There's no one in the open-concept living area, and nowhere for someone to hide. The bedroom is the only room that's really separated, but it's empty, too.

There's no way an adult human could fold themselves up into Gunnar's tiny closet, but I look anyway. When I tease open the door, there's a single moment where my brain screams at me that this must be it. He must be in here, because he isn't anywhere else. It's enough that I almost think I see him.

Then, when I see nothing but fancy-ass suits and air, I feel even more ridiculous.

I should sit down. Before I collapse, or my foot falls off, or something. I want to.

Except, the thoughts and images tugging at my chest won't let me. I pace around the apartment one more time, drawing all the open blinds after looking at everything I can see. I worry that I catch a glimpse of him in the tree line a couple of times, but nothing comes of it.

Besides, I don't think he would hide like that. If he knew where I was, he would just come for me. He has no reason to hide. There's nothing here that he's afraid of.

I check that each window is latched, along with the doors. I freeze for a minute when there's another distant creak from the stairwell outside—the one I dragged myself up, disoriented and desperate, just a few hours ago—but it stops. When I head for the couch a second time, I feel the brief urge to check the windows again, but it's so stupid I don't let myself.

'Collapse' would be a polite way to describe how I get from standing up to slumped on Gunnar's sofa. Once I'm ensconced in his deep, worn cushions, I realize I should have brought an ice pack or ACE bandage or something.

Oh, well. It's too late now. I'm definitely not getting up anytime soon unless the building is on fire.

If Eamon does get in, I'll be easy to find and we can get it over with quickly.

I sit here, too drained to think or move or be afraid of anything. But the longer I do, the more the sensation of dread seems to work its way into each one of my cells and make itself a home. I hate it. My mind is resigned to whatever is going to happen. I don't see why my body can't get on board.

But no. Instead, I continue to jump and tremor at every noise I hear like a frightened wild creature until my patience with myself is about to snap. I need something—anything—to soothe myself with. A distraction, at the very least. It's getting later, so the low rumble of people from the bar below is kind of helping. But it's also pushing the thought that he could be in there deeper and deeper into my brain.

What would have happened if I'd gone down with Gunnar like he'd suggested? When Eamon came in, which way would be the quickest to run out of the building from behind the bar? If I ran to the back, it would be faster, but with fewer people to potentially help me. In the front there are more people, but I can also picture each one of their faces as they looked between me and him, trying to decide who to believe.

The crazed one who still looks too young to even be in a bar, or the gangster who is always calm and collected and will inevitably be prepared with some rational explanation.

I'm his boyfriend. I'm fucked up on drugs. My homophobic parents kicked me out. He's trying to help me get straight. You can't believe the words I'm saying. The doctors said this would happen. I'm overdosing on psych meds. Just leave me with him. He knows how to keep me safe from myself when I'm like this. You can trust him. He's the most trustworthy gangster there is, for some reason.

And on and on and on.

Gunnar would believe me, but get himself hurt in the process. Same with Sav. Kasia would believe me, but I think she hates me too much to do anything about it, probably. Plus, I think she has kids. No one should be getting orphaned because their mom tried to help save me from a situation I was never going to escape. No way.

The rest of the people down there are strangers. None of them would take my side. They'd grab me for him while I tried to duck down a hallway or find any exit, thinking they were being good Samaritans or some shit. Like always.

The images play out in my head on a loop. Each time, my body flushes with adrenaline like it's really happening, keeping me tingly and tense. Poised for flight, even while I remain slumped—alone—on Gunnar's couch.

I'm aware that this is wasted mental energy. I understand that it's actively exhausting me to think about it for no reason, considering it's never going to happen because I'm not fucking going down there. This is all pointless. But none of that means I'm able to pick up my brain and remove it from the carousel of hypotheticals that it's created for me.

A little part of me is afraid that if I stop thinking about what might happen, I'll start picturing what's already happened, which seems infinitely worse. And not thinking about any of it is clearly not an option.

I need to do something. There's a TV in the corner. The silence is officially fucking killing me, so I dig around for a remote and turn it on.

Gunnar has fewer subscriptions than my lola, apparently, but whatever. He has Peacock. Maybe he likes weird niche sports, along with his love of weird, fancy clothes and playing savior to damaged men who invite themselves into his home.

My eye is instantly drawn to the long row of mediocre horror films that it's offering me, each with nearly identical dark posters. The repetitiveness of it is already soothing me. I scroll through them absently until I find an old one I've seen a million times: *Candyman*.

I hit play and crank the volume as loud as I can without it potentially being heard over the music downstairs. I've been jumping at every creak and groan in this old building for an hour and I need it to stop.

As soon as the ambient noise and worse—the deafening fucking silence of this empty apartment—is drowned out by the haunting music of the opening credits, I feel my muscles unclench one by one. Once I stopped moving, all the aches and pains of my body became more insistent than before. They're pulsing and throbbing from my head to my toes, making it impossible to truly take my mind off why I'm here, but the sound of the movie is intense enough that I can let it pull my focus.

I'm still fizzing with a low-level, whole-body anxiety, but it's manageable now. I fold myself and my attention into it before throwing all of that at the movie, and basically counting down the minutes until Gunnar might get home.

I'm tired. So fucking tired. But no matter how much more relaxed I am now than before, the idea of sleeping while I'm the only one here and anything could happen still doesn't seem right.

Instead, I let myself space out as much as possible. My consciousness drifts, rolling from side to side like I'm riding a gentle wave, not moving frantically, but still too quickly to let any single thought get purchase.

When *Candyman* finishes, I put on *Halloween*. Then I skip the early sequels, because the comedy to horror ratio is not in my favor there, and go to the requel. Then the requel sequel.

I'm not sure exactly how deep I am into the franchise when Gunnar finally comes home, but I'm numb enough to my surroundings that it doesn't make me crawl through my skin to hear him open the door. Besides, it's Gunnar, so he has to be unnecessarily considerate. He knocks gently before unlocking the door to his own apartment and then slips inside while calling my name.

I lean up from the couch to look at him, but that's as far as I'll move. I've been lying here for so long I'd be surprised if there wasn't an imprint of me. I haven't even gotten up to pee, but I also haven't had anything to drink since the coffee Gunnar poured me fourteen hours ago, either. It's fine. The less I consume, the less I have to move and wake up the beast that has its teeth in my ankle.

It's dark in the apartment. Only the TV screen is lighting the space, because it's dark outside as well and I doubled down by drawing all the curtains, and on the TV it's also night. Michael Myers is dragging some wayward teenager by the hair across her front lawn with his stabby-stabber in his hand, ready to go, undeterred by her feeble kicking and screaming.

I know how she feels. Well, not really, because I keep my hair as short as Eamon will let me—he still likes to be able to grab a handful—but still. Vibes are the same. I can empathize, fictional screaming girl.

"Are you okay?" Gunnar's voice cuts through my mental meandering.

I shrug. It's quickly becoming my default answer.

"Yeah. My ankle hurts, but everything else is fine. How was work?"

"Y'know, the same. Drunk people. I taught Sav how to make a margarita, though. You should have seen it. He was pretending not to be excited about it. It was real cute."

He's answering me, but I can tell by the dim tone of his voice, as well as the crease between his eyebrows that I can just about make out in the dark, that his focus isn't on his words.

"Are you sure you're okay?" he says slowly, moving closer to the couch.

"Yes? Why?"

His eyes flick to take in the TV. "Can I turn on some light?"

I shrug again, but when he turns on a lamp, the brightness hits me hard and I have to squint.

"That's better. Are you sure you want to be watching this?"

He's looking between me and the screen again, but I'm too fucking tired and dozy to figure out what he's talking about.

"I love these movies. Except the ones in the middle. Why?"

Gunnar doesn't answer me. Instead, his frown continues to deepen, almost comically exacerbated by the deep shadows the lamp is casting across the room. He looks me over from head to toe, now that he has the light on, and for a second, I think he's going to reach out and touch me.

He doesn't, though. I'm catching on to a pattern. Gunnar only touches me when I'm on the cusp of vibrating into little fragments and his hands seem like the only thing that can stop it. Or, if he thinks I'm going to fall over like some clumsy toddler and break my neck in his apartment.

"Tobias, your ankle! Have you been like this the whole time?"

"Wha—" I start, but his brisk movements are already cutting me off.

Gunnar is fired up, moving around me. He touches me now, but only to carefully lift my foot off the floor, where it was resting, and rearrange it up on a pile of pillows. The whole process makes me gasp, but when I look at it, I realize it does look even worse. I guess I'd been too lulled to notice all the blood pooling around the joint.

He grabs more ice packs from his apparently endless supply in the freezer, wraps them in unnecessarily fluffy little hand towels, and then arranges them carefully as well. When he's done, he stands back to regard his work. I swear, a full minute passes before he seems satisfied.

As an afterthought, he brings me two more ice packs for the biggest bruises on my face, then he finally sits down, parking his ass on the little ottoman next to the coffee table.

I immediately notice that it's different from before, when he seemed happy to share the couch and rest my foot in his lap. I also notice the sudden tension he's carrying and the way he's avoiding looking me in the eye. He's looking at me, sure. But it's always my body, and always in a clinical way. Like I'm a problem he's trying to resolve. Not like he did this morning.

"Tobias, I think we should talk about something."

Yep. There it is. I'd get up to pack my bags if I had any.

Although it's kind of a dick move to get me all cozy and shit right before he kicks me out.

"You want me to go."

It's a statement, not a question.

"What?" His gaze snaps to mine, but after a few seconds, he looks away again, running his hands over his face. "No. Not at all, Tobias. You can stay here as long as you need to. I want you to stay here where you're safe. That's not what I'm talking about."

Well, now I have no idea what he is talking about, but whatever it is still can't be good, based on his expression. I keep my mouth shut and wait for him to continue.

"Last night. And this morning. And... All of it, really. I don't want you to get the wrong idea." He's tripping over his words more than I've ever heard from him. Normally, he has this whole suave, secret agent vibe going on. But right now, it's closer to 'high schooler reading his oral presentation to the class'. It'd be endearing if it weren't so patronizing.

"I think I've already crossed a bunch of boundaries," he continues. "You're in a difficult position, and I don't want to confuse you. Or make you think you owe me anything. Or that anything is more complicated than it is."

He's barely even making sense now, but I've put together the pieces. Despite what he must think is my childlike, innocent intellect.

"You don't want to *confuse* me?" I repeat, my voice dull. "You think I might be *confused*?"

I'm drawing out the word, not because I don't know what he meant by it, but because I'm honestly astounded he had the fucking balls to say that to me.

"You've been through enough, Tobias. I don't want to make it worse."

For some reason, it's so much more annoying when people are rude with a full-ass, genuine look of compassion on their faces. It kindles the spark of anger in my chest into a low flame. I'm still too broken to get up and move, but there's no mistaking how I feel when I speak again.

"Let me get this straight. You think that because I'm so fucking stupid that I ended up in a situation where I got my ass endlessly abused... Where I chose to stay instead of facing the consequences of leaving until the consequences of staying got even worse... You think that because of all that, I'm just some helpless, hapless thing. That I'm so used to being a whore that I can't delineate kindness from violence, and I'll never understand that you're not expecting sexual enslavement in return for my safety. Am I getting that right?"

Gunnar's eyes widen. "Fuck, no. That's not what I meant. You know that's not what I meant."

I ignore him and continue, because the fire in me is burning hotter by the second.

"Or is it that I'm so much younger than you, and my face makes me look even younger than I am, so I must be all innocent and desperate? Bound to immediately fall in love with you for showing me a little compassion. Like a puppy. Or a duckling."

The last words come out slowly, letting each consonant pop to get my point across how ridiculous it sounds when you actually say the inside thoughts out loud. Gunnar was shocked at first, but now his face is hardening.

"Stop putting words in my mouth. You know that's not what I mean."

"Do I? Because it's definitely what you're saying. Oh, poor Tobias. Oh, the poor victim. Oh, he must be protected from himself because he's too foolish to make his own good choices. Did it ever occur to you that I might have been fully aware that Eamon was a terrible choice this whole time? But a terrible choice is still a choice when there aren't any others?"

Gunnar sighs but doesn't interrupt.

"And besides, even if Eamon had tricked me. Even if I used to think I loved him or whatever, it still wouldn't justify you talking about me like I'm a child. I'm an adult. Help me or don't help me, but don't treat me like I'm too stupid to know the difference between generosity and coercion, just because I've experienced it. I think that makes me especially fucking qualified to know what coercion looks like."

For the nth time this conversation, Gunnar runs his hand over his face, looking as weary as I feel.

"I'm sorry. It's not what I meant. But you also don't get to piss and moan when this horrific thing happens to you, and I'm trying to put boundaries in place to keep anyone from getting hurt. Either of us. It's an unusual situation."

Part of me wants to flag at that, because he's not 100% wrong. But my anger is still leading the charge, and I have enough bottled up to last a while.

"So help me god, Gunnar, if you say the word 'boundaries' one more time, I'm going to scream."

Gunnar shakes his head. "I need to take a shower. And sleep. It's been a long day. Would you rather sleep out here or in the bed?"

He stands up as he's talking, making it clear this part of the debate is over.

I roll my eyes at him, even though I know it's petty. "I'm fine here. You can sleep in your bed." At least here I have the TV to fill the gaping maw of silence.

"Are you sure? Because you're still pretty—"

"Fuck, Gunnar, yes. I'm fine. All I've done all day is lie on this couch and it's probably all I'll do tomorrow. You went to work and you're also twice my size. Sleep in the damn bed."

He nods, turning and heading toward the bathroom. I pretend not to see the sadness in his eyes, even as I shove my own into the box that contains all my other undesirable emotions. We can fight about this more tomorrow. Or never. Or until he kicks me out. I'm genuinely almost past caring.

Chapter Eight

GUNNAR

Tobias isn't sleeping. It's been three days since he showed up at my apartment, and I don't know if he's slept more than a couple of hours in total. In fact, ever since he installed himself on the couch so I could have my bed back, he's barely moved at all. The TV is on twenty-four hours a day and it's always turned to the most gruesome, traumatic shit he can find. There's only light if I turn them on. He eats and ices his injuries and takes ibuprofen if I make him, and other than that, he lies there.

Every single day I want to at least ask him to put on a sitcom or something, before he slips deeper into whatever dark place his mind is in. But I don't want to risk another verbal takedown.

He continues to insist he's fine. We don't have any other incidents like we did the first day, where he let some of his emotion and vulnerability break through. Which I suppose makes it easier for me to stick to all those stupid rules I made for myself while I was down in the bar the first night, not thinking about my business.

No touching other than to help him move around.

No looking more than you have to.
Nothing that he could misconstrue as flirting or romance.
No pet names.
And don't fucking kiss him, you idiot.

They seemed simple enough, but they've been harder than I'd like to follow. Even if Tobias has continued to be distant with me since we had that fight.

The fight that I still don't totally understand. Was I really being that much of a dick? It didn't feel like I was. I want to protect him. It doesn't mean I think he can't protect himself. I just... want to.

I want to protect myself as well, before I become even more fixated on someone that I can never let myself get involved with. I have a business to run and a lifetime's worth of issues to continue mostly avoiding. Tobias can recover from this, and then he still has his whole adult life ahead of him.

The thoughts continue to swirl until it's so frenetic in my head that I realize I'm clenching my jaw and have to manually make the effort to unclench.

"How you doing, boss? Boy troubles got you down?"

Kasia looks at me with an exaggerated pout, as if I couldn't already tell she was making fun of me when she called me 'boss'.

"Your disapproval is scathing, as always."

Some of the smarminess drains out of her face. "Give me some credit. I don't disapprove of you helping him. He deserves all the help he can get. You know I'll barricade that staircase with my own body before I'd let anyone up there to hurt him more than he's already been hurt. I'm just pointing out that getting overly involved with broken things you promised to stay away from is definitely your calling card."

I stare at her. I still can't tell if she wants to tease me or make a serious point here.

Kasia takes a step toward me, lowering her voice so there's no chance anyone could overhear.

"Seriously. What are you going to do when he decides to go back? Because the chances are, he will. And it will completely break your heart."

Now that I'm looking more closely, I see the strain around her eyes. She always wears heavy, sort of gothic makeup, so it's difficult to penetrate down to the real her. Which, I assume, is the point. But once I noticed it, it's impossible not to see how worn out she looks.

"Are you okay? Because this doesn't sound like you. You should know better than anyone that it's possible to get out of a terrible relationship. You never went back. And now look at you." I wave my hand at the bar. "Queen of all this glory."

I'm trying to make her laugh, but it falls flat. Instead, she averts her gaze and stares into the distance with dull eyes before sighing.

"Yeah, well, I know better than anyone that just staying away isn't enough. No matter what, that ex is going to keep finding ways to ruin your life until he finally gets what he wants. We all die in the end."

The morbid take doesn't sound like her. I've never known anyone who can speak so eloquently on the complexities of domestic violence as Kasia, both from a survivor's perspective and an academic one. I want her to eventually take the hint and become a social worker or something, once she's crawled out of the debt her ex left her with and her kids are a little older.

This isn't her talking.

"What happened? Did he come to the house?"

She shakes her head and takes a step back from me.

"Nothing happened. It's fine. I'm just feeling morbid."

I don't believe her. And I'm also getting to the point where I want to ban the word "fine" from my presence.

But I also know my friend well enough to know that if I push, she'll only push back.

I watch her for a few seconds. "I'm always here, Kasia. Never forget that. Even if it seems like I have my hands full. Screw it, we can put you, your sister and all your kids up there too and then turn that apartment into a fortress. Maybe put in a drawbridge and install Sav as the guardian who makes you answer riddles before you can cross over."

It doesn't get a laugh, but half of her mouth lifts in a smile.

"You're a moron."

"Yeah, I know." The words come out softer than I mean them to. The moment feels tender between us, mostly because it's surrounded by all the pain we survived together and the weight of our history. It drowns out the din of the bar, that it isn't until Kasia finally turns away to serve someone at the other end that I realize I have a new customer.

"Oh hey," I say, pleasantly surprised to turn around and see Micah leaning against the bar. "Fancy seeing you here."

"I don't feel very fancy," he says with a sigh, looking down at some dirty, rumpled scrubs. He leans in to give me a kiss on the cheek, anyway, and something about it lightens me.

I made this place to be welcoming and inclusive. But there's an inherent neutrality in that, which we needed to have in order to survive in an area that didn't exactly treasure queer-owned small business. And while I left all my 'straight', fake macho bullshit in the past a long time ago, that hasn't stopped me from forcing a lot of neutrality on myself.

Not hiding. Not lying. But always so, so neutral. Voice a little lower. Gestures careful and a little smaller. Nothing with even the slightest touch of lavender. At least when I'm in a mixed group. Combine that with my build, and people are going to assume what they're going to assume. I don't have to lie about myself to pass.

But I went from deep in the closet here, to the polar opposite when I moved to Chicago for school and threw myself as hard as I could into every stereotype in existence to overcompensate. Then I finally came back here to this careful, inoffensive blandness. It makes me hyper aware of the fact that I've never really known where I would lie on the spectrum if I weren't always performing for a crowd.

All I know is that being around people like Micah, who are from here and get it, but are also queer and about as safe as can be, makes me relax. It makes me relax muscles I didn't even realize I had.

Definitely all the bullshit code-switching muscles, which get a daily workout.

"Can I get you a drink?"

"God, yes," Micah says as he slumps on the bar. "I'm never covering for a day shifter again. I hate days. There's so much talking. It's all the work, but you also have to follow dress code as well as deal with all the high-up doctors who think they deserve to get their ass kissed just for showing up. And, I swear, the clickety-clack of anyone in management following me down the hallway 'for a quick word' will haunt my fucking dreams. I would like approximately seven margaritas and a large-bore IV to dump them into my veins."

I can't help but smile, because Micah has that effect on people. Even though he never really stops rambling.

"Hey, Sav!" I yell the words into the ether, because he's always lurking somewhere. And even if he's (hopefully) not still doing whatever crime he used to do for a living, his situational awareness is still unimpeachable.

"Yes?"

He steps next to me, silent and graceful in his motions, even though he had some kind of terrible injury when he started here that I don't know if he fully recovered from. Sav's standing next to me, but he's looking at Micah, who is still leaning on the bar and giving his brother the warmest smile.

"You look terrible," Sav says.

"Well 'hello' to you, too. I feel terrible. I need a drink, but Gunnar's stalling. Will you break his kneecaps for me? Pretty please?"

He's fluttering his eyelashes at Sav while I sputter out a laugh and hold out my hands.

"*Wait wait wait*. I need my kneecaps. Sav, your brother—"

"Stepbrother." They both cut me off in unison, just like they did back at the apartment. It's becoming a thing, but I decide that's a rock I don't need to look under.

"Micah asked for a very large margarita. Why don't you show him what you learned?"

Sav's face freezes like I just asked him to recite pi to ten decimals, but Micah's grin only widens.

He lets out a quiet squeal. "Look at you! Learning big boy normal job shit."

That earns him a glare from Sav, but it at least cuts through his momentary glitch of panic. The glare is kind of terrifying, but Micah is completely unperturbed.

"Show me-show me-show me!" He stretches one long arm out over the bar and touches Sav softly on the wrist, and I swear for a few seconds I can see the man *blush*.

"Whatever," he grumbles before reaching for things and ignoring us.

I don't look at him, because I know that won't help when he's trying to pretend he doesn't care about impressing his stepbrother. I'm watching Micah, who is watching him rapturously as he fumbles around behind the bar, but the lull in conversation makes me realize something.

"Can I ask you a question?"

"Hmm?" he answers, dragging his gaze over to meet mine several seconds after he makes the sound. "Yeah, what's up?"

"I'm worried about Tobias."

Micah tilts his head from side to side and blows out a breath. "I mean, that's to be expected. Is there something specific you're worried about?"

"Everything, obviously. But he stopped getting up and moving around a couple days ago. I know he needs to rest, especially with his ankle looking so bad, but is it really good for him to lie completely still for twenty-four hours a day? It's been three days, and I'm worried he's going to be absorbed into the couch. I feel like he should be moving at least a little. Sitting up. Talking to me, even if it's to yell at me. I don't care. Just something."

I can see all the words being absorbed into Micah's brain and then run through whatever mental nursing calculator he has that tells him how to fix people like a wizard.

"Yeah, that's not great. I'm not surprised, though. Being in an abusive situation takes a huge toll on your body, even when you're not actively being physically harmed. It's being constantly on edge that wears you down. Now that he's somewhere safe, it makes sense that he'd need to recoup a lot of that. But not moving at all isn't going to help. Especially if he's lying flat all the time. He needs to sit up and breathe like normal or he could eventually fuck up his lungs. And at least be moving the ankle, so it's not freezing up."

I turn the problem over in my mind. I'm pretty sure, after the last conversation we had, that if I try to tell him what to do, he's going to tell me to shove it up my ass.

I'm not sure what I'm about to say, but it doesn't matter, because that's when Sav finally finishes making the world's slowest margarita. It's pretty, though. It is, in fact, an excessively large serving, on the rocks with a tidy little salt rim and a nice garnish.

The whole thing makes me disproportionately proud, because it's such a small thing and he's a competent adult. But I feel less ridiculous when I look at Micah's face. Because he is gazing at Sav like the man really did break my kneecaps for him and it's the most amazing gift he could ever have received.

He doesn't say anything, but he gives his stepbrother a wide smile that has him blushing all over again before taking a big sip. As soon as he does, he acts like he's going to swoon sideways before taking another one.

"Yes. Thank you. You have brought me perfection. I'll take one million more, and you can also start making these for me at home. Much obliged."

Even while he's sipping—gulping—his drink, you can tell he's smiling by the crinkle in his eyes, and Sav continues to squirm silently under the praise.

I don't understand anything about their dynamic, and I'm not sure I need to.

"Wait. Gunnar, let me ask you a question," Micah says when he remembers that I exist again. "What's your goal here?"

"Where?"

He tosses his head in the direction of my apartment. "With him. Helping him. What do you want to get out of it?"

I don't like the feelings that phrasing brings up in me.

"I don't want anything. He needs help."

Micah waves his hand at me as if he can brush my words away.

"Yeah, obviously. And you're a decent human being. We all want him to be safe. But do *you* want to be the one to help him? Or do you just want him to get help, however's easiest? Like, how involved are you in this process?"

Not a single word in the English language exists for me right now. And even if they did, I still wouldn't be able to string together an answer to that question. Either because I don't know, or I'm not willing to admit it. Maybe both.

"Look, I'm fried. He isn't sleeping, so I'm not sleeping, and I can't think straight anymore. It's quiet tonight, so I'm going to go upstairs to check on him. Sav, can you watch the bar for me? Kasia's closing tonight. Maybe you two could swing by before you go home and you could check on him, Micah? He might talk to you."

Micah nods. His expression is neutral, but he's watching me with a level of attention that definitely isn't.

I don't want to talk about this anymore. I dig around until I find my spare key and give it to Sav, then tell Kasia I'll be upstairs tonight unless they need me. She seems to have it under control, though.

It's more proof that she's stressed out by something. Whenever she is, all she wants to do is work. She suddenly has the capacity to be three bartenders at once, as well as bossing the rest of us around about not cleaning enough or stock levels or anything else she decides to throw her anger into.

It's barely a few minutes before I'm trudging up to the apartment and letting myself in. The lights are off and the curtains drawn, as I expected. I'm not sure which horror movie is on the TV this time, but it's really fucking gross. I think a woman is sawing at her own neck with piano wire.

I don't know what to do about any of this. I feel completely powerless in a way that I never have before, and this is hardly my first rodeo.

"Tobias?" I whisper, in case he is asleep.

Of course, he's not. His head pops up so he can look at me over the back of the couch as I move closer. He wears the same blank, withdrawn expression I've been seeing on him for a while now. There's no way this kind of exhaustion isn't eating away at him, even if he's not moving around.

I want to touch him. Hug him. Anything to bring him a little more back into this reality, but I agreed with myself that all that contact would only cause problems.

"Hey," he says. Nothing else. He doesn't ask me why I'm back so early, because I'm sure he has no idea what time it is.

A sudden surge of anger hits me.

Not anger at him. Anger at the situation and my incredible impotence in it. Anger that I'm not helping him, no matter how hard I try. And definitely anger at that asshole for putting him here in the first place.

"Are you okay?" His mouth quirks as he looks at me, but just like earlier, I have no idea how to put my torrential emotions into words.

"I hate that you won't stop watching this shit. It can't be good for you. Your life was nothing but violence, and now you're spending all day, every day, watching people get dismembered. It's morbid. Why are you doing this?"

His face hardens. For a second, I think he's about to yell at me. I almost want him to. When I opened my mouth, I didn't intend to complain about this because I'm aware that it's probably none of my business. But it's also been irking the shit out of me for three days, so apparently my brain decided now was the time for my petty thoughts to spew out like hot bile.

When he finally speaks, it catches me off guard. His voice is quiet, but there's no mistaking the ire in his tone.

"Why don't you just tell me how far we're taking this daddy kink of yours? Because you won't fucking touch me, so it can't be sexual. Unless you wish it was, but you're too disgusted by me and my life of 'violence' to bear it. But you fucking love telling me what's best for me. What's next? Are you going to give me a speech about my moral character or the dangers of violence in media leading me astray and then go jerk off over your own self-righteousness?"

I'm beginning to sense a pattern in our arguments, and it isn't me winning.

I make a conscious effort to keep my posture soft, trying to de-escalate the tension that's already filling up the room.

"I'm asking, not telling. And I'm not getting off on it. I know you're suspicious of anyone who acts like they care about you. That makes sense. But I would appreciate it if you didn't use everything I said to make me feel like a piece of shit."

Tobias laughs, and it's a cold, dead sound.

"I'm just pointing out the obvious. I'm too tired to dance around the truth with you. Kick me out or don't kick me out. I don't care anymore. I'm fucking exhausted. And I'm completely alone here. Just me and all my fucked-up thoughts. So, yeah. You may think my horror movies are all macabre and shit, but I promise they're so much better than what's in my head. It relaxes me. I don't know why. But I do know that if I tried to watch a rom-com right now, I would put my busted ankle through the fucking flat screen. You wanted me out of your orbit, so here I am. I'm taking care of myself. It's not your problem to worry about that."

I can't stop rubbing at my temples, because now I definitely have a tension headache of some kind forming, tugging at my thoughts and my will to exist in equal measure.

I always thought I was so good at dealing with people who were in their darkest moments, but when it comes to Tobias, I'm incapable of doing anything but mis-stepping.

"I didn't say that. I didn't mean that. I don't want you out of my way. I just don't want to fuck you up by being too close."

He doesn't answer. Instead, his head dips down, so I can't see his eyes anymore behind the back of the couch. I move around to perch on the edge by his feet.

Fuck it.

I can already see my rules teetering in the face of all this sadness surrounding him. He looks so alone. And I saw how tired he was—how fragile, I thought—but I don't think I really saw how much he was pulling into himself to get away from me because of the arbitrary boundaries I tried to set.

Without letting myself second-guess it, I pick up his hand. He fights me, but it's weak.

"You're not supposed to touch me, remember. I'm young and impressionable. Who knows what I'll start thinking? And then I'll get my damage all over your perfectly moisturized skin."

"I'm sorry." I grab his hand again, although not too tight that he can't pull it away if he really wants. "I'm sorry. I fucked this all up. I was trying to treat you well, and I think I just made it worse. I'm sorry."

The words keep coming out on repeat because it's the only thing I'm thinking clearly.

Tobias isn't looking at me. He's staring forward with a stony expression, but his eyes are shining in the dim light of the TV screen. It gets worse and worse until he finally wipes at them with his free hand and sniffs.

"I'm fucking sick of this. I feel insane," he mumbles, his voice thick. "I feel a thousand times worse now than I did before. It doesn't make any sense."

It does, but I don't think now is the right time to explain that to him. He looks so fucking tired.

"I'm sorry. It's awful and I made it worse. I shouldn't have left you so alone."

He nods, still not looking at me. On the TV, credits are rolling with some creepy music over the top. I'd absolutely love to turn it off, but I manage to control my asshole urges for once.

I can't tell him what to do. But I can encourage him. So, I tug his hand a little, pulling him in my direction. That makes his gaze snap to mine, a question in his eyes.

All it takes is a small nod, and then he's climbing across the couch to me. It's the most movement I've seen from him in so long, it already feels like I made the right choice for once.

Tobias climbs on top of me as I move more of my weight onto the couch until I'm sprawled out. He hesitates a little, but as soon as he seems convinced I'm not going to push him away, he nestles into me. It takes a minute, but I end up lying against the arm of the old sofa with his entire body laid out on top of mine, his face in my chest and his arms around my sides.

I don't deserve anywhere near this kind of trust, but I can still feel the way his body relaxes into me. I'm able to snag the blanket that's tangled around his legs and pull it over him, then I start rubbing my fingers gently up and down his back.

"You don't owe me anything," he says, the words muffled by my body.

I don't say anything. Only my actions are going to convince him, anyway. Pretty words are worthless.

When the movie finishes, it autoplays onto something else equally horrific. But it's dark and the volume is low, so I don't want to risk disturbing whatever equilibrium he's found. I focus on stroking his back as steadily as I can, and it doesn't take long for him to fall asleep.

Idiot.

I can't believe I convinced myself that this would be bad for him.

I don't fall asleep, but I'm lulled by the steady rise and feel of his chest on mine. Time passes, which I vaguely keep by the movie I'm trying not to look at. I'd put my phone on the counter when I walked in, so I can't check it.

The first hint of noise coming up the stairs makes my blood run cold, but it only takes me a few seconds to connect the dots. It's confirmed when I hear the key that I gave Sav turning in the lock.

I completely forgot that I'd asked them to come up. They step inside quietly, although Micah must have had a few more margaritas while he waited because he is visibly swaying, and I can see Sav reaching out to hold him steady.

As soon as they walk around to see both of us on the couch, I'm staring at two sets of raised eyebrows.

I put one finger to my mouth and shake my head.

"Don't wake him," I whisper, barely audible. "This is the first time he's slept in days. Maybe come back tomorrow?"

They don't speak. They do look at each other, and have some kind of silent communication through eye contact that I can only begin to guess the meaning of. But then Sav shrugs and Micah smiles at him before turning the warm expression to me.

He raises his hand in a silent little wave, and Sav nods at me politely before guiding a very wobbly Micah out of the apartment. I can hear the door close behind them, Sav locking it behind them, and then we're alone again.

I just need him to sleep. I can worry about the rest of it tomorrow.

Chapter Nine

TOBIAS

It's been so long since I've actually slept deeply that waking up feels like climbing out of a tar pit. At first, everything is thick and heavy. Peaceful. Then, my mind comes online a little at a time and realizes that my limbs are weighed down.

This isn't right. I'm supposed to be light and agile at all times. Ready to flee. This feels like a trap.

My brain is still struggling to shift from asleep to awake, so it feels like my body hits me with an internal defibrillator to kick-start the process. My blood buzzes, my limbs tingle, my heart goes from slow to racing with a lurch, and panic floods every crease and crevice of my brain.

"Whoah."

I hear his voice, but the part of my mind that processes things like that is still slow, because all the adrenaline went to the *fight-flee* portion of my gray matter.

There's something on me, so I jerk away from it. It tightens its grip, so I jerk harder. The movement is uncoordinated, an external repetition of the electric-volt-jumpstart that I just went through internally.

The second jerk obviously does the trick, because I don't feel trapped anymore. But then pain explodes over the length of my body on one side, including my head, and my eyes open to a bloom of color filling my vision.

It only takes a few seconds for everything to become clear, but those seconds are numbing. I'm lost in time and space, with only this fresh pain to convince me I'm alive.

"Gunnar?"

I can see him hovering over me looking panicked, his hands frozen in mid-air like he was reaching for me and stopped halfway. The room is dimly lit, but not dark. The last thing I remember was him pulling me into his arms sometime in the night. Early in the night, I think.

Then I remember feeling peaceful. Kind of, at least. Peaceful enough that I didn't have to constantly watch my surroundings.

Now I'm here, and it looks like daytime, so I must have slept for a *while*.

"What happened?"

He stares at me, still looking shook. "I'm not sure. You were sleeping, and then it seemed like you woke up and just launched yourself onto the floor. Are you okay?"

I rub my head where I smacked it. It's throbbing a little, but I'm sure it'll pass. Slowly, I try to get my hands under me and lever myself upright, internally inspecting myself for damage as I move.

As usual, everything hurts. I may not have been entirely forthcoming with Gunnar about how much Eamon fucked me up this time, because there's no way he would want to know the gory details. I wouldn't.

The aches and pains of bruising are mostly fading. But my ribs are still fucked, and it's hard to take a full breath, especially when I try to walk. My ankle seems to be getting worse, not better, and the downstairs situation is just the last humiliating straw in a stack of humiliation.

The silence between us feels heavy, but at least he's not pushing me for an answer.

"I'm okay," I say once he's helped pull me to my feet, and we're both rubbing sleep from our eyes. "I just dinged my head on the coffee table, I think. It's fine."

Gunnar frowns, reaching for my face so he can tilt my head and take a look at where I hit it. "I swear, I'm going to ban that word from your vocabulary."

I can't really hear the words, though, because I'm too distracted by the feeling of his very fucking large, very warm hand tenderly moving my head from side to side. It makes parts of me flutter that I thought were long-calcified from disuse. He holds me gently, like a child picking up a bunny for the first time when they're terrified to hurt it.

There's a moment where he grazes his fingertips over the bruised patch of my scalp. Just barely—just enough to ruffle my hair—and it makes my gut clench while my breath catches in my throat.

It's so close to the vulnerable prey feeling that I'm used to, but not quite. Because it's not bad. It's exhilarating. I didn't think I could be exhilarated without also being scared half to death, but here we are.

It makes me realize I'm breathing too heavily. My lips are parted, and he's standing close enough to me that I can feel everywhere his body brushes against mine. He's still wearing his work clothes he must have slept in—his fancy slacks and a formerly crisp white button down—while I'm drowning in the same oversized PJs I've been wearing for days.

I must be gross. I can't believe he's willing to stand this close to me, let alone let me snore on top of him for ten hours.

Gunnar seems to realize how close we are at the same time. His eyes meet mine, and I don't think we've ever been close like this without one of us trying not to look at the other or me being in the middle of a meltdown. Or drunk. Or all of the above.

I always thought he had brown eyes. But now I notice he has that thing where a portion of one is blue. I don't remember what it's called. But it's like a quarter of that little ring has been flooded with dye, or something. I guess that's the kind of thing that's supposed to be a flaw, but really just makes someone even hotter.

It makes him seem more real and also more unattainable at the same time. He's this solid, sturdy thing right in front of me. Like four inches taller, of course, so I have to look up, but he's still right there. I can see all the little imperfections in his skin, as well as the rise and fall of his chest that makes him real.

That doesn't mean he belongs anywhere near me, though. None of that has changed, just because I've been afflicted with the pining sickness, in addition to all my other injuries. He's still in the world of people who have it together, and I'm still in the world of people who crash on those people's couches.

"Come downstairs with me," he says, apropos of nothing.

"What?" I stare at him, leaning back. "You know I can't."

He snags my elbow. Still gentle, but like he's afraid I'll jerk away again and go ass over until I hurt myself.

"It's Wednesday. On Wednesdays we—"

"Wear pink?" I interrupt. I don't know why. My brain can't stop being obnoxious, even when the rest of me is exhausted, apparently.

Gunnar doesn't laugh, though. He looks confused, like he doesn't get the joke.

"What? No. On Wednesdays we open late to deep clean the kitchen. There's no one down there but us, and the doors are locked. What... pink?"

He is so un-fun sometimes. "Man, how old are you?"

"Thirty-six. Why?"

"You're literally the perfect age for that reference! Did you grow up in a cave?" I know this isn't the point, but my thoughts have been derailed. "Also, I thought you were much older. If you're not even forty yet, then why do you wear all these fancy-ass grown-up clothes? And why do you have so much gray in your beard?"

The side quest that my brain has taken me down must have taken over my senses, because without thinking, I reach up and paw at the beard in question. I've been low-key obsessed with it for a while. Thick and always perfectly trimmed, giving him this weird air of authority that kind of compliments his soft-spoken, 'aw, shucks' personality.

It's soft to the touch, and the playful gesture immediately turns into my hand resting on his face the way he was holding mine a minute ago. Except I don't have a purpose here. I'm only touching him because I've been itching to forever, and now that I'm allowed—kind of, when he's not being a dick about it—it feels like the floodgates have been opened.

Gunnar doesn't answer. He doesn't move my hand away, either, which is progress. But I feel his cheek lift under my fingers as he smiles at me.

"Maybe I'm just old at heart, and my beard knows that. And my pop culture references, apparently."

"*Pffft.*" I'm trying to keep it light and not let it show that I'm caught up in staring at him like someone in a Shakespearean tragedy, but I'm not sure if I pull it off.

"Come on," he says, his voice practically a whisper into the tiny space between our faces. "Micah says you need to move around a little. And I hate leaving you up here alone. You can sit out of sight and keep us company while we clean. Please?"

He looks so imploring; I can't remember all the reasons I should probably say no.

There's a decent amount of hallway in between the little kitchen/storage area at the back, and the bar itself. Conveniently, it doesn't have any windows. It's right by the door that leads to Gunnar's apartment and about as far from the main entrance as you can get. Which is where I'm sitting, drinking something fruity that Kasia handed me wordlessly. It's delicious, but tragically doesn't seem to have alcohol in it.

Alcohol would really settle my nerves right now. I would drink Everclear. Not a lot. I don't need to be drunk. But just enough to take the edge off this squirrel-like urge to constantly check and recheck my surroundings would be fantastic.

Booze isn't good for a lot of things, but it is excellent at making you care less about both yourself and the world around you. It's pretty much the only thing it brings to the table. My body cares way too much about every single aspect of existence, even if my mind is telling it not to.

Because realistically, this was a good idea. Damn Gunnar and his stupid wisdom. I'm just as secure here as I was upstairs, and it is kind of nice not to be fusing into the couch all alone. Although I'm now much more aware of how much I need a shower, and the thought is making me want to hunker in on myself.

The guys are all busy doing stuff that looks relatively tedious but important. Cleaning things. The kitchen—if you can call it that—is basically just a place where they deep fry shit, throw nachos into plastic trays, and cut up fruit. But it's nice to see they keep it clean, which is more than I can say for most bars I've spent time in.

No one really talks to me. I get the feeling they're treating me with kid gloves, but I don't feel like talking, so I'm not mad about it. Sav hardly talks anyway, but he does watch me. Not in a creepy way, though. More like he's checking I'm still here.

Kasia has never been anything other than tepid toward me. Now, she's giving me these looks that I think are about as empathetic as she gets, but thank fuck she's not trying to become friends. She is, however, oozing stress from every pore and seems to be throwing that stress into cleaning ferociously. I don't love myself a lot, but I'm going to choose to love myself enough to assume her stress has nothing to do with me.

Gunnar is the only one who does speak to me. Mostly making very dorky jokes whenever he walks past, which I also don't hate. The whole thing is peaceful, and ridiculously normal, and it lulls me into a semi-relaxed state. About as relaxed as I'm going to get, I assume.

Until I hear raised voices coming from the bar. For a second, everything freezes, because I assume the worst. But the doors are locked. I made Gunnar check like a billion times. As the fog of panic recedes a little, I try to pick through the angry sounds and see what it actually is.

Kasia and Gunnar are fighting. Not yelling, exactly. But terse.

My ability to pretend this isn't about me is waning, but I'm still holding out hope. Not everything is about me, I remind myself.

Curious, I set down the bag of tortilla chips that someone handed me at some point and carefully lower myself off the stool. My ankle throbs whenever it's not raised, especially when I put weight on it. It's also starting to feel more stiff than swollen, like a lump of painful rock sitting on the end of my leg. But I'm used to powering through a little pain, and I need to know what's going on.

"I can deal with it myself, Gunnar."

"You shouldn't have to, though. Why won't you let me help?"

Their voices are clear, because it's a relatively small space and there's only quiet music playing right now. I was planning to stay out of sight, but I think this is confirmation that it really isn't about me.

It's a misstep. As soon as Kasia sees me limping around the corner, driven by morbid curiosity, she points at me.

"That. That's why." Ok, rude. "You have your own problems to deal with. I'm a big girl. I will take care of it."

"Uh, I'm fine, thanks. I don't need a babysitter."

I don't totally believe the words even as I say them, because I can't even seem to sleep unless Gunnar is eight inches away from me, but still. The battered remnants of my pride want me to say something.

Kasia's expression tells me she's not buying it, anyway.

"It's not a bad thing, kid. It's fine. I've needed help too, but my days of handholding and weeping into my pillowcase are behind me."

Gunnar sighs more dramatically than I knew he was capable of. "Jesus Christ, Kasia, no one outgrows vulnerability. You don't hit a certain birthday and become totally self-sufficient. I don't know what you're trying to prove here."

Apparently, that's when Sav notices the very loud snark-fest and decides to get involved.

"What's the problem?"

"Kasia—" Gunnar starts before she cuts him off.

"Don't!"

"No. If you didn't want me to be involved, you wouldn't have told me. You know me better than that. For better or worse, we are all a very weird, fucked-up team and we are going to help." He pauses, waiting for her to interject again, but she's silent this time.

His mouth opens like he's about to speak, but then he looks at me again and gets distracted. Moving across the room with long strides, he passes me, grabs my stool from the hallway and then brings it over to where I'm currently leaning against the wall. Then, without hesitation, he wraps those giant hands around my waist and hoists me up onto it like a child.

It absolutely, 100%, in no way turns me on.

I swear.

"You need to stop standing," he says, pointing at me before he walks back to where he was before.

"I'm fi—"

"Don't even." His expression is so fucking stern, I don't even bother to mess with him right now. "Anyway, as I was saying. Kasia's piece of shit ex is trying to drag her through family court for custody. Not because he wants custody, but because he knows she can't afford it, and he wants to fuck with her. Correct?"

Kasia nods, still sulking—like she's being called out for secretly wanting help—but not interrupting him.

"You guys weren't here when all of this went down, but Jorden is actually more than just your average abusive shitheel." I wince at the words. I'm not sure why. Gunnar is very much on his soapbox, though, so I manage to keep the weird reaction under his radar while he keeps talking. "He also turned out to be a pedophile."

If anyone wasn't paying attention before, they are now.

Kasia rolls her eyes, like she's been over this a million times before and is sick of the sound of the same words being repeated over and over. I can picture what that might feel like.

"I was trying to get away from him anyway, and then I found him talking to teenage girls online. It was bad. I took the kids and left, reported him to the cops and everything, but somehow that slippery fucker managed to keep what he was doing under the radar. He couldn't hold down a job the entire time I was married to him, but when it came to proxy servers and anonymous internet use, he was suddenly a Mensa candidate. He only got some bullshit battery charges and probation, in the end."

"So, him trying to get custody is a very big deal. Which is why it is a *team effort*." He stares at Kasia while he says the words, and she seems to soften for him. "Sav, Tobias, congratulations. You are now on the team. Please start brainstorming solutions. Preferably ones that don't include murder. Not that anyone here would do something like that."

He looks at me and Sav, and it's so dry and unexpected, I swear to god I almost laugh out loud. Sav doesn't look offended, at least. He seems to consider it for a second before responding with his trademark shrug.

"Excellent," Gunnar continues. "We'll talk about this again later, then. Sav, can you help Tobias get upstairs so we can open please?"

A little piece of me is upset that he's not going to take me himself, but that feels too pathetic to even acknowledge. It's a thirty-foot walk.

Plus, before we're even out of sight, I catch Gunnar leaning in to wrap Kasia up in his arms, and she actually lets him. I know from first-hand experience how comforting it is having that big, solid body wrapped around you. It would be selfish of me not to share.

Just this once, at least.

Chapter Ten

GUNNAR

It doesn't take long for things to go back to normal after our dramatic interlude. My subconscious can't decide which it wants to worry about more—Kasia or Tobias—so it settles for doing both in excess.

I'm running on autopilot as I open the bar and start serving. Because it's later than we usually open, Wednesdays tend to start with a rush instead of a trickle, and within half an hour we're pretty busy. Kasia is focused, as always, but I keep an eye on her, anyway. None of this stuff with her ex is new. That doesn't mean it isn't awful every time it rears its head.

Sav left, because tonight is one of his nights off before the weekend and he only comes in to clean if he wants extra money. So, between the two of us, we're at least not given the space to get too deep into conversation.

Instead, I let myself keep tearing apart the problem in the back of my mind while I work. How we could convince the courts he's a piece of shit without having any new evidence. Or how we could convince him to drop it without doing anything super illegal. Nothing comes to mind, but I'm determined.

I'm so focused on it, instead of what I should be focused on, that I don't see him until it's too late.

"I'm hoping you can help me find something I lost."

Eamon managed to walk in and push through the crowd until he leaned against the bar and spoke to me, all without me noticing.

Idiot.

I'm not sure what my face does. Several variations of shock, if his quiet glee is anything to go by. He always seems to look happiest when the people around him are freaking out.

My first instinct is to tell him to get the fuck out and call the cops. I can already feel the anger rising in me, and the words are on the tip of my tongue. But then I remember the most important thing.

He still doesn't know where Tobias is.

He might suspect, but he doesn't know. If he did, he wouldn't be in the bar, he'd be upstairs. The angrier I act, the more it's going to confirm that I know exactly what he did to Tobias and, at the very least, know where he is. Which would probably lead to him beating the information out of me.

I have to remain neutral.

My favorite.

"What can I get you?"

Pushing out the words in a flat tone is excruciating, but I manage it. I even look him in the eye. And it's not like we were buddies before, so at least my general air of contempt is nothing new.

Eamon orders the same overpriced whiskey he normally does, and for a minute, I think I'm going to get away without a conversation. But once his drink is poured, he starts at me again.

"Like I said, I lost something recently. And this was one of the last places I had it. Do you feel like pointing me in the right direction?"

If I were better scripted as a human being, this would be the moment I pulled out a lost and found box and put it on the bar in front of him.

But we don't have a lost and found box and I am so far past finding any of this funny, even in the darkest possible way. I am completely out of patience for his bullshit.

"You know what, Eamon, if the boy ran away from you, I really hope he ran so far you'll never be able to touch him again. Because you're a scumbag and he doesn't deserve any of it, and I'm sure I only see the tip of the iceberg when you're dragging him around here and getting him suspiciously wasted off one drink. But no. If that's what you're asking. I don't know anything. So we can skip to the part where you threaten me and then I'll continue to not know anything. It's actually a very important part of a bartender's job to not know anything. As long as you want to stay alive, that is."

I hope I hit the right tone. It's entirely possible that mine and Tobias's lives both depend on it. Eamon has to believe me.

"You're pretty rude for a customer service worker. Did anybody ever tell you that?"

"I'm only rude to people I loathe."

He's leaning on the bar and so am I. We're roughly the same height, so we're eye to eye, and he seems completely calm, while I'm trying not to vibrate with barely contained rage. The weird staring contest goes on for way too long, and I imagine all the ways he's thinking up to stalk and kill Tobias right now.

"I can't help you, Eamon. I'm just a bartender." He hums a little, but continues to stare at me. "Can I get you anything else to drink?"

"One more," he says, before draining the glass.

I pour him another one. Generous, in the hopes that it'll make him slow and weak. Although who knows if it'll have the opposite effect? Just when I think he's about to start the whole thing over again, he silently pushes back from the bar and walks away.

Of course, I don't get away with it that easily. He finds a small booth in a corner and sets himself up in it, sipping the second whiskey slowly and not moving from the spot for the rest of the night. The crowd thickens and then finally thins while he sits there through all of it.

When it finally gets to closing time, I'm worried I might have to kick him out. But as soon as the last few patrons are on their way out the door, so is he.

Slowly. Like he's not in a rush and is making sure I know it. He leaves, though. I see him get into his car in the parking lot, but he doesn't turn the engine on yet.

I could call the cops and have him trespassed. Technically, the parking lot is privately owned commercial property. But part of me thinks that might be what he wants me to do. If I start something, he'll keep one-upping me until shit gets violent and if that happens, he's the one holding all the cards.

Instead, I decide to act like everything is normal. Do nothing to arouse suspicion. Close like normal, go upstairs like normal, and then have my freak out where he can't see me. Where I can see Tobias is safe with my own two eyes.

That only leaves Kasia. We continue to move around the space like nothing is wrong as we clean up and close. Maybe a little slower than normal, but nothing that someone would clock through the window as unusual. Nothing that looks like we're huddling together, talking out of concern. But every time we pass close enough, we exchange a few words.

"What are you going to do?" she asks.

"Nothing. I don't want to give him any reason to think he's got our scent. I'll close, go upstairs, lock every door and window, and then wait."

"Okay. So what am I gonna do? What do we think the over-under is that this guy follows me halfway down the highway and then runs me off the road or something?"

I grimace.

"Yeah, I'm not crazy about the odds. I would take you home, but there's no way it wouldn't look suspicious. Don't go out to your car at all. Especially because he might not know that it's yours if he hasn't watched you before. I'm gonna have Sav come pick you up."

Kasia doesn't say anything for a while, because she hates feeling like a burden to people and it's easy for this all to seem like an overreaction.

It isn't, though. We both know that. "Yeah, okay."

I step into the kitchen quickly to call him and explain the situation, and he agrees to come over. He lives close. It won't take long, so we go back to our very slow and steady cleaning.

Part of me is almost too scared to take the trash out like normal, but then I really do feel ridiculous. The dumpster is right by the door. I don't even have to step outside.

All in all, we make it through without incident. By the time Sav shows up and I'm ushering them out, the ratio of embarrassment to fear has tipped in the favor of embarrassment. But then the lights are off, the security system is on and the doors are locked, and I'm heading upstairs.

The sinking, twitching fear I felt before is back in force. I practically race up the stairs, desperate to get to Tobias now that there's nothing standing in my way. I knock, like usual, before I let myself in. So he knows it's me.

Like always, the TV is on and the lights are off. But Tobias isn't on the couch. The fear gripping me squeezes tighter, and I almost call out. He has to be here. If Eamon did something, he wouldn't still be sitting in my fucking parking lot like a ghoul.

No, screw it, I can't see him anywhere.

"Tobias!"

There's a sound. A rustling; then the bathroom door opens and Tobias steps out, making my entire body sag with relief.

"Yeah?" He looks me up and down and his face falls. "Oh shit, are you okay?"

My hands are on my hips, and I take a few seconds to concentrate on just breathing and releasing all the irrational thoughts that have been buzzing around my head for the past couple of hours.

"Yeah, I'm okay. I'm sorry, I didn't mean to scare you. I got freaked out and overreacted."

I take another deep breath and make a point of looking him in the eye like a normal human.

Which is the first time I notice that he's not dressed. He is, in fact, only wearing a towel. His hair is so wet that the dark curls are dripping onto his face, and his skin is flushed from the shower. Well, the parts of his skin that aren't still covered in bruises.

I've always thought of Tobias as small. Not in a metaphorical way, but just like someone who I could fit my hands around. As much as I've tried to suppress that thought. But I think it's actually a combination of the fact that he's several inches shorter than me and has a tendency to wear baggy clothes he drowns in, even before he was borrowing from my wardrobe. As well as the way he often huddles over and makes himself smaller, shrinking into the background of any room he enters.

The night he first showed up, everything was so chaotic that actually looking at him was the last thing on my mind. Especially considering how swollen and bloody his entire body was. But now, apart from one huge, angry looking bruise covering most of his ribs on the left side, the rest of his chest looks mostly normal.

There's more muscle to him than I would have expected. Not bulk, but definition. The same water droplets that were rolling down his face are also dripping off the curve of pecs and abs and biceps. Proportional to his body and still slender, but all giving a real impression of strength that I wasn't expecting.

What other parts of himself does he hide away from everyone?

It's a long, convoluted train of thought that careens me completely off course from what I was supposed to be focusing on, and as soon as I realize that, all the fear rushes back in.

"Shit," I say, for lack of anything better forming in my brain. "Your ribs look terrible."

Tobias squirms, and I immediately feel bad for drawing attention to it.

"You look good, though. Overall, I mean. It's just that bruise." The words spill out like I can somehow walk this whole thing back, but it definitely makes it all more awkward.

Tobias continues to stand in the doorway to the bathroom, half-naked and seeming caught between wanting to run away and move closer.

"I'm sorry. I'm apparently only capable of putting my foot in my mouth whenever you're around."

That gets a little smile out of him. He leans his head to the side, clearly agreeing with me, before moving a few steps toward me.

"So, why did you come in here looking all pressed?"

"Is there any chance you'll let me not tell you, and accept it's for your own good?"

"If you want me to put your dick in a blender," he deadpans while I flinch at the imagery.

"Yeah, I didn't think so. Get dressed and then we can talk about it."

He shifts his weight from side to side, his unease obvious. The windows are covered, like always, but his gaze still flits toward them.

I realize I have to rip off the Band-Aid.

"Eamon came to the bar tonight." Tobias doesn't move, but I can hear the uptick in his breathing, so I move slowly and steadily toward him as I continue to talk. "Don't be scared. It's okay. He was looking for you, but I think I convinced him I don't know anything. He stayed until close and then went and sat in his car in the parking lot. I did everything exactly like I normally would—locked everything, set every alarm, and then came upstairs."

Tobias wraps his arms around himself, hunching in. His face is impassive, though. I think I can see a faint tremor in his hands, but he's not letting any of it travel to his face.

"It's fine. I'm fine. It's not, I mean. But it was always going to happen. Thanks for taking care of it."

My brow furrows. I don't know exactly what reaction I was expecting—shock, fear, even anger at me for trying to baby him. This blank stoicism wasn't on the list.

"It's okay to be scared. It's only me here. You can be whatever. I don't care." I watch him, but he doesn't respond. "As long as you don't put my dick in a blender."

Tobias snorts, shaking his head at me and bringing back that ghost of a smile. I think a little hint of a tear slips out, because he quickly swipes at his eye and sniffs a little, but I pretend not to notice.

"Alright. Bet. I'm fine, though."

"Okay," I nod. "Do you wanna watch a movie? I'll let you traumatize me."

"Sure."

He walks into the bedroom reluctantly, I'm assuming to get dressed. I let myself do a very quick, silent sweep of the room, double-checking the windows are locked. Not that you could get to them easily, anyway. I know I'm being paranoid.

I make sure I'm on the couch before he gets out, because I don't want my anxiety to set off his own. He walks over to me but pauses before sitting down.

"Are you hungry?" I ask.

He shakes his head. Then he looks at the couch, and I realize that this couch has kind of become a minefield for us. It's entirely my fault, because I'm the one who keeps changing the rules. But as much as I don't want to overstep, I want to deprive him of something he clearly needs right after I just freaked him out even less.

"Do you wanna sit with me?"

I lean back as I say it, trying to look relaxed and inviting. Tobias doesn't speak, but he nods. Once the offer is out there, he doesn't hesitate to make himself comfortable. He climbs into the narrow space between me and the arm of the couch, so most of his body weight is on my lap and he's half-facing the TV, half-leaning against me. Then he works his way closer and closer against my chest until he finds the spot that apparently works for him.

The whole process sinks into me like a weight, filling me up and tying me to the spot. As I hand him the remote, I realize how completely laughable it was that I might ever have been able to stop myself from having this.

Not that I have any idea what *this* is. Not that it should ever be more than what it is right now. But even that is already too overwhelming to be something I could possibly give up.

Hopefully, Tobias will sleep again. I'll sit, and wait, and watch for Eamon. So he can sleep safe.

Chapter Eleven

TOBIAS

I feel more rested than I have in a very long time, and I could definitely get used to this. The twitchy, nervous energy that controls me whenever I'm awake is still there, for sure. But it's dulled. Like there's a piece of fabric sitting in between me and the electric sparks that power that part of my brain.

The awkwardness that I've gotten used to is missing when Gunnar and I wake up. And all through the normal morning—well, afternoon technically, but morning for us—things like teeth-brushing and whatever, it never makes itself known. We're both quiet. But it's a peaceful quiet.

I keep eying Gunnar for signs that he's about to freak out. There's been a constant sense of push and pull with him from the start. Which I get. I kind of crash-landed into his life, and he doesn't owe me shit. Especially not just because no matter how much I deny it, I really do follow him around like a desperate teenager with a crush.

It's humiliating but inexorable, so I've learned to accept it. And if he's going to insist on standing there in the kitchen, barefoot but still wearing slacks and that stupid wrinkled button-down, with the shirtsleeves rolled up to his elbows so I can see the way the muscles and tendons in his forearms flex as he gently cracks some eggs into a frying pan... All deep olive skin and the kind of dark body hair that isn't overwhelming but reeks of masculinity...

I can't be held responsible for my actions.

I'm only human. And not a very strong one at that.

So, I sit at the table in the oversized loungewear that I've come to live in permanently, openly ogling whenever I get a glimpse of the veins protruding from the side of his forearm.

I've suffered in life, and I deserve a little something in return. The horny police can't stop me.

"Tobias?"

The voice snaps me out of my daze. Apparently, I wasn't paying attention to Gunnar actually speaking to me while I was too busy objectifying him.

"Mm?"

"Do you want coffee?" He's staring at me like I'm being weird, so I probably am, but what else is new? At least I don't have drool on my face.

I think.

"I can get it. You're fine."

Hopping up, I busy myself with getting coffee for both of us. Focusing on the physical task helps me order my thoughts and pull them back in line. Away from the pervy place, which is harmless but also a little pathetic. Especially considering it's not like I have a chance with someone like Gunnar for anything more than pity snuggles until he eventually releases me back into the wild.

And also away from the paranoid place that still sees Eamon lurking in every corner. Which is less abrasive now than a few days ago. But I think that's because I've acclimated to the constant sense of dread, not because it's actually lessened. I still think I see him, hear him, smell him, or whatever, a hundred times a day. But my body was already used to coasting on the jagged edge of an adrenaline rush from one minute to the next, so shifting to this particular kind of adrenaline rush hasn't been too much of an adjustment.

It's fine. It's a feeling I know how to work with. If it never goes away, I can deal with that. As long as *Eamon* goes away.

The reality of that happening isn't great, but I'm not ready to seriously think through that yet.

I do, however, have something else to distract the both of us with for a little while. Something where I can be useful for a change.

"I was thinking last night while you were at work."

I turn around and lean back against the kitchen counter, resting on my hands while the coffee sputters and percolates behind me. Gunnar continues to poke at the eggs and sausage, which are apparently the only non-microwavable foods he keeps in the house, but he gives me a wary look all the same.

When I don't get a verbal response, I take that as a sign to continue.

"I think I have a plan to help Kasia."

Gunnar frowns. "That's not what I thought you were going to say, but okay. Hit me."

"You said he was a pedophile, right?"

"Yeah," he says, his frown deepening as his gaze returns to the eggs. "She found awful shit on his phone. I know she still feels guilty about not being able to do anything to stop him, but she did everything she could. She filed reports, tried to get other people to file, made anonymous complaints. There was never enough evidence. And she couldn't exactly stalk him when she filed for an order of protection that prevented contact between them."

I nod along, because all that tracks.

"Totally. I get it. I probably would have felt responsible, too, if I were her. Because he's this piece of shit, and she's been the one serving him breakfast all those years. Knowing he was a scumbucket and having made her peace with the repercussions that had for her, but not realizing how much farther it went."

Gunnar is staring at me instead of the eggs now. I'm not sure if it's because the breakfast comment was too on the nose considering he's currently cooking for someone who is technically a criminal squatting in his apartment, or because

I let too much of my own thoughts slip out like an unstoppable moron, but I'm going to power through.

"Anyway," I shake my head, as if that'll help me focus. "The point is, I get it. But there really was nothing she could do that probably wouldn't have led to him killing her. People like that protect their secrets closely, because they know how bad it would be if it got out. But also, because they always, always, *always* have evidence. I think it's something about the way their minds are broken. They can't let go, even if they know it makes them more likely to be caught. There's always evidence if you look hard enough. I've seen like a thousand documentaries on sex offenders, and it always ends the same way."

Gunnar's eyes narrow at that. "So, in addition to watching every piece of fictional cinema that's been designed to deep-fry your brain cells in human misery, you also watch documentaries about pedophiles. That's what you're telling me? Is that the next stage in how you're planning on taking my television's virtue?"

It's not really funny because of the topic of the conversation, but it kind of is. Also, he just looks so fucking serious as he says it. Spatula in one hand, the other on his hip, those forearms still working hard to distract me, and just a teeny tiny bit of sweat beading on his forehead from the oven. One of the only imperfections I've ever seen on him, and it still looks like spray on. The perfectly formed sweat droplets of someone who always has their shit together.

So fuck it. I laugh. I laugh and turn to pour us the coffee before I finally get to the point.

"I'll tell you what, if you go along with my genius plan, we can watch something boring about baby panda bears or whatever normal people like. Promise. But hear me out first."

"I know I'm not going to like this," he grumbles, but doesn't object.

"There has to be evidence. That's my point. And he knows that she can't touch him and she's also the only one who probably knows this about him, or at least believes it. So, he thinks he's safe. Arrogance is also a common theme with these guys."

Gunnar rolls his eyes, but I'm assuming it's directed at Jorden and everyone like him rather than me.

"So, let's go get it."

Now I have his attention.

"What the fuck do you mean, 'let's go get it'?"

"Exactly that." I put his coffee on the counter next to him while he unfreezes his brain enough to plate up the food. "Let's go get it. This man cannot possibly live in a fortress. He'll have evidence of his horrific federal crimes somewhere in his home, I would bet anything on it. And I'm literally a professional cat burglar."

Gunnar stares at me. This isn't new information to him, but for whatever reason—either the fact that I'm acknowledging it out loud, or maybe just the playful enthusiasm I've got going on now that I finally don't feel like baked shit for once—his mouth is hanging slightly open, and his synapses can't seem to form a sentence to reply to me.

I do the only natural thing, clawing the air in front of me very slowly and hissing like a cat to get my point across.

"See?"

Gunnar blinks.

"You want to break into Kasia's abusive ex's house to steal evidence of his underage sex-abuse crimes? While you're currently on the run from your own abusive ex?"

The words come out very slowly, like he knows he has several objections, but he can't quite articulate them yet.

"Yep." I nod. When he doesn't make a move with the plates, I grab them out of his hands and put them on the little table before returning to stand right in front of him. "It'll be fun. Use my evil powers for good, or whatever. Besides, I'll have you by my side to protect me, right?"

My tone is teasing, and I tug at the front of his shirt and bat my eyelashes at him coquettishly while I say it, which seems to snap Gunnar out of his shocked daze.

He bats my hand away from his shirt gently, looking at me with a powerful combination of annoyance and indulgence that I kind of want to soak up like a sad, underwatered little houseplant.

"You're terrible. I can't decide which is more concerning: the catatonic version of you that makes me worry so much I might drive into a ditch, or this version," he says, gesturing at me vaguely. Then he smiles, leaning into the ever-shrinking gap between our faces. "You're dangerous, little one. You know that, right?"

My stomach flip-flops. I may be the one who started flirting, but I wasn't expecting to get it back in such a real way, and my body was totally unprepared for it.

I've been appreciating Gunnar in both a personal and an aesthetic way for months now, and it's only intensified the last couple of days. But my dick, unsurprisingly, has not been interested in the conversation. He's been preoccupied with sad shit, and I was happy to let him mope. It's not like I really needed him for anything.

But right now, with Gunnar looking at me from a few inches away and my clothes still smelling like him after spending the whole night sleeping in his arms, some things are waking up. The chipped and dented connections in that part of my body are finding ways to line themselves back up again, and while the feeling is very fucking abrupt, it's not unwelcome.

I have completely forgotten what we were talking about. Is it my turn to speak?

Gunnar seems to break from his own lascivious trance around the same time and takes half a step back from me. His face falls, and he scrubs one hand down it.

"Let's just eat. We can talk about it afterward, okay? I'm not crazy about the idea of putting you in danger, but I'm also very aware that I can be overprotective, and when it comes to catching a child predator, I might need to have some perspective. But first..." he trails off, hesitating for a second before reaching out to touch my cheek. Just for a second. So lightly I can barely feel it. "Fuck it," he sighs. "Let's just eat first, and then you can talk me into it."

I feel like I've been spun around and turned inside out, but the smile comes to my face, anyway. I'll win this fight. He knows it; I know it. It's only a matter of time.

Six hours later, we're parked in Gunnar's car down a shitty back road behind Mishicot. Mishicot is not far from the bar and is essentially the trailer park version of a 'town', with a population of 196.

I've managed to avoid it the entire time I lived in Possum Hollow, despite being a fifteen-minute drive away. And now I'm here, because this is my stupid plan, and I talked Gunnar into going along with it approximately four and a half minutes after we finished breakfast.

Kasia and Sav are watching the bar. Kasia knows we're doing something, but doesn't have the details, so she can't be implicated. Sav, we decided, got all the details, just in case we needed rescuing. Then it took a long time for me to piece together something from Gunnar's closet that I could actually do crime in—very old, too-small black work-out pants that he should have thrown away a long time ago, with the cuffs rolled up, along with a t-shirt I will be daring him to still fit into later and a black sweatshirt that Kasia lent me. Because if you account for my broader shoulders and her heftier chest coming out in a wash, we're kind of the same size.

"It's not too late to change your mind, you know."

Gunnar looks at me from the driver's seat, the same grave-but-kind look in his eye that I've come to recognize. He almost always seems to pull that expression when he's more worried *for* you than *about* you, but it's cute either way. I'll take it.

"I'm not changing my mind. This is important. I'll get whatever I can find, like a laptop or a secret hard drive. They always have a secret hard drive. Leave it out, leave the door open and call the cops. He gets busted, goes to jail, Kasia lives happily ever after, and I get rid of a tiny little percentage of my karmic debt. It's simple."

"And what if you can't get in?"

I snort. "Please. The man lives in a trailer. If I can't break in without leaving a trace, I deserve to get caught."

The skin around Gunnar's eyes tightens, but he doesn't say anything.

"You're my look out. Don't worry, everything's going to be fine."

He pauses before turning even more in his seat to look at me and reaching out like he's going to touch my cheek again, but then quickly pulling his hand back in.

"Then why do you look nervous?"

I freeze for a second, but then let out all my tension with a huff. I guess I can tell him? Otherwise, he'll just assume it's about this, which it really isn't. This is kiddie-league level theft.

I roll my eyes, because I know it's going to sound so stupid when I say it, but I also know he won't leave it alone until I tell him.

"It's nothing. I'm not nervous about this. I've just never been to Mishicot before. I've always avoided it because it's where my shitty sperm donor is from."

Gunnar raises his eyebrows as the information sinks in. "Is he still here?"

Shaking my head, I avoid his gaze. "No, he bounced a long fucking time ago. I don't think anyone knows where he is. I've never even met him." Gunnar is waiting for the other shoe to drop, clearly, so I give it to him. "But I do have a half-brother that I've also never met, and he lives here."

There's a long silence. It's fine. I wouldn't know what to say to that either.

"Do you wanna meet him?"

That was the last thing I expected him to ask, and the question makes me freeze.

"Um... I don't know. No? I don't hate him or anything. He's just some random guy whose mom also got knocked up by a scumbag. It's not like we mean anything to each other, though. And there's a chance he could have turned out just like our father, which means he's not someone I want to be around. What's the point?"

Gunnar seems to take his time considering this. When he finally speaks, his voice is low, and his words seem to be carefully chosen.

"I'm not one of those people that believes you owe your family everything just because you're blood related. Family is more complicated than that, and no one should have to keep people in their life that are hurting them. In whatever way. But," he takes a deep breath and then he really does touch me, tilting my chin up to force me to look at him. It makes me feel small and shivery, but in the best possible way. "Just because he doesn't mean anything to you now doesn't mean he couldn't one day. If you did want to meet him eventually, there's nothing wrong with that. Family can be thin on the ground sometimes, and it's not embarrassing to want a little more."

The words tumble in my head out of order, not totally making sense. The thought makes my gut twist, though. I don't have the capacity for this right now. I file it away as something to deal with later.

Much later.

"Yeah, sure. Maybe." I shrug. "Come on, let's get this show on the road. We have some sneaking to do before we get to his place, and I think you might be too tall to be stealthy. If you're not a good look-out, I'll have to fire you and replace you with Kasia. Just saying. She seems like she would be an excellent guard dog."

Gunnar really does roll his eyes at me this time, but he drops the subject. We both seem to take a few more seconds to look at each other before finally, silently, slipping out of the car.

Chapter Twelve

GUNNAR

It's been too long. Way too long. This can't be the normal amount of time it takes to break into someone's home. Everyone would get caught if that were true.

I look at my watch, but the time tells me it's actually been about eight minutes since Tobias and I parted ways. Not the forty-five that it felt like.

Kasia thought there would be a good chance her ex wouldn't be at home right now, because it's a Thursday night and he normally goes 'bowling' on Thursdays. Which sounds like it's code for getting drunk and doing meth, but bowling might also be involved.

She was right. We scoped the place out, and confirmed that he's not here, at least. It's a long single-wide on an unincorporated lot, so the neighbors are far enough away that we were able to get in on foot without being noticed. It seems like he values his privacy.

Which isn't surprising, but plays in our favor right now. I'm crouched in the yard behind a lean-to that might pass for a utility shed, watching to make sure he doesn't come home. If he does, I'm close enough to make it to the building under the cover of dark, bang loud enough for Tobias to hear, scramble around the back, and then hopefully get both of us the fuck out of here.

Not that I made a single solitary part of this plan. It was all him. It didn't even take him long. He dropped the whole thing in these fluid, unhesitating sentences full of technical jargon that I only half-understood. It was so impressive; I forgot to check my enthusiasm for a skill he only has because of the crimes he's been forced to commit.

Is he really not done yet? How hard can it be to find a laptop?

I wait and wait and wait. It's so dark out here that my eyes keep playing tricks on me, making it seem like a figure is emerging out of the tree line. Every minute that passes, my heart rate continues to mount, and I swear I can feel my individual blood vessels tightening in my body.

This is absolutely the last time we do something like this.

Never again.

Every sound that hits my ears is tires crunching over cold earth until my brain realizes it's not. Over and over and over again, while I picture what would happen if we got caught. If Jorden tried to beat the shit out of Tobias. If he wasn't alone when he came home, and we were so outnumbered, I couldn't even hope to protect him.

If—shit, what if—Jorden is even more of a scumbag than I thought and has connections to the Banna?

That's the thought that chills me right down to my bone marrow. Hot to cold in an instant, like I got dipped in liquid nitrogen.

I can feel my thoughts begin to race out of control, just like my pulse. It's so overwhelming that I barely notice the noise behind me, and Tobias is forced to tap me on the shoulder.

Whipping around, I move so fast I clearly startle him. It's not enough to wipe the grin off his face, though.

Grin. He is full-on, gleefully grinning. I honestly don't think I've ever seen it before. He looks gorgeous even when he's miserable, but this is something else.

I'm choking on relief and unfettered anxiety and this sudden wave of adoration for him, which I still don't know how to address, so I don't think it through and let myself throw my arms around him.

"Whoah," he says, but doesn't pull away. After a few seconds, he relaxes into my too-tight grip and puts his arms around my waist. "Are you okay?"

"We're never doing this again. That was terrifying." I blow out a breath, leaning back to look at him but still not letting go. "I don't like it when you're in danger."

He raises his eyebrows, looking a little confused but still smiling.

"Technically, we were both in danger. And we still are, because we're standing at the scene of the crime. But it's cute when you go all protective on me, Gunnar."

He's teasing me a little, but there's also sincerity running underneath it. I pull him back in and hold him tight, squeezing him hard for just a moment until my body is satisfied that he's okay. Tobias doesn't seem to mind. He presses his face into my shoulder, in the same spot he always finds, like it was made to fit him perfectly, waiting until I get myself under control.

When we pull apart this time, I take a big step back, so I'm not tempted to keep clinging to him.

"Ready to go? You can call the cops on the way. Unless you wanna hide in the bushes and watch it all go down."

I shake my head. "No way. We've been through enough mortal peril for one day. My heart can't take it. There's a reason I'm going gray this young, and it isn't because I've lived such a stress-free life."

Tobias snorts but acquiesces, and together we head away from the trailer. He's still limping, but it isn't worse than before, which was another worry I had about this expedition. He doesn't object when I wrap an arm around his waist so he can lean on me, though.

We walk through the woods toward the car as he tells me what he found. And while I'm glad he found it so we can hopefully get this guy arrested, it's even worse than I thought.

One normal laptop sitting out that had Instagram chats with teenage girls open. One not very well hidden but encrypted laptop that probably had the really bad stuff. And one very, very well-hidden hard drive that he obviously didn't bother to encrypt because of that, which Tobias hooked up to the regular laptop and found a horde of photos of underage girls.

All disgusting. All of which he relates to me with a sad but matter-of-fact expression. He left the pictures open on the one laptop, left the other laptop next to it and then left the door open with everything in plain view, so the cops can come in when they get here.

Sav even gave me a burner phone to make the 911 call with, which I would not have thought of. Clearly, I'm not cut out for this.

By the time everything is wrapped up, we're back in the car and on our way home. We should feel happy. We got away completely unharmed. Not even any close calls. But Tobias's grin is long gone, and instead of being elated, I feel like something's missing.

All that adrenaline and frenzy from earlier is floating around inside me, and it's as if it has nowhere to go. There was no big dramatic chase sequence or a fight to end the situation. One minute, I was on the edge of a heart-pounding panic attack. Then everything was just... fine?

It doesn't make sense.

I'm in a daze when we get back to the bar, but not so much that I can't keep an eye out for Eamon. Sav and Kasia both promised to call if they saw him. I circle the whole place three times in the car before actually pulling into the parking lot, and even then, surrounded by dead space, I can see the nerves that Tobias is trying to hide.

It was the same when he left the apartment earlier—for the first time in days—to hustle into the car, despite us checking the surroundings as many times as possible. No one acknowledged it. It makes sense to be scared.

"Ready?"

He nods, stealing a glance at me. I see him reach for the door handle, but before he can, I grab his other hand to pull his attention back to me.

The atmosphere has completely shifted from earlier when he was so elated for once. I hate that, but at least he's not bothering to hide from me. That feels like progress.

"I know it's pointless to say, 'don't be scared', because you can't control it, and being scared is a logical thing to feel after everything that's happened. But no matter how scared you are, I need you to remember that I'm here. I'm here, and I will do anything I can to make you feel less scared. Whether that's actually physically protecting you, or just falling asleep on the couch with you and your awful movies. Whatever it takes. The fear will pass, but I'll still be here."

I don't know how I expected him to react. I wasn't planning what I was saying. The words just tumbled out of me. But Tobias's mouth twists, and he seems to go through a convoluted series of emotions before he speaks or moves.

Instead of saying anything, Tobias slowly and carefully shifts in his seat and leans toward me. My hand is still resting lightly on his arm, but he's careful not to dislodge it.

He moves closer and closer until there's a fraction of the space left between us, and he still doesn't stop. Before I have the chance to breathe, Tobias slides his other hand against my neck, his skin cool and soft compared to where I'm overheating with stress. He leaves it resting there as he closes the last few inches, and then he kisses me.

It's tender. Closed-mouth, but there's a heat behind it that would never let me mistake the kiss for anything other than what it is. Time seems to unspool as my body relaxes into it, all his softness leaning into me.

He's the one who breaks away, but he moves just as carefully and deliberately as he did when he came closer.

His voice cracks a little when he starts to speak.

"I know you're going to think that was about some kind of misplaced gratitude or hero worship. I know you've been tying yourself in knots over it. Which is dumb, but also not. You're a good person. But I need you to hear me very clearly when I tell you that I didn't kiss you out of gratitude. I am grateful, but that's not why I kissed you."

Tobias is still hovering close to me, and he smells like spearmint and my soap that he's been borrowing. It's simple, but it's still intoxicating enough to threaten to distract me.

"I kissed you because I've wanted to for a very long time. And the more time I spend with you, and the more you say things like what you just said, the more I realize that I deserve to do some of the things I want to. I'm not going to feel guilty about it and neither are you. Got it?"

I nod slowly, feeling like I'm in a trance. Like the brief taste of him was enough to work its way into me and send every part of my body slithering to a slow stall.

"Good. Now let's go inside."

He holds my hand for the short, tense walk across the parking lot. We go upstairs using the back entrance, my head whipping around the entire time to make sure we're not being watched. As soon as we make it inside without incident and the door is locked, though, the tension bleeds away.

"What do you want to do now?" I ask because we're standing awkwardly in the middle of the apartment, close enough to but not touching, hovering in each other's orbits like satellites about to collide.

"Kiss me."

It's a command, even if it's soft-spoken. All my doubts from before are still in my mind, but they've grown quieter and quieter the more time I've spent with him.

He was right, after all. Worrying about taking advantage of him is one thing. Depriving him of his own autonomy, especially when he's shown how fiercely protective he is of it, would be unforgivable. If he wants me to kiss him and I want to kiss him, I can't decide against it because I think it's better for him in the long run.

I have no idea what he really needs. I can only be here for him when he asks for it.

This time we're standing, so I have to step close before leaning down to kiss him. It makes me want to curl around him protectively, so I don't fight it. Within a few seconds, he's wrapped up in me, and his warm mouth opens under mine with a hint of desperation that I undeniably return.

My hands roam over his back, not pushing any boundaries, but exploring the smooth planes of muscle hidden under his clothes. Like I've done before, I lean over, looping one arm under his ass before hoisting him up into my arms with his legs bracketing my hips.

Tobias makes a small squeak of surprise when I do it this time. It's an incredible sound, and I want to devote a serious amount of energy to making him repeat it.

With him on my front like a koala, still eagerly swapping messy, breathless kisses, I stumble over the few steps to the couch and then drop us both onto it.

This couch is beginning to feel like the origin point of everything that's ever changed between us. I'll never be able to replace it now.

Once we're there, we can both sink into it. We alternate between frantic, intense kisses and languid making out. It's all glorious, and it seems to go on forever. I've been hard from the start, which I'm sure Tobias can feel underneath him. I'm careful not to move too much or grind into him, though, because I don't want to push.

I touch him everywhere that seems safe—his back, his arms, his face and his incredible, strong thighs that are straddling me, over and over. He pushes into the contact every time. It takes him longer to get hard than I did, but before long

I can see his erection tenting his borrowed pants. He doesn't really acknowledge it, so I don't either, but the longer we continue to tongue-fuck each other's mouths, the more I feel him writhing under my hands.

Eventually, he's rocking his hips into me. Delicately, not enough to be considered grinding, but more like an afterthought. Like his aching cock is seeking friction.

I break off the kiss for a second—both of our mouths spit-slick and swollen—but hold him in place by the back of his neck so he knows I'm not going anywhere.

"Can I touch you?" My eyes flick down to the tent in his pants. "It's okay if you don't want to. There's no rush. But if you want me to, I'd like to. It doesn't have to go any further than that."

Tobias is panting, his eyes flicking from side to side for a minute while he seems to gather his thoughts.

Finally, in a single breath that turns into a whine, he says one word.

"Please."

Arousal pulses through me just at the thought, and I have to be very conscious not to grind up against his ass where my own erection is lying snug against his crease. It's an incredible tease, but I also know without a doubt that it's a line not to cross, no matter how distracted I get.

Instead, I focus on him. I kiss him deeply, not wanting him to get in his head, and begin to rub his cock through the fabric. There's already a damp spot, and he's completely rigid against my palm. His cock is slender, like him, and average length.

I tug down his pants and briefs in one movement, not removing them all together but enough that I can reach him. His entire length is a blushing pink color, cut, and fits perfectly in my hand. I wrap my fingers around him and stroke him a few times, slowly and gently, to get a feel for his reaction, only to have his hips buck as he moans into my mouth.

Keeping the slow pace, I'm a little shocked when Tobias breaks off the kiss. It's not to pull away, though. There's already redness crawling up his cheeks, and he's digging his fingers into my shoulders like he's clinging to me, but his mouth is hanging open to pant. His eyes are half-closed, thin lines of honey-brown gazing at me from under dark lashes.

"Does that feel good, baby?" I ask, when he still doesn't say anything.

Tobias nods, then gasps when I roll my thumb around the head of his cock before continuing to stroke. He's so hyper-sensitive, it's like every touch is setting off a chain reaction in him, and he's already overwhelmed.

"It's been—" he pants in between words, "—a long time."

I steal another quick kiss, his lips already parted for me, and then lean back to watch him come undone.

It's beautiful. He doesn't move a lot, like he's trying to keep himself small, still. But everywhere his hands are on me, I can feel the intensity in his touch. His fingers dig into my skin through my shirt, refusing to lean more than a few inches away.

"Take this off," he breathes.

I comply quickly, whipping off my shirt and then going back to stroking him. I can see that lust-drunk gaze roaming over me, taking me in, and I don't quite resist the urge to flex while he watches me.

Tobias makes a quiet moaning sound, one that draws out with the rhythm of my hand. I lean in closer to his mouth, as if I could steal the moan from him.

"Still good, baby?"

"Yes," he says. "Don't stop."

I don't. I keep the pace steady but gentle, and he continues to groan and mutter soft curses. His hips fuck up into my grip and his cock continues to weep over my fingers. Gradually, he seems to get closer to the edge. His breathing gets harsher, and I can see his muscles tense, while his length keeps flexing in my hand, like he's right on the cusp of coming.

"Fuck," he mutters, but it's more tense than dreamy this time.

"It's okay, Tobias. There's no rush."

I keep jerking him but use my other hand to cup his head. He opens his eyes to look at me, then screws them shut completely.

"It's hard..." he whispers. "I wasn't allowed to..." I see what he's getting at, even if he's not saying it. And I have to shove away the surge of anger that threatens to overtake me. "It's hard sometimes now."

He said enough. Consciously unclenching my jaw, I keep my hand moving softly over him and cradle his head as I lean in to whisper in his ear.

"You're here with me now. None of that matters. Nothing matters. You can take as long as you need. Now be a good boy and relax for me."

His eyelids fly open again at that, and I'm close enough to see his pupils dilate and his mouth move a little like he's about to say something.

I don't give him the chance. I kiss him again. Shallow, just lips against lips as we both pant and sigh, but distracting him.

"That's my good boy," I whisper directly into his mouth, feeling him shudder in return.

Letting go of his head, I move my free hand down to tug at his balls. They're tight, right up against his body, so I gently roll them around my palm and enjoy the feeling of him falling apart in response.

His breathy moans become sharper, so I pick up the pace of my strokes a little, although still with a loose grip. With one hand on his cock and one on his balls, I continue to work him while I whisper in his ear.

"You're doing so well, baby."

Another gasp.

"You're close. I can feel it. Let go for me. Be a good boy and make a mess all over my hand."

Sharp nails dig into the skin of my back as he starts to cry out—short, loud little cries in time with my strokes.

"Ah-ah-ah-ah-ah—"

His muscles tense, and then his body quivers over mine as wetness finally pulses out of him. It starts so slowly; just one long, arduous, bow-string-tight arch of his back with a cry, but then his hips are jerking and he's releasing more and more cum into the air.

It coats my fingers and chest in long stripes, while Tobias continues to shudder and contort himself through it.

"That's it," I keep whispering. "Such a good boy. You're doing so well. Don't stop."

I'm not really jerking him anymore, but I keep touching and stroking the hot skin of his cock until he finally pulls away from me with a gasp. He's a little wild-eyed, looking around him, so I pull him close and press his head against my neck the way he likes.

It doesn't take long for him to get on board. The shuddering continues, although he squeezes me so tight I can barely feel it. For a second, I think he might be crying. But he doesn't make a sound. Just heavy breathing as his body gradually comes down.

Minutes pass. Then more minutes. I fall into a contemplative space that feels like it's outside of time. My own erection waned, which I don't care about right now. I'm content to stroke and tug at the strands of hair curling around his ears and rub the overheated skin of his back, one of my hands shoved up inside his t-shirt.

Eventually, he leans back to look at me. His eyes are dry, but he looks worn out and dazed.

"Are you okay?"

Tobias bites his lip, looking smaller than I've ever seen him. But not scared. Not anxious or exhausted or overwhelmed. Just... soft. Like he's allowing me to hold him.

It's perfect.

He nods, though.

"You?" he asks, his voice raspy. "Did you?"

I shake my head. "I can do that later. It's fine. Right now, I want this."

Tobias doesn't argue, thank fuck. He shifts back into the position he was in before, but his posture is more relaxed this time. His fingers trace their way through my chest hair as he tucks his head under my chin and places the occasional kiss on my neck.

Yeah, I'm fucked. I could never come again, and this would still be all I wanted.

Absolutely fucked.

Chapter Thirteen

TOBIAS

Waking up in a bed for the first time all week is surreal. I'd gotten used to the couch. The comforting flicker of the TV chased away the kind of still darkness that I always find unnerving. And once Gunnar had started joining me there, it was a done deal. I was actually sleeping.

After last night though, he convinced me we needed to sleep somewhere fully horizontal for a change. He was right, of course. It couldn't possibly have been comfortable for him to curl up on that thing with me lying on top of him and him still in his fancy-ass street clothes. That doesn't mean that all this space isn't a little disconcerting.

As soon as wakefulness begins to filter through my synapses, I make the conscious decision not to open my eyes. I do, however, reach for Gunnar. It's warm underneath all these blankets, and my face is buried in the soft edges of them. My hands grope around underneath until I find the thick, solid lines of him before shuffling closer.

He's dressed. He insisted on putting on some buttery-soft sweats and a t-shirt to sleep in last night, even though I told him he didn't have to. He was undeterrable, though. It's hard to tell which of his sticking points are about him being weird in general and which are about him thinking he knows what's best for me, but I decided it wasn't worth the fight on this one.

I'll get him naked, eventually. Just the glimpse of him shirtless last night was not enough. I was too in a daze, lost in the struggle between intense pleasure and whatever else I was feeling to put my focus where it really belonged. But everything about him is just as inviting externally as internally.

He's muscular and strong, probably from years of lifting heavy shit at the bar, but he's not cut. I like it. Soft skin over a body that's just... firm. Solid. There. And everything about him contributes to his overall impression of size.

Gunnar seems larger than life to me most of the time, and watching him sweaty and panting in the low light, like a dark, shadowy version of himself that's all intensity, didn't do anything to change that.

But the feverish way he looked at me and kissed me had nothing on how he touched me. That was light—gentle, but not like I'm fragile—this incredible counterpoint to the rest of it.

I could swim around in a vat of all those endorphins and images for hours until I drowned, and I'd die happy.

"Are you awake, or are you just burrowing in your sleep?" Gunnar says when I find his arm and thread my head through it, fully ensconcing myself in both his body and the covers.

"I'm not awake."

"Ah." His voice is just as thick with sleep as mine, but he turns a little onto his side, throwing his other arm and one leg over me, as if he could pull me any closer. "That's what I thought. An unconscious burrower. Of course."

I huff into his warm skin, but then focus on letting his scent wrap around me in exactly the same way his body is.

I never put any stock in the idea of someone 'saving' me. I wasn't the type of person to sit around daydreaming about being swept off my feet by some guy who would keep me safe. Because there's no such thing. 'Safe' is a fragile, fictional concept and people are inherently unreliable.

Even the good ones who want to be there for you. Even Gunnar.

You never know what circumstances are going to hit.

But right now, I feel pretty safe. It's just not in the way I thought that fantasy was supposed to be selling me. I'm just as scared of Eamon as I was yesterday. The idea of him creeping up the stairs to break in still sends my nervous system into a fractious, incendiary meltdown. And while I know it's unlikely, if he really did burst in through those doors, I don't think Gunnar would physically make a damn bit of difference in the outcome.

In fact, it would probably just be worse. I'd have to watch Eamon hurt Gunnar before he finally shoved me back into captivity.

The reality of my existence hasn't changed, and my perception of it hasn't changed.

So why do I *feel* safe?

It doesn't make any sense. I'm not going to argue, though. I'll hang on to this feeling for as long as it lasts.

Gunnar is more than that, anyway. I'd want him even if he didn't make me feel a damn thing other than the same pervasive fascination I've always had with him. His understated but obvious intelligence, his gentle brand of strength, his misplaced bleeding-heart compassion. All of it. It sucked me in too hard and I refuse to be spat out anytime soon.

These are the thoughts that work their way through the layers of my sluggish mind as I press kisses and scrape my teeth over every part of him I can reach. Most of it is through the cotton of his t-shirt, but it makes him squirm all the same.

It barely takes a minute to get him breathing heavily, holding me close in the cage of his arms. His erection brushes against my thigh and he doesn't hide it from me, but it's not insistent.

I keep waiting for him to freak out. To baby me and tell me that I don't know what I'm doing, or the age gap between us is unethical, or whatever. Instead, he's been quiet. Contemplative, maybe. But peaceful. Not fighting it for once.

It seems the obvious choice to seize the moment. At the same time as Gunnar's big hand finds my face and pulls me into a filthy good morning kiss, I wrap my fingers around his length and stroke him. The moan he makes directly into my mouth is like crack.

After a little gentle groping, I let go of him so I can slide my hand into his pants and put my skin on his. He told me he was fine last night when he didn't get off. Of course he was, because he's just that self-sacrificing kind of guy. I was in too much of a daze to really worry about it, but it's time to make that up to him now.

Immediately, I get down to work. The feeling of his cock in my hand is waking up more of my own arousal that I was beginning to think was desiccated beyond the possibility of restoration. It's thick and weighty—solid, like the rest of him—but not so big that it's intimidating. I know there are plenty of size queens in the world who pride themselves on being able to take a porn-star sized piece of equipment, but that's not for me.

Shocking, I know.

The skin is velvety soft, and feeling the subtle changes in how he continues to firm up under my touch is making more heat pool low in my gut. I take a second to press my free hand to my crotch, because I need something to relieve the pressure, before I go back to stroking him in earnest.

Gunnar is fully on board. I wasn't expecting it, but I'm here for it. He's practically fucking my mouth with his tongue, his hands firm around my waist to hold me close. I can tell he's holding back at least a little, probably not thrusting his hips against me the way his body is telling him to, but that's alright.

I'll get him to let go, eventually.

Gunnar breaks off the kiss, panting, and I worry that the stray thought about him potentially freaking out jinxed me. Instead of backing away, though, he slowly finds the waistband of my pants with his thumbs and tugs it down until my aching cock is freed. Then he pushes back the covers so we can both see each other fully and repeats the same action with his own pants.

Once we're lined up next to each other, Gunnar readjusts my hand, so it's wrapped around both of us, and then covers my hand with his larger one. He has us both completely enveloped, and the feeling of warmth and pressure when he gives a slow, firm stroke is almost overwhelming.

I groan, and he rolls his hips to fuck his cock into mine as he continues to stroke. He keeps going, his movements slow and sure, just like last night. His free arm circles my waist to hold me close, and also just like last night, I start to come apart in his hands. Occasionally, we exchange open-mouthed kisses, but neither of us can concentrate enough for more than that.

The pressure between us continues to grow until it feels like the room is filled with nothing but the sounds of bitten-off moans and Gunnar's soft cursing. I'm close. I'm so close. It wasn't the same battle as it was last night. More of a normal, slow build until I feel like the crest of an orgasm is almost within my reach.

Then Gunnar shifts. It's not a lot, and I don't think he's even aware he's doing it. He presses closer, but his larger bulk means that I fall back, and instead of lying on our sides facing each other, suddenly I'm mostly on my back, lying under his weight.

Lord help me, I freeze.

There's no conscious thought of feeling afraid. Nothing connects in my brain from a to b to c that makes me decide to feel this way. It's like my brain is totally left out of the loop on the decision, and one minute my body is screaming at me on the brink of a mind-blowing orgasm, then it's completely still, waiting to see what will happen next.

I just want it to be over. It was amazing, but now I need it to be done before Gunnar notices so we can move on, and I can pretend this humiliating interlude never happened. These are the thoughts that circle my consciousness as I focus on not letting any of the sudden catatonic terror that slapped into me like a rogue wave show on my face.

But it's Gunnar. Of course he has to fucking notice.

"Tobias?" His lips are a few inches from mine, and his hand is still wrapped around both our cocks, although he's stopped moving it. "Honey, what's wrong?"

I don't say anything. I don't know if I can say anything. But I can feel my lip trembling, and as much as I want to avoid being seen by him at all, not looking at him right now sounds so much worse. I stare into his eyes, focusing on that little chunk of blue, while his expression crumples and he searches my face for clues.

It's probably not that hard to put together. I grasp the logic, but when he seems to understand and abruptly pushes away from me, it feels like he's ripping some of my skin off with him. Like he was the thing holding me together and without him, I'm left even more raw and exposed.

"No!" My voice is louder than I expected, and I hold him when I say it, tugging at his t-shirt that's already sweaty and stretched out from my grabby hands.

He freezes, then lets out a slow breath through his nose. His eyes are a little wider than they should be, but I can see the wheels turning as he tries to calculate his plan of attack.

He's leaned back far enough, so he's not on me anymore, which helps me take a full breath. I concentrate on doing that again and again, and then make myself blink. It's a weird sensation, having to consciously decide to do something your body normally does without your input. Like all your human parts have been replaced with mechanical ones that technically work, but none of them know how to talk to each other, so you're just a brain in a rust-bucket begging each body part to do its fucking job.

"Hey," he says it in a whisper this time, but he isn't moving farther away from me. "What's wrong? What happened? Talk to me."

"It's, um. It's okay." My tongue feels like it's too big for my mouth, and I'm hyper aware of the fact that my jaw is hanging open in an awkward, unnatural way. "It was just a weird moment. I'm not sure why. My brain went weird."

Well, those are words. Some of them are kind of in the right order, I guess. It's better than nothing.

But Gunnar is nodding solemnly, like everything I said makes total sense. Then I can almost see his thoughts turn inward again, like he's chewing over the situation until he gets to the center.

"Did everything feel good until right at that last minute?" he asks, reaching out slowly to stroke his hand up my side. His touch gets firmer when I push into it instead of pulling away, and it settles some of the anxiety still fizzing inside me.

I nod, and he thinks for a few more seconds.

"Did I touch you somewhere you didn't like? Or too hard, or do something that hurt?"

I think about it, my mind percolating like sludge, but I can't think of anything, so I shake my head 'no'.

More thinking.

"Was it because I rolled on top of you?"

I involuntarily hiss in a breath, and Gunnar nods. We both realize it at the same time. Even as the thought hits me, I can feel the ghost of his body weight on mine, crushing me into the mattress.

Which isn't right. He wasn't crushing me; he was barely leaning on me at all. But apparently that part of my brain decided to be way, way, way out of pocket and take its paranoia to the extreme.

"Okay. Okay," he repeats, almost to himself. "That makes sense. I won't do that again."

Gunnar pauses and looks at me—really looks at me, holding my gaze as if he's trying to inject me with whatever weird zen he seems to be full of.

"What do you want to do now?"

Ugh. Choices. Why is he giving me choices? I'm not good at organizing my thoughts at the best of times. This feels like a punishment.

I can't gather enough words together for a sentence, so I shrug. Then I make sure to tug at his shirt, so he knows I don't want him to go any farther away, which pulls a small smile out of him.

"Don't worry, I'm not going anywhere. Do you want to try to sleep some more?"

I shake my head. Fuck that. Like I need the extra nightmares.

"Do you want to get up and go do normal-people things until you can reset?"

Again—ugh. This time I answer with a whine that I hope is more adorable than annoying, throwing myself toward him and rubbing my face all over his shirt. It's practically wrecked at this point from all my manhandling and I'm a little proud of myself.

A soft chuckle escapes his lips, and he puts both his arms around me, letting one of those warm palms smooth up and down my back.

"Ok, we're not getting up yet. I'm out of ideas. Do you wanna just lie here? Snuggle?"

I snort, because the word sounds ridiculous coming out of his beardy, manly mouth. But it's also pretty sweet.

Climbing up the last few inches of his body, I press my mouth against his. It's chaste, but I don't let him pull away. After a few seconds of tension, we both relax into it.

Eventually, we end up exactly where we were before—lying on our sides, clinging to each other while exploring each other's mouths. His thick leg is in between mine and I'm riding it like a desperate teenager, while he's making these deep, reality-shifting, mind-numbingly hot moans every time I touch him basically anywhere.

Once the arbitrary panic has finally fled my body, my hard-on is back in force. All my thoughts of embarrassment are gone, and I'm chasing that high from before. Gunnar is hard too, although I notice that he's being very careful about where he touches me, and to not hold himself too close against my body.

I hate it. I understand it, and the kindness behind it is kind of heart-wrenching, actually. But right now, I just need to come, and I want him to be holding me when I do.

"More," I beg in between kisses. "Touch me again, please."

"Are you sure?"

I nod, looking him in the eye as our breath mingles between us.

"Please."

There's a flicker of hesitation. Only a flicker.

Then it's replaced by resolve. Gunnar rolls onto his back, leaving my heart lurching after him like I'm being abandoned. But his hands quickly reach out to grab me. Even from the awkward angle, he lifts me so easily. In a few seconds I've been rearranged to straddle his lap, while he scoots up until he's half sitting, propped against the headboard.

"How's this?" he asks, while he grabs my ass with one hand and encourages me to grind against him.

"*Hnng.*"

It's not a flattering sound, but it makes my feelings clear. I grab onto his shoulders for dear life while he squeezes my ass with his other hand as well, and soon he's built up a rhythm. It's like I'm riding him, but he's guiding me, controlling the movement with his firm, tender grasp.

It's incredible. But I still need to feel his skin against mine.

With fumbling hands, I tug down my sweats to tuck them under my balls and then do the same to him, just like before. The elastic is more restrictive in this position, but I kind of like it. Everything feels tight and intense, like I'm being held against him by a rubber band.

Once we're both free, I use one hand to jerk us off and the other to lean against his chest. He's still controlling my movements by rolling my hips against his, and it's all coming together with a synchronicity I never would have expected.

It's so luxurious. What is really just a quick and dirty mutual jerk off on the outside somehow feels like the most intoxicating, indulgent sex I've ever had. I don't bother to hold back the noises that I want to make, no matter how loud or over the top. I commit every noise he makes to memory.

"That's it, little one," he says, his voice strained. "You're doing so well. Look at you riding me, making me come with your perfect hand."

I let out a whine, because whenever he says these things, it makes my stomach clench with embarrassment while my dick gets even harder.

"Perfect. That's it. Don't stop touching me. Such a good boy to make me come so hard. Come with me."

The last sentence is said on a gasp, and then I feel his cock pulse against to mine. Thick ropes of cum spurt out, so much more cum and with so much more force than I was expecting. Gunnar is completely tense from head to toe, his fingers digging into the muscle of my ass while I work him through it, his chest and my hand both coated in his load.

He lets out this raspy, broken groan that fucking does me in. With another stroke, I join him. My cum streaks across his t-shirt, mingling with his, and I clutch at the fabric to hold myself up as all the blood in my body floods away from my brain.

I'm panting so hard I can't think straight. The buzz of orgasm is still in my veins, and I'm not ready to let go. Without thinking, I drop both of our cocks and lean forward.

There's cum everywhere. Gunnar's ruined shirt, his beard, the hair-covered portion of his stomach that was exposed where the shirt rode up. I want it.

I start licking at every stripe of cum I can find. The need to have him inside me—like this, not in the way I can't think about yet—is sudden and overwhelming. Gunnar freezes, but he doesn't stop me. He moans when I lick across the skin under his belly button, and when I get to his neck, he lifts his chin to give me better access.

It's perfect. Simple. I lick and suck and devour every drop of him that I can find until I finally collapse on top of him; my spent dick still hanging out and more exhausted than I have any right to be.

Now I might consider trying to go back to sleep.

We lie there for a long time. Cleanup is needed. Food as well, probably. Getting up and doing real-people things. But right now, this feels good, and also like the maximum amount of things I'm willing to handle.

"Tobias?" Gunnar breaks the silence after a long time, his arms still wrapped around me as I lie on top of him, his fingers tracing patterns over my back.

"You know you say my name a lot. I kind of like it. It sounds prettier when you say it, for some reason."

"It's a pretty name," he says.

I shrug. I guess, but I've never really had feelings one way or the other.

"It's Polish. Or popular in Poland, or something. My deadbeat dad picked it, apparently. According to my mom, he was very insistent, which is weird for a kid you have no intention of ever meeting. At least she gave me her last name. I'd look dumb as hell walking around with a Polish last name."

Gunnar pauses for a while, frowning before he responds. "Maybe he intended to meet you, but then something happened. Or maybe he just changed his mind and started making shitty choices. It's nice that he cared a little, right? Even if it was only for a minute?" Then he smiles, touching me on the cheek. "I don't think you'd look dumb with any kind of last name."

Another shrug. "Whatever. It doesn't affect me." Because I have nothing to do with that man, and the fact that he named even a part of me is bad enough.

Gunnar tenses, like he's about to say something else, but nothing comes out.

"Sorry, wait," I add. "You were going to ask me something?"

"Oh, yeah. I was just going to say... I'm sorry I pushed against this. I was wrong. And a dumbass. I'm not letting you go anywhere."

Now I lift my head enough to look him in the eye. It's hard to keep myself from feeling the storm of emotion forming in my head, but I do my best to push it all down.

"Yeah?"

"Yeah," he says, running his fingers through my hair. "We gotta get you out of all that shit, though. You can't be trapped up here like a princess in a tower forever."

We both laugh at that, but it's forced. Probably because neither of us has any idea how that's going to happen.

At least Gunnar wants to try. That's more than I've ever gotten from anyone before. It's a fucking start.

Chapter Fourteen

GUNNAR

"You are so smitten," Kasia says as she pushes past me to reach for more napkins. "It's disgusting. I think it could be contagious and anyone who gets too close to you is going to walk away looking like an anime character that's nothing but heart eyes. Who are you and what happened to my lonely, insular friend who buries himself in work and other people's problems?"

There's a pause, because I'm not sure which part of that ramble I'm supposed to tackle first.

"Don't hold back, Kasia. You're too demure sometimes. Tell me how you really feel."

She huffs a laugh but continues to talk and polish glasses at the same time.

"So, what happened to all your boundaries? I see he didn't magically age ten years since last week."

Sighing, I turn to look at her. I feel a twinge of extra guilt on top of the low thrum of constant guilt that's pretty much been my companion since all this happened.

"I don't know. I keep going back and forth on whether I'm being mature and respectful of his autonomy as an adult, or if I'm just making fancy excuses to soothe myself because I gave in to what I wanted, even though I should have put a stop to it. Am I being a gross old man? Or is this not a big deal and I need to stop infantilizing him?"

Kasia rolls her eyes for what feels like the hundredth time so far today. "I swear, you are the most dramatic person I know. And that includes people I met before I gave up on dating."

"That's not an answer."

She freezes, pinning me down with a look. "What do you want? Absolution? I'm not your priest; I don't have any authority here. Just because I hold a membership card to more oppressed social groups than you do doesn't make me in charge of right and wrong. Figure your shit out."

Her tone is sharp, and it's matched by her movements when she goes back to wiping the glasses. I feel yet another twinge of guilt then, because I didn't mean to piss her off.

"I'm sorry. I know I'm being self-involved. I can't stop thinking about it, and I don't want to do something that Tobias looks back on in a decade with a different perspective and hates me for."

The biggest, most exhausted sigh comes out of her mouth, but at least some of the fight seems to go out of her.

"Christ. Okay, I'm going to give you exactly one piece of wisdom, because I still owe you in that department. But then we're talking about something nice, because I'm fucking weary." She pauses, clearly for dramatic effect. It works, though. "In my experience, the kind of guys who get into gross age-gap relationships are doing it specifically because they want someone they feel like they can control and manipulate. They sought out someone young for that purpose. It's different from just ending up there. And the people who want that power imbalance in a relationship are not sitting up at night contemplating the ethical ramifications of it. 'K?"

I tip my head from side to side, because I do see what she's saying. It doesn't resolve my conflicting emotions, but there's logic there.

"Oh, and if you imply that being in your thirties makes you objectively old, instead of just older than him, one more fucking time…"

She doesn't finish the sentence, but between the rabid look in her eye and the wine glass she's pointing in my direction, her point is made.

"Oh, that's right," I say, a slow smile spreading across my face. "How close are we getting to your birthday? It's what—a month? Are you excited? Should I get you some cardigans so we can match when you start joining me every evening to sit by the fire and read? Would you like to hear about the advantages of joining the AARP?"

Now she really does shove me in the chest. It's hard enough to make me hit the counter, but she's fighting back her laughter the whole time, and so am I.

It feels good. After all the drama of the last couple of weeks, I already feel lighter. And seeing Kasia managing to not get pulled under by the riptide of her own drama is something I think I needed.

When she arrived today, she'd given me a brief rundown about Jorden—he'd been arrested, her lawyer told her things were looking positive for him getting a real sentence this time, and her custody issues were hopefully about to dry up. Which doesn't cover all her issues, but helps. Then she'd thanked me for my help, and said if I ever mention it again, she'll put laxative in my whiskey.

I understand. We all need to move on from the sad things before new sad things show up. Which is why I'm pretty proud I've got her laughing out loud at me barely an hour after that conversation.

"I've never had a real job, but I don't think you're supposed to laugh this much at work," Tobias says, his voice cutting in as he appears from the back.

We're not open yet, and he's been here since I came down. I didn't even have to convince him. He is already a world of better than just a few days ago, and watching him interact with people instead of being forced to hole up in the apartment twenty-four hours a day is a relief.

The bruises on his face are almost faded, just a sallow yellow tinge to the skin under his eye and around his jawline. I know the big one on his ribs is bad, but it's improving, at least. He's still limping, but it's not dramatic anymore. Although that doesn't make the urge to carry him everywhere any less overwhelming.

Stop it, brain.

"Some normal jobs actually don't require you to be miserable all the time. I promise. I know it sounds fake, but it's true. I'm a good boss, right Kasia?"

She throws a napkin at me instead of answering, but I take it as a yes.

"We're going to open soon. You should probably head upstairs."

A little of the mirth drains from Tobias's face when I say the words, but not all of it. He nods, resigned, and we hold each other's gaze for a beat too long. I want to go over there and do something. Touch him. Anything to remind him that this is only temporary. But I'm not sure if we're doing that in front of other people, yet. Even if Kasia already sniffed out the truth of our situation like a bloodhound.

"Yeah." Tobias shifts his weight for a second, his gaze running up and down my body in a way that makes a curl of arousal take root in my gut. I try to ignore it, but it's undeniable. A flash of memory bursts into my brain—Tobias riding me, jerking both of us off, finally relaxed as he lost himself in his own pleasure this morning.

I hope it's the last thing I picture before I die.

"Have a good shift," Tobias says before he turns and heads for the apartment.

The awkwardness in the room is palpable. I can't tell if that was my fault or just an awkward situation, but it was bad. When I look at Kasia, the thought is confirmed. She's making an over-the-top *yikes* face at me, amusing herself, I'm sure.

"That wasn't great, right?" I ask.

"I know I just said I was going to stop giving you advice, but no. That wasn't great. You should probably figure out what the fuck you two are doing before you interact in public again, or the rest of the world is going to be so uncomfortable all our genitals will collectively shrivel up and run away."

"And I'm the dramatic one." Although she may have a point. Whatever.

We have to open the doors, and I can already see some of our more devoted afternoon lushes filtering into the parking lot. All of this is a problem for me to address after. If I keep letting Tobias pull me away from my fledgling business, it'll go under. Then we'll both need a new place to live.

All night, I can't concentrate. My thoughts flit back and forth between Tobias upstairs, the possibility of Eamon showing up, and why I still don't have some kind of master plan yet.

Every time the bar door opens, I jump a little. My adrenaline pumps, ready for a confrontation with him, and every time it's just another customer. I'm beginning to see why Tobias looks so drained, just from being on edge all the time. I understood that before, of course. But there's a difference between being cognitively aware of how someone feels and getting a taste of the experience for yourself.

The night is slow, thankfully. I avoid conversation wherever possible, which earns me a few looks because I'm normally on the chatty side. I'm too busy counting down the minutes until I can finally go upstairs, though.

It's the final stretch. Everyone is on their last drink, and in a few minutes, I'm going to kick these remaining stragglers out and lock the doors. Then someone walks in. Not Eamon, but someone that also doesn't look like they're coming with good news.

Tristan. I don't know Tristan particularly well. I know he works shift work on an ambulance, partly because he's shown up here for a couple of the minor bar fights and incidents we've had since opening, and partly because he sometimes shows up to day drink when he's not working but his internal clock is still all jacked up.

Although that was before he settled down. I try to avoid gossip, but it's physically impossible as a bartender. So, the fact that a hot, eligible guy like Tristan hooked up with the town pariah—also a man—when no one knew either of them was even queer, has been buzzing through here ever since.

All I know for sure is that I see him less, and I hope that means he's happy. Or at least busy. He still comes in here to drink with his friends sometimes, but now is not one of those times, judging by the grim set of his face.

"What's up? We're about to close."

I don't bother to beat around the bush.

"Yeah, that's why I'm here." Tristan finishes his walk to the bar, leans on the dark polished wood, and lets out a deep sigh. "Can I talk to you in private? I can wait until everyone leaves, if you need."

The furrow between my eyebrows deepens. I catch Kasia watching us from a few feet away and toss my head in the direction of the back, while she nods. It's quiet. She can finish up here. It's not like I'm going to be able to concentrate with Tristan's doom and gloom saturating me.

Tristan trails me as I lead him to the kitchen. It's small, but far enough away from the bar that no one will overhear us if we're quiet. He takes in his surroundings briefly, adjusts his position so he has one eye on me and one on the only entrance, then leans in.

"Whatever you say stays between us. I know just enough to be able to grasp the shape of the situation, but none of the details. But I thought about it and thought about it, and there's nowhere else to look that I haven't tried already. So, off the record—do you know where Tobias is?"

I freeze. I should have realized some people would be able to make an educated guess he might come to me. As far as I can tell, he doesn't have any friends. It's a rural area with barely a cluster of very small towns to begin with. He can't go to any of the Banna guys. His family lives out of state, and the only thing he does apart from work and take care of his grandmother is drink at my bar.

"Why?" I ask.

Tristan huffs, but nods. "I get it, but I promise I'm not a spy. I'd rather lose a testicle than turn him over to Eamon. Who has not been quiet about the fact that he's looking for him, if you were wondering. He's saying all sorts of crazy shit, probably in the hope that something will shake loose. But I need to find him. I just took Anika—his grandmother—back to the hospital, and she's not looking well, man. I know how close they are. If he doesn't go see her and the worst happens, I think it could be something he won't recover from."

My entire body sags, and I take a few seconds to scrub a hand over my face. Exhaustion is already setting into my bones at the thought of dealing with the overwhelming number of ways to potentially deal with this situation.

Tristan is right, though. I still don't know that much about Tobias, but it's clear how much he cares about his grandmother.

Screw it.

"Yeah, okay. Follow me."

Tristan narrows his eyes at me, obviously confused, but I just turn and wave him after me. He follows silently behind as we work our way through the building and up to the apartment.

My initial urge was to stay downstairs and talk to him about it. I wanted to make a strategy before presenting the information and the plan to Tobias at the same time. But I'm quickly coming to realize that my first instinct with Tobias always involves wrapping him in cotton wool and hiding him from the world, and that instinct is normally wrong.

I have to keep him safe. That's not optional. But I can't keep steamrolling his ability to make decisions for himself, or I'll turn into the kind of man that Kasia was describing.

The thought makes me shudder.

I knock quietly on the apartment door and then let myself in. Tobias is on the couch as usual, although this time he looks more sprawled out and half-asleep. I think that's a good sign.

He sits up to offer me a smile, only to freeze when he sees Tristan standing behind me.

"What's going on?"

Tristan takes a few steps to brush past me. "Don't worry, kid. I'm not here to rat you out. We need to talk."

Tobias seems to gradually shake himself out of the frozen position and relaxes, bit by bit. Then he takes in the words and his narrowed gaze turns to me.

"Gunnar, did you bring Tristan in here to break up with me for you?"

The laugh that I bark out is unstoppable. Fuck me. I was not expecting him to crack a joke, but every twenty-four hours that gets inserted between him and the last time he saw Eamon reveals him to be more and more hilarious. Dry. Sort of biting. But definitely hilarious.

Tristan is looking between us with a smug little smile, like all of this is what he expected.

"No. Can you not be ridiculous for two minutes, please?" The words don't land though, because I'm biting them out through my own smile.

Tobias scrunches his nose at me in this adorable, facetious way that makes me want to kick Tristan out and immediately start defiling all my furniture. But then my brain resets and I remember the point of this conversation.

With another sigh, I let the mirth drain away and walk over to the couch. Tobias is propped up on the back like a meerkat, but his smile turns downwards when he sees me get serious.

"Something's wrong," he says.

"Honey, I'm sorry." I wrap my arm around his waist over the couch back, because apparently, we're not caring if Tristan knows anything, and hold him close. "Tristan just took your lola to the hospital. He's here because he wanted you to know."

Tobias's eyebrows raise, but he doesn't say anything. Tristan takes the opportunity to move closer as well, keeping his movements small and his voice gentle. Like you would around someone fragile.

If only he knew how tough Tobias has already been. Had to be, but still.

"Anika just went to the ED, and I checked with the nurse before I left. There's no way she's not getting admitted. She's got a wound on her foot that's pretty bad. That's why she called me. But she's hypertensive and throwing arrhythmias like last time as well. There's a lot going on."

The sympathy on Tristan's face is clear, but not condescending. Tobias doesn't move, though.

"What do you want to do?" I ask.

It's a long time before he answers. When he does, I'm taken aback by how fragile he really does look, compared to all the other times I've seen him break down in this apartment. Even compared to when he first showed up, barely able to walk.

"Can I go?" His voice is quiet and wavering when he asks me.

Oof.

I keep holding him up, but stroke his cheek with my other hand. He leans in like he needs the contact right now.

"I can't decide that for you. I want to, but I can't. Do you want to go?"

Tobias huffs and chews at his lip for a minute. The brief flash of unrestrained weakness is gone, and all his exhausted resignation takes over his face again.

"Yeah. I'm not leaving her alone. I can't not go." He pulls away from me and stands up. "Let's go now. The longer she's there, the more likely it is he might find out and come looking for me."

"Okay."

I take a step back as well. Tobias has slipped into this brusque, uncaring version of himself that I recognize as a protective shell. That's fine. I don't have to hold him for him to know I'm still here.

"Come on, guys. We can take my car. I'll keep you company."

Tristan nods as he speaks, and I appreciate the gesture.

It'll be fine. I'm probably exaggerating in my mind because we've been dwelling on it for so long. What can realistically go wrong in a public place, with both me and Tristan there for company?

Everything's fine.

Chapter Fifteen

TOBIAS

I'm generally a fan of silence, but the tension sitting over the three of us as we head to the hospital is unbearable. I'd almost prefer it if one of them was scolding me for something. I feel like that's generally what happens when I get pulled into someone else's car—either a scolding or a sympathetic 'maybe we can help' speech that's fucking useless.

I would take it. Anything other than this silence. Because all I'm thinking about right now is how this could possibly end for us.

Eamon finally kills me. Gunnar gets sick of me, so I go back to the Banna and Eamon, or something identical. Eamon kills Gunnar and then me. Lola dies alone, because I'm too busy dealing with this clusterfuck to take care of her like I'm supposed to.

My mind spits out dozens of scenarios, but none of them have a happy ending. It's not feasible. Wherever I go, whatever I do, Eamon will hunt me. He gets too much pleasure out of it, and there's no downside for him. I come back; he wins. I run; he still gets to chase me, so he wins.

He always wins in the end.

Even though there's not a single rational part of me that *wants* to go back to him... The thought that it might be better for everyone else if we just cut to the chase is lingering on the periphery of my awareness.

Part of me thinks it's the pessimism talking, but part of me thinks it's realism. And if getting the messy, horrible ending over with now instead of later saves Gunnar some grief or potentially keeps him out of danger, isn't it worth it?

I'm selfish. I want this time with him. I still barely know him, but the feeling of being around him is intense in a way I never knew was possible. I want to crack him open and examine all the parts inside, knowing the whole time that he'll stay quiet and still and patient as I peel back his layers, one by one. Knowing that he'll not only allow me to really look at him, he'll want me to.

It's exhilarating.

I want one stupid, selfish thing in my sad little life. Just for a little while. I'm aware that it probably makes me even more pathetic. I should be holding onto hope. Having faith in my inner strength or the value of my existence or the potential for a future I could have.

But I'm so fucking tired. From before I was even born, my existence was a problem for people. Filling up that void with my own positivity has been an uphill fucking battle. I've tried. I have. It's just a lot. In the midst of all this chaos, I feel like I deserve to be weak for a little while and hang that feeling on someone else.

If caring about Gunnar makes it easier for me to also care about whether I live or die, then fuck it.

I'm doing my best.

This is the inner monologue that runs on a loop the whole thirty-minute drive to the hospital. Maybe I'm really trying to distract myself from thinking about Lola.

She's been sick for a while. This isn't news. But lately it's felt like she's in the hospital more often than she's out of it, and I don't know what else I can do. I started working for the Banna so I could get the money to pay for her insulin, and she still ended up having to ration it. Only now I'm on the fucking lam and can't even be there to take care of her.

If I'd been there instead of lying around Gunnar's apartment having butterflies and trading hand jobs, maybe this never would have happened.

Or maybe Eamon would have killed us both already.

I swear, I can feel my brain thrumming like a tuning fork that's been struck, desperate to halt these chaotic, painful thoughts for a little while. As if on cue, Gunnar turns around in the passenger seat and looks at me, that hangdog expression on his face.

"If you've changed your mind, we don't have to do this now. We can go home. Make a plan and then come back tomorrow. Maybe during the day when there are more people around."

I look out the window for a minute, seeing nothing but trees that look gray under the headlights and black, black emptiness beyond it.

"It wouldn't make a difference," I say with a shrug. "I need to see her. The longer we wait, the more likely it is one of his contacts will tell him she's been admitted, and he'll start skulking around." I shake my head from side to side, trying to put something into words that's almost impossible to express. "I mean... He's going to find me. If he wants to bad enough, he'll find me in the end. He has all the power here. The only thing I can do is wait and hope he gets bored in the meantime, but the chances of that happening are pretty fucking slim."

Well, that successfully increased the already intolerable level of tension in the car. Tristan's driving with both hands on the wheel and his arms locked, not saying anything but obviously locked into what we're saying. And Gunnar looks like he's about to turn this car around, whether I want to or not.

He manages to restrain himself. I'm sure it's not easy, but he keeps quiet for the rest of the drive. By the time we get to the hospital, it's sooner than I expected, and a sudden rush of nerves hits me.

The parking lot is dark and quiet, only illuminated by evenly spaced streetlamps. There are a few cars sleeping peacefully, but no people standing around as far as I can see.

One ambulance is sitting by the ER loading bay, but that's the only real movement. Everything else is as silent and still as the woods we drove through to get here.

It doesn't help my nervousness. In fact, it makes it worse. Realistically, I know that if Eamon comes for me, it won't make a difference if people are around or not. He'll take what he wants. But Gunnar's earlier offer to come back in the light of day is more and more tempting.

The process of getting inside all passes by in a blur. Tristan seems to know this place inside and out, which makes sense. I let myself numb out to everything, following along in his wake as he nods to nurses and turns down a gazillion different corridors. Gunnar is by my side the whole time.

He times his steps to match mine, like he's pacing me so we can never be more than an inch apart. He doesn't touch me, but he's always close enough that I can feel the warmth coming from his body. I could stretch out my pinkie finger and touch his skin if I needed to. And he doesn't watch me. He looks around us, his demeanor calm but his serious eyes everywhere, taking in every face and dark corner as if assessing for a threat.

It makes an emotion swell inside me. Something powerful and turbulent that I can't possibly put a name to.

I catch his eye for just a second, and in that moment, I know he feels it too.

By the time we reach her room, I feel a little better. Tristan cracks open the door for me, but a thought crosses my mind.

"Are we even allowed to be here?" My voice is a stage whisper.

It's not silent inside the hospital. Nurses and other staff are still walking up and down the halls, bustling to do their jobs, and there are some patients walking back and forth. But I had forgotten just how late it was until this moment.

Tristan shakes his head at me. "Not all hospitals have official visiting hours. This one I think it's only labor and delivery. Maybe the ICU? Whatever. It's fine. Just don't cause a ruckus. I know how loud and outgoing you can be."

Uncalled for. I don't bother with a comeback, though, instead giving him the derisive look he deserves while I push past him into the room.

It's dark inside. There's a computer monitor glowing in one corner and a whiteboard with some notes on it reflecting the glare. I was worried I would find her surrounded by tubes and wires and beeping machines, but it's not as bad as I expected. She has an IV, and the pump blinks softly in the darkness. There are a few wires surrounding her, some of which attach to a little gray box lying beside her in the bed.

It's not that bad. It's not that bad. *It's not that bad.*

Gunnar and Tristan both follow me into the room but hang back as I approach her. For a minute, I think she's unconscious. Her eyes flutter open though as soon as I get close.

"Apo," she says, reaching for my hand.

Her expression is laden with more emotion than I ever want to see her burdened with. She's happy to see me, but underneath that I can see all the hurt and worry that I'm sure has gone hand in hand with my abrupt absence.

"Are you alright?" she asks.

"I'm fine. I'm fine. I'm so sorry I had to leave. How do you feel?"

She lets out a long, weary sigh. "It's okay. It's just more of the same. I had my handsome medic there to save me again." She smiles at Tristan where he leans against the far wall, and he grins back at her.

They've always had a weird kind of friendship. I don't get it, but I'll take it. She needs all the friends she can get to make up for her shitty, neglectful grandson.

Then she cocks her head to the side, and I realize she must have noticed Gunnar in the room.

"And who's this?"

Gunnar moves forward until he's standing close enough to the bed that she can get a good look at him. He looks so calm. I'm almost jealous. I've thrust him into a weird, uncomfortable situation and he's just standing there, giving her a warm smile and introducing himself.

"My name is Gunnar, ma'am. I'm Tobias's friend."

There's a beat of silence while she seems to evaluate that. I'm not sure what she's thinking. Maybe she's wondering if he's one of the people she knows I probably work for but shouldn't. I wish I could spill everything right now. I want to tell her how Gunnar is the closest thing to a real person in my life, outside of her, that I've ever had. I want to tell her how much she'd love him and how I'm desperate to make him a permanent part of my existence.

But now isn't the time.

I'm about to ask her about her health when there's a sharp knock on the door. Without waiting for an answer, a woman in scrubs lets herself in and takes in the sight of the three of us.

She's older than most of the nurses I saw in the hallways, with the kind of tanned, weathered skin you get from decades of cigarette smoke and too much sunbathing in the eighties. Her blonde hair also looks damaged, and it's pulled back into a severe bun. Everything about her gives the impression of sharp, harsh angles and it sets me on edge for no particular reason.

"Are you the grandson?"

She looks directly at me as she asks, but her tone implies that she couldn't possibly care less. I nod, and then she tosses her head in the direction of the hallway.

"Perfect. Doc wants to speak to you about her case. I'll take you to him."

"He can't come here?" Tristan interjects, but the nurse is unfazed.

"We're slammed tonight. He's got too many unstable patients in ICU to come over here right now. We're shuffling some things around. It's easier if we go to him. It'll only take a minute."

Gunnar looks at me, drowning out the noise in my head with his stare. "Do you want me to come with you?"

I think about it. There's a tingle of fear running through me, like always, but there's nothing I can do about that. I can't only exist with Gunnar as my shadow for the rest of my life.

And like I said before—if Eamon really wants to take me, he'll take me. Gunnar can't stop him. He'll only get hurt trying.

I'm about to tell him I'm fine when the nurse interrupts.

"Sorry, sir. HIPAA. You can wait here."

Gunnar turns a baleful glare on her, matched by Tristan's expression behind him, but she doesn't back down. She's not wrong. And thank fuck Lola made me her medical proxy months ago for exactly this situation.

"It's no big deal," I tell him. "I'll be right back."

I lean down, telling Lola the same thing and kissing her on the cheek before following the nurse toward the door. Gunnar's fingers graze the small of my back as I walk past him, but I don't let myself look. The more I give into this feeling that every step I take is a step toward my funeral, the more it sinks its claws into me.

The nurse moves down the hallways at a brisk clip, unconcerned about whether I'm keeping up. I've been here so many times since I moved back, but I still can't keep it all straight. Especially at night when the patient hallways and nurses' stations are all dimly lit. Before I know it, I'm completely turned around.

Is this the ICU? I don't think she's ever been in the ICU, so maybe I've never been here before. It's all kind of a blur. Wait, what's the CVICU? Was that where she went last time?

I have no idea why I'm on internal ramble mode. Maybe to keep my thoughts from straying down the darker paths. Turn off and do as I'm told. Follow the nurse. She badges open a random door for me and indicates for me to go through, still looking like she'd rather be anywhere else than helping me.

I thank her anyway, but my attention is so far away from the present. It takes me a good fifteen seconds to realize that once the door clicks shut behind me, also with that little black box that means you need a badge to open it, I'm not in a room.

I'm in a stairwell. A dark, empty stairwell.

Well, empty except for the one person standing a few feet away from me, leaning casually against the railing.

My stomach drops out, but it feels like a physiological reaction. The adrenaline, the fear, the fight-or-flight. All of that is there in an instant, like it always is.

But my mind is calm this time. I'm not sure why. Maybe enough of me was expecting this, that I was genuinely prepared. Or maybe I've worried over it and tossed and turned so much that I don't care anymore.

"Hello, lover," Eamon says as he slinks toward me. "I thought I might find you here."

I don't move. I don't breathe. I wait and I think and I keep myself as unobtrusive as possible, already conserving my energy for whatever is about to come next.

Eamon sidles up next to me before running his fingers through the longest part of my hair.

"This little vacation is over, pet. We have work to do. And you have a lot of things to be punished for. Understood?"

I don't answer straight away, because my vocal cords feel as frozen as the rest of my body. When he doesn't get an answer, he tightens his grip on my hair and yanks my head back.

"Understood?"

His voice is low and his breath is hot in my ear. I thought I might feel an extra kind of repulsion to have his hands on me after all the softness of Gunnar's touch, but I don't. It's the same as it ever was. Blankness. My body is suspended in time as it waits.

"Yes, sir."

They're the only words I can choke out, but it does the trick. He lets go of my hair and gives me a small shove to get me walking down the stairs.

I wonder how far away Gunnar and Tristan are right now? How far had I just walked? Would they hear me if I screamed?

Then I shove the thought away. Like I thought before, there's no point. He was always going to find me in the end. At least this way, nobody gets hurt but me.

Chapter Sixteen

GUNNAR

Unease sits heavy in my gut. It's so profound I almost feel seasick, as if the hushed hospital room were swaying from side to side.

He's been gone for too long. I know nothing significant has happened to him in the middle of a busy hospital, even if it is the middle of the night. But what if the doctor gave him bad news? What if he's freaking out, and he needs support? We haven't had the chance to talk about his family a lot, but I get the strong feeling that he thinks his grandmother is the only person in the world who loves him.

She seems lovely. She's out of it right now, alternating between whispering quietly with Tristan, who is crouching next to her bedside, and dozing in the darkness. I'm glad he has a relationship with her, because I'm not sure I have the bandwidth to be good with new people right now.

All I can think about is counting the seconds until Tobias comes back and my heart can stop trying to beat out of my chest. I look at Tristan, assuming he'll give me one of his prepackaged-but-reassuring paramedic smiles and take the edge off all this anxiety.

Instead, he returns my look with one just as concerned. Anika is asleep again, and Tristan's hands are clasped tightly in his lap, while his gaze flits between mine and the door.

When he stands up, we both know why without having to say anything. We quickly move into the hallway toward the nurses' station. The halls are all dimly lit, but the station is full of several nurses sitting at computers, their faces all illuminated by the screens as they tap quietly on the keyboards or talk amongst themselves in low voices. I don't see the nurse who took Tobias anywhere, but she could still be with him. The thought doesn't settle my nerves at all, though.

There's a woman sitting at the desk facing the front. She's middle-aged, with bronze skin, intense but flawless makeup, and a slick, dark ponytail, who gives off a general air of authority.

"I didn't get called about a direct transfer, Tristan. What are you doing up here?" she says, looking preoccupied but not unkind.

"I'm actually off shift, Maricella. I came to check on a patient and give her grandson a ride. Anika Tanikon. Do you know where her nurse is? She took the grandson to talk, and they've been gone way too long."

Maricella looks at me, probably to figure out how I fit into this equation, but then shrugs it off. She glances at her screen quickly, but I immediately notice the crease that forms around her eyes.

"That's weird. You said the nurse that talked to the grandson was female? Your patient has been assigned to Jameson since she arrived, who's both male and has been on lunch for the last half hour. Who did you talk to?"

Tristan and I look at each other, but we both move slowly, like a moment out of a horror movie. Which isn't a comparison my brain would have pulled until Tobias made me start watching the stupid things, and now I have even more horrific images running through my brain of what might be about to happen to him. As if my imagination needed the help.

"Go," Tristan snaps, before reaching for the desk phone. "What's the extension for security?" This question is for Maricella, who is clearly taken aback but locking into Tristan with the same kind of emergency hyper-focus he seems to have for situations like this.

I don't hear her answer, because I'm already running. I have no idea where I'm running to, but at least I'm finally doing something.

Hopefully, Tristan is getting security to lock the place down. Or, if he can't convince them to go that far, at least start looking for where Eamon took Tobias.

If that's what's happening. Is that what's happening?

It has to be. There's no other explanation for it.

The 'nurse' said something about the ICU, so I follow the signs overhead at a brisk jog, ducking around slow-moving patients and even slower phlebotomists with their giant fucking carts, doing my best not to plow anyone down in the process.

When I finally make it, I can't get in without a keycard. But the unit is small, just a hallway with bays on either side, and the doors are transparent. I can see far enough to know Tobias isn't in there unless he's being held in a corner somewhere, which seems unlikely. If he's trapped, it would be farther away from all the real doctors and nurses.

"Fuck!"

I'm loud enough that I turn a few heads from the sleepless people around me, but I don't care. Why didn't I get him a fucking phone yet? Why did I trust him to be safe just because it was a public place?

Why did I trust myself to keep him safe in the first place?

I've screwed this up from the start. I'm just another person in the long series of people in his life letting him down. Now he really needs rescuing, and not only am I not there, I don't even know where to look.

The next hour is a blur. I think it's an hour, at least. I keep moving through the hospital, looking over every floor inch by inch, begging nurses to look wherever I can't go. Tristan got ahold of security at least, because they're searching, too, but their enthusiasm is lukewarm at best.

They keep asking if there's an order of protection, or to confirm that the person isn't a child. And I'm saying 'no' every time, but it doesn't seem to land.

As soon as they wrap their heads around the fact that it's an adult man who we believe has been taken against his will by another adult man, it's like they shutter closed. They don't care, or don't believe us, or don't think it's in their jurisdiction to get involved. Some combination of the above.

I don't know and they're not explaining. But the more we look, no matter how much energy Tristan puts into barking orders and calling in any professional favors or personal influence he has, it becomes clear that they're not interested in helping us. It's not a child, it's not a patient, and it's not someone that they're legally obligated to care about.

Call the cops or get out, is the end result.

I equivocate for about a minute and a half before I decide to call the cops. I know Tobias wouldn't want me to. I know he'd be pissed, but we're past that now. Eamon has him and is now fully aware that he's capable of running. Fuck knows where he's hiding and what he's planning to do to him.

Tobias's grandmother is as safe as she can be while she's here, at least. Tristan dealt with that, talking to the charge nurse from before about limited visitors until Tobias is found.

I feel like I'm going to unravel. I've never felt this impotent in my entire life. Not during all the times I've tried to help people get their lives back together, with varying degrees of success.

Not even the first time I experienced this kind of disaster, when my family imploded before my eyes, and I did absolutely nothing to stop it. Memories of all that violence and misery—ones I'm normally so good at stuffing into the dark crevices of my mind where they belong—are trying to peek out at me. I don't have time for it, though. I can't change anything that happened back then.

I can't change what's happening now, either. But I can pretend. I wait for the cops and I look at every person walking through the lobby to see if maybe—if there's even the slightest chance—I'll snag Eamon and Tobias. Over an hour since he went missing. Wandering around in front of everyone.

At some point, I call Sav and wake him up. He doesn't know anything but promises to do some digging. Tristan seems to make some calls of his own in the same vein. I want to go back to Possum Hollow and look for him, but where? It's a small town, but not that small. Where can you look if someone wants to hide a *person*?

It's a good thing I don't, though. Because boy, do the cops have some questions for me.

I know Tobias wouldn't believe me, but I hate cops as much as he does. I'm only doing this out of desperation. As soon as they arrive at the hospital, they want to take this conversation to the station. Tristan and I begrudgingly agree, but once I step into the station, the flashbacks hit me with brute force.

I was nineteen years old when I spent twenty-two hours being questioned about my father's murder. The whole thing is a blur, but somehow also etched into my memory. Like something that's been scrubbed down and faded with time, but still permanently warped the surface there.

The memories aren't linear. It's more impressions. The coldness inside the holding cell was a big one, as well as the hunger. It was long enough ago that they fingerprinted me with ink, not digitally, and I remember how the ink managed to coat every last inch of my hands. It almost seemed deliberate, like another way to dehumanize me. It didn't have to be that messy, but they were so determined to make it impossible for me to get clean.

Getting poked and prodded and harassed was bad enough, but for some reason that ink was the worst part. I hate being dirty, and it cast this film over my fingers that I was constantly aware of, which contaminated everything I touched. Eventually it got on my face and my clothes, and the rest of my skin, making every part of me nearly burn with this tacky, grimy, indelible sensation. It became so uncomfortable, it even overrode my grief, after a point.

Although maybe that was just the easier way to think about it.

"So, you're not related to him?" Officer Bumblefuck asked.

His real name isn't *Bumblefuck*, but I don't remember, and I don't care to squint hard enough at his badge to figure it out. It's close enough.

"No, he's my friend. He was staying with me to get away from his abuser."

The officer makes some more notes with an impassive face.

"Yeah, I'm familiar with Eamon. I've seen the two of them together before. I've seen the kid hanging around all those guys a lot. Also high as a fucking kite at your bar." He gives me a serious look. Not unsympathetic, but the condescension in it is undisguised and I bristle before he even speaks. "How do you know he didn't just leave? You know what these guys are like. A kid like that is going to be flighty. He runs, he stays. Is Eamon really abusing him, or are they just getting high and fighting? There's no way to know what's going on in these people's heads."

The layers upon layers of things he just said that make me enraged… I want to flip the table. I want to flip the fucking table and then pin him to it by his throat while I explain—in explicit detail—how cruel and incorrect his attitude is.

Instead, I take a deep breath, and I try to release a tiny bit of tension with it when I exhale. I know I have no power here. I already know how this is going to end.

"When he came to me, he'd been beaten half to death. I know him. He's been physically, sexually, and emotionally abused by this man for months at the least. It's getting worse. Eamon is a violent criminal. Tobias chose to leave him, and now Tobias is missing. This seems pretty cut and dry."

The condescension I'm getting from the cop doubles, but now it's coated in a layer of misplaced pity. Like I'm some poor schmuck who got the runaround and is too naïve to know it.

"Young, damaged guys like him change their minds. From where I'm standing, they're both criminals. I've got no crime scene, no evidence of violence, and you're telling me he was so badly abused before, but there's no hospital record and neither of you bothered to file for a protective order or even an assault charge. What am I supposed to think?"

I slam my fist on the table. It's a burst of anger, white-hot and then immediately smothered, like all the other emotions raging to come to the surface right now.

"He was too fucking scared," I snap. "He begged me not to."

The cop takes it in stride, though. He clearly doesn't see me as a threat. Instead, he just holds out his hands, like I'm a horse he's trying to settle.

"I understand where you're coming from."

I beg your finest fucking pardon, Officer Bumblefuck, but you clearly don't.

"I know you're worried about him. But I have to go by the evidence, and there's no evidence to say this is anything other than interpersonal squabbling among some low-level criminals and you getting caught in the crossfire. Are you sure you and Tobias didn't have a fight? Something that might have pissed him off and sent him running back to his old friends?"

I snort. No matter how many times I describe Eamon and Tobias's relationship explicitly as intimate partner violence, he keeps defaulting back to whatever language he's used to. Friends. Buddies. Criminal associates. It swings back and forth, but he's incapable of calling anything what it really is, because that wouldn't help sell his theory that this is all just one big misunderstanding, and Tobias is an indigent criminal who can't be expected to stay in one place under any circumstances.

"Look, Officer," I say, steeling myself to appear as rational as humanly possible. "Tobias isn't a drug addict. If you've seen him high, it's because Eamon forced him. He's only associated with criminals because Eamon forced him." Okay, that's technically not true, but we're going for the big picture here. "He's an adult, but he's been manipulated and controlled by a powerful, violent criminal since he was still a teenager. He's refused to leave my apartment because he's so terrified of this man—so terrified that Eamon will kill him the next time he sees him—and the only reason we left tonight was because his grandmother is in the hospital. He barely even got to see her before he spoke to a nurse who wasn't really a nurse and then disappeared. How is this not evidence of foul play? He's been taken. He's missing. He's being held against his will, and god knows what is being done to him. He could already be dead, and you—"

My voice cracks, and I trail off. I was getting more heated the longer I spoke, but nothing was stirring in the demeanor of the man opposite me.

Nope. Nothing. This was still a big waste of his time, as far as he was concerned.

I can't do anything else, but I will at least spare myself the indignity of breaking down and crying in front of this fucking waste of oxygen.

Officer Bumblefuck sighs and leans in, furrowing his brow in a way that he's probably practiced to try to look sympathetic.

"Look, pal. My hands are tied. I can't file a Missing Persons Report with no evidence, especially if the person is gonna pop up at the sight of a robbery or a drug deal in a couple of days. Keep an eye out, keep asking around about him, and next time he comes back to see you, encourage him to file a report so there's a paper trail. Until there's a paper trail, nothing's going to happen. It is what it is."

I'm flipping the table in my mind's eye. Papers are scattering and hot, bitter coffee is splashing over his pock-marked, doughy face. Then I'm cracking his skull open on the linoleum and leaving him here while all the blood and spinal fluid slowly drains out of his body, before going to find Tobias myself.

In reality, I nod. I don't thank him or accept what he's saying, because I'm not that weak, but I do accept that I'm not going to change his mind. There's a record of me trying to make the report, at least. I'll try the same thing tomorrow, and the day after, and the day after. That, and have everyone I know harass everyone *they* know to see if anyone's seen Eamon or Tobias.

I don't have the power to do anything else. It's that, or wait to hear that Tobias has been killed. Which is not something I'm willing to contemplate right now.

Chapter Seventeen

TOBIAS

The only bright side right now is that I haven't been away from Eamon for that long. It's been long enough for my brain to get used to freedom, but not for my body to completely reset. My internal defenses are still there. I just have to dig them out. Or maybe they'll always be there no matter how long I'm away for them, like my DNA has twisted and warped to be shaped around him, and him alone.

The thought makes me shudder with revulsion. I wish I could crawl into a brand-new body as well as a new life. I want a vessel he's never touched. Neither of those things are in the cards for me, though, so I need to focus on surviving the here and now. If I can.

It helps that a part of me always knew this was coming. Instead of having to cope with feelings of rage or loss or despair, it's just resignation. And exhaustion. These are emotions I know how to handle.

"I hope you know how disappointed I am in you, pet," Eamon says. He grabs me by the hair and shakes my head possessively for what feels like the thousandth time since we got in the car, and we've barely been driving for ten minutes.

I block it out. The pain of him pulling my hair, the sound of his voice, all of it. I drown it all in the synthetic white noise that I'm trying to fill my skull with. Don't think about anything. It's all out of your control now.

Eamon has been driving over the speed limit with one hand on the steering wheel and a cigarette between his fingers the whole time. He keeps forgetting to smoke it for long enough that the cherry dies and he makes me pull out a new one for him, throwing his out the window. His jaw is tense, and his normal babbled ownership crap is even more nonsensical than usual.

So, not only is he taking me back, he's fucking high. Great. Eamon doesn't get fucked up that often. He prefers to be in control, and he especially prefers to drug me into a state of passivity and then exercise that control without any obstacles. Whenever he does get truly fucked up, though, it's not good.

Everything gets amped up. The rage, the aggression, the crippling insecurity that's clearly underlying it all. These are the times when I'm the most afraid of him, even though it's also when he's most likely to pass out and let me make a run for it.

I make a decision in that moment. If he gets weak, I'll run. If he doesn't, I'll stay. I can't fight him. It's too dangerous. As long as he stays awake and alert, I have to wait with him. If he kills me before I get the chance to leave, that's just how it is.

"Are we going home?"

I know I shouldn't speak or do anything to provoke him, but I can feel the exhaustion overwhelming me. I need tonight to be over. Let's get where we're going so he can do what he's going to do, and it can all be done.

Eamon grins. I catch sight of it out of the corner of my eye, but even that glimpse is enough to make my stomach churn. I don't want to know where we're going anymore.

Of course, he doesn't drop it, now that I've brought it up.

"We're going somewhere much better. Don't you worry," he says. I can hear how reedy and strung out he sounds, like maybe he's been high for a while. I don't know if I've ever seen him quite like this, and it pushes my consciousness deeper and deeper into the dark place at the back of my brain where I can wait for it to all be over.

Eamon reaches across, grabbing me by the jaw and yanking me toward him. A gesture that would feel like the purest, most scintillating show of possession from Gunnar makes my skin crawl instead, and I switch to consciously trying to shut down every single nerve ending I have.

I don't want to feel his skin on mine. I don't want to breathe the acrid scent of him in the air or hear his panting breaths that are making me itch internally. I want to twist myself until I'm inside out and there's nothing but blood and viscera coating me, so everything he touches is slick and wet and so revolting he never wants to touch me again.

Instead, he kisses me. Forcefully, pushing his tongue into my mouth until I open for him. It's rough enough and long enough that I'm worried the swaying car is about to jump a barrier or hit a tree, but he finally disconnects before we collide with anything.

Regret trickles through me when I realize we're not going to crash, which is quickly followed by shame that I was thinking about it in the first place. As if I have the power to control whether we have an accident.

For the rest of the drive, it's all I can think about. Grabbing the wheel and jerking it so hard we collide. I picture his body smashing through the windshield and shredding itself on the road while I survive. I picture him being injured, and how I would manage to finish him off before the ambulances arrived, but no one would ever know. I picture him being tangled in his seatbelt with a broken leg while I slowly, meticulously strangle him to death with a tire iron.

Endless iterations of it flick through my brain, but for all of them, my body stays completely still. I barely breathe. Nothing to draw his attention. I know I'll never do any of it, but picturing it all on a loop is as cathartic as it is upsetting.

Maybe it's wallowing in the shame of not being able to finally do something and save myself that's actually cathartic.

Fuck knows.

I just want to go home.

As soon as the thought crawls through my brain, I have to blink and do a double-take, because we're pulling into the Feral Possum. I wasn't completely conscious that this was what I meant when I thought about 'home', but now that it's sitting in front of me... it is. This is home.

So why the fuck are we here?

The parking lot is empty, and all the lights are off. It's well after close, so everyone else is gone, and I'm sure Gunnar is still out looking for me. The thought makes me ache with guilt, but there's nothing I can do about it now, so I try to shove it aside.

"Come on, pet. It's time to earn my forgiveness."

Eamon practically scampers out of the car, slamming the door behind him hard enough that my window vibrates, and I jump in my seat. I stay frozen. It's too much. Whatever he wants here, he's going to take it from me. I don't have the capacity to figure it out first and offer it to him.

My door swings open just as roughly, then those fingers are back in my hair and I'm being dragged out of the car. It's a struggle to get my feet under me, and Eamon is moving fast to fuck with me. My knees are dragging through the parking lot gravel half the time I'm drag-marched over to the bar, long enough to shred the denim of my jeans and get to the skin underneath.

I'll never understand why he loves pulling me by my hair so much. Maybe it's how utterly dehumanizing it is. Either way, by the time we get to the back door, I feel weak and worthless, like I'm about to be slung over his shoulder or traded like a piece of damaged livestock.

"Eamon, please," I gasp, desperate enough to beg. I don't like that we're here, and there's no way hurting Gunnar isn't the point. If I can appease him, maybe I can keep Gunnar out of it. "Let's go home, baby. I missed you. Let me show you how sorry I am."

The words are ash on my tongue. My hand feels like ice as I reach for his cock, still on my knees in the gravel, but it's clear he sees right through me. He pushes me toward the door, undeterred by my attempts to distract him.

Eamon fishes around in his pockets for a minute, then my lock pick kit is deposited at my feet with a soft thud.

"Get us inside. If your boyfriend wants to act like he's hot shit around here, I need to show him who really runs this town. I told you I was going to make an example of someone until the others fell in line and started paying me for protection. It could have been that fucking feed store if you hadn't bitched out. But now we're here because of you. And he's the one who needs to be the example."

Eamon reaches down, grabbing me by the jaw and pulling me half up to my feet again.

"Break in, destroy everything he loves, and then we'll show him exactly who you belong to."

I don't cry. This would be the perfect moment for one single, cinematic tear to roll down my cheek as Eamon's fingers crush my throat, and I accept just how much my presence in Gunnar's life is about to cost him.

But the capacity to feel sadness is well and truly in my rearview mirror. Everything inside me is hollow and numb. This is smart. Eamon is making me destroy the one place I have to run away to.

Now there's really no point in fighting him. All I can do is wait to die.

It doesn't even look like the Feral Possum anymore. Normally, Eamon uses me to rob places. Even if it's a smash and grab, or something a little more destructive. This was a brutal, systematic dismemberment of the building.

I don't even know how long we've been here. An hour, maybe two. The alarm was turned off, so it was easy to get in, probably because we left in such a hurry, which is also my fucking fault. There's a single blinking security camera that has a wide angle of the bar itself, which has watched me the entire time without moving.

It feels like it's judging me, even though it's an inanimate object. Which is ridiculous. I'm judging myself enough for everyone. I know how disgusting I am for this. I felt it with every piece of expensive equipment I damaged or mess I made. The floor is slick with liquor, every surface is disgusting to the touch, and there's not a wire or line that's uncut in the entire place.

Eamon, of course, has been wearing a gaiter whenever he's in view of the camera. Only I'm taking the fall for this one, obviously. He didn't help, either. He stood there, leaning against the bar, drinking Gunnar's liquor and smoking more fucking cigarettes, pointing out every time I missed something and threatening encouragement when he felt my destructive energy was lacking.

Finally, once I feel drained of every drop of energy and the room looks like it was in the wake of a hurricane, I'm exhausted enough to be bold.

"Are we done?" I ask.

Eamon chuckles, before very dramatically snorting a little powder off the declivity between his thumb and forefinger, then lighting another cigarette.

"I don't know, pet. Do you feel like his life is sufficiently ruined? Do you think this is enough of a price to pay for stealing from me?"

My gaze falls to the floor as my shoulders droop, weighed down by something neither of us can see.

"Yes."

"I don't know. I think I need one more thing to make my point." He crooks a finger at me. His gaiter is pulled down so the cigarette can dangle between his lips, and his back is turned to the camera.

I move toward him even though it feels like I'm dragging my feet through tar. When I get to arm's reach, he snatches the front of my shirt and pulls me close to him, making my stomach drop out like I just crested the top of a rollercoaster.

I'm waiting for him to do something, but he moves slowly. Like he has all the time in the world. It's as obnoxious as it is menacing. The cigarette gets thrown on the ground and stomped out, and it's a small miracle he doesn't set the fucking floor on fire with how much high-proof liquor is soaked into these floorboards right now.

He pulls his gaiter back up before spinning me around and slamming me gut-first into the bar. All the best memories of sitting here and being with Gunnar are knocking at the edge of my mind, but I do my best to shut them out. They're ruined, of course. But I don't have to physically watch them taint and warp in my mind's eye as Eamon paints this place with the same disgusting brush he's painted the rest of my existence with.

"Look at the camera, pet," he says, his voice husky in my ear in a sadistic attempt to be seductive.

My stomach drops again as I realize what he's about to do. I never fight him. Not anymore. I know it only makes things worse. But the realization makes so much fear and shame flare inside me that for a second, I don't think straight.

"No, no, no, no, no, please, Eamon," I say. My words are a jumble and the panic in my voice is obvious.

Not here. Not where Gunnar will eventually see. It's bad enough for him to know exactly what's happened to me, let alone actually see it.

I already have to fight with the constant voice in my head that tells me this is all my fault. I can't do that if I'm picturing Gunnar watching me, questioning every moment where I choose submission over more pain, or compliance over death.

Fuck. Please don't make me do this.

"I always told you what would happen if you disobeyed me, Tobias," he says as he pushes me harder against the bar. "Stop acting like all of this isn't your fault. You should have known exactly what to expect."

He's right. Well, he's wrong, but he's right. It's not my fault that he's a fucking psychopath and happens to have set his sadism sights on me. It's not my fault that I got dealt so many shitty hands I fell from one bad decision to another until I ended up being a chew toy for a lunatic, trapped in a cycle of violence that there's no escape from.

But I shouldn't be surprised that this is where we've ended up. Allowing myself to hope... That was my fault. That was dumb. All the shame and disappointment that I'm feeling right now are because I let myself have too many hopes and dreams for a future that could never possibly exist.

I shut it down. All of it. Gunnar, the future, my own precious humanity. None of it is real anymore.

Before I was upset that Gunnar would be disappointed to see me not fight enough. Well, he's about to see me not fight at all. I consciously make myself as limp and pliable as possible. I put a simpering expression on my face, and I focus on doing whatever I can do to end this as quickly and painlessly as possible, especially considering how long it took me to recover from the last time we did this.

Letting myself act like a human was my first mistake. I won't make that again. Let's just get this fucking over with.

Chapter Eighteen

GUNNAR

When I finally get home, the cold, blue-tinged dawn light is breaking over the horizon and I'm fucking exhausted. Tristan drops me off in the Feral Possum parking lot before heading home to catch some sleep himself, promising to call me in a few hours.

The cops were useless. I was useless. No one's seen Eamon. Tobias is in the wind, and right now I'm trying to figure out how to sleep in my shitty apartment without the sound of his breathing beside me.

The first thing I notice is the door hanging ajar. It's too early for anyone else to be here, even staff. I know we left in a rush last night, but not that much of a rush.

My brain immediately spits out the idea that it must be Tobias. It's totally illogical. The chance of him escaping this quickly is slim. He doesn't even have a key to that door, so it's not like he could let himself in. But none of that stops me from barreling across the parking lot, cold gravel flying behind me in a spray, until I burst through the open doorway in the desperate hope that he'll be standing inside.

Instead, I see... I'm not even sure what I see. It's too much. It takes too long to filter through all the sensory information I'm receiving right now and put together a complete picture of what the fuck happened to my bar.

The floor is sticky when I shift my weight, and I look down to realize it's covered in something. Probably booze.

When my eyes flick back up and look around the room a second time, more of it sinks in. The place is trashed. Just wrecked.

Every single piece. I picked each inch of this stupid decor myself. The dorky little coasters, the sandwich board with drink specials written in chalk that everyone says looks too hipster, all of it. And it's all turned into rubble.

I'm not sure how long I wander around, taking hesitant step after hesitant step through the space that used to be my favorite place in the world. There's a shattered barstool that I remember Tobias sitting on while he got shit-canned the day before he showed up at my apartment.

I don't know what to do. I'm always the person who stays calm when shit gets real, but right now, I have no idea what to do. I need to call my insurance company. I need to call the cops, although my body revolts at the thought of seeing them again after I just got finished with them. I need to call Kasia and Sav.

I need to...

I need to...

I need to...

I need Tobias back.

I wish my dad were here.

As pathetic as it is, the intrusive thought makes something inside me snap, and I start crying. Not dignified crying, either. Crying like a little kid who dropped his ice cream. Crying like I can push all the stress and sweat and fear and misery out of my body through my eyeballs, so I don't have to deal with it anymore.

It sweeps me up like a wave, buckling me at the knees until I'm sitting on the disgusting floor, leaning against the bar with my arms bent on my knees and my face buried in them.

I get myself under control after a minute, thank god. I can't remember the last time I cried like that. Not that I think adults shouldn't express their emotions, but that was too much. I don't like feeling like my body is carrying me away with it and I don't have a choice.

I swallow hard, my throat feeling thick and choked even though the whole situation was over so quickly.

Get it together, Gunnar.

If by 'get it together', I meant control myself enough to swallow so I can start drinking on the floor, then that's what I do.

There's a bottle of Tanqueray, with a thick layer of dust covering all that green glass from how little it gets used. It's on its side on the ground, rolling around but with the lid still closed and the contents intact.

I reach over—grateful for my long torso and arms because fuck getting back up—and snag it. It's warm and god knows how old it is. Definitely not stock that I've replaced since I first opened this place. But right now, I don't care. I'll drink the sickly sweet, herbaceous liquid as long as it makes my chest burn and the rest of the world dim at the edges for a while.

Every time I look at the destroyed bar, it's overlaid by the image of my father's body in his destroyed store, and every time it makes my heart clench. It feels like my brain and the alcohol are in a race to see who can take control of my consciousness first. I'm desperate for those awful memories to roll back, because stirring up old trauma isn't going to help me face this new one. That's why I'm drinking at a pace I haven't in years.

Eventually, I feel better. Well, not better, but more numb. The invasive memories of my childhood are rolling back and I feel like I can breathe. I still miss Tobias every second. The worry about where he is and what's happening to him isn't going anywhere. I know that. But there's nothing I can do for him right now.

It's not the first time I thought it, but the realization that the bar being destroyed is most likely connected to Eamon hating me suddenly hits me with total clarity. I've drunk enough to feel like the world is something I can exist in, but not so much I feel like a zombie. And as soon as I put the pieces together, the rest of me begins to wake back up and my focus sharpens.

Eamon did this. It's the only explanation. Why else would I be targeted? Normal criminals might have robbed me, sure. But no one else would have gone to the trouble of causing this level of destruction. I feel like an idiot for not putting the whole thing together the second I stepped in the door, but I guess I was distracted.

Then I feel like even more of an idiot, because I completely forgot about the camera. The new camera that I recently installed because of Tobias. The one that is still sitting above the bar, blinking green, when I crane my neck to look up and over the wooden barrier.

I pull out my phone. The battery is at 12%, but hopefully it's enough to see what happened before I have to get up to find a charger. The app is already downloaded and logged into, even though I've never needed to use the damn thing, so it takes me a few minutes to tap around and see how it works.

I should have paid for the alert system. But I thought it was unnecessary, because I have separate perimeter alarms to let me know if someone breaks in after hours. Of course, that only works if I remember to turn them on when I leave, which I obviously didn't. Because Tobias was with me, I didn't care what happened to anything else.

Once I pull up the grainy footage, it buffers for a while. They also trashed my Wi-Fi, so I'm working on the tenuous 5G coverage that kind of exists out here. Every moment that the buffering drags on, I get more anxious.

Load, motherfucker. Show me his fucking face.

I know he did this. Or his friends. Someone was trying to send a message. The only upside is that maybe this footage could be used to put him away, or at least get him more shit from the cops. Or even a clue about where he took Tobias. Or a sign that Tobias is still alive.

Equal parts of horror and relief hit me when the video finally buffers, because Tobias is alive. Or at least, he was a few hours ago. Here he is, grainy and black and white, but still so beautiful I want to reach through the screen and pull him back to me so I can clutch him tightly and keep him safe.

He's the one who trashed the bar. Well, he did it looking like a dead-eyed automaton under the supervision of a man with a covered face, but who I would still recognize anywhere. So, it's safe to say it wasn't his idea.

I can't look away. I set the playback speed as fast as it'll go, but it's still heartbreaking to watch. Tobias looks utterly numb. He works through it all methodically, destroying everything piece by piece, occasionally turning to Eamon for instruction, or maybe a question.

My poor boy. I can only imagine how much this must have hurt him. Knowing how deep the rabbit hole in his head goes, I bet he spent the entire time wondering if I would be furious with him as well.

I'm not angry with him, obviously. But my anger is very real, and very present. It's also accompanied by a kind of hopeless despair that I haven't felt in a long time. Maybe I've spent too much of my life trying to dig people out of these situations, only to be shut down. Maybe it's because I'm being forced to confront how unrealistic it is that I could ever really help Tobias get free, no matter how much I care about him.

I loved my brother more than anything and trying to help him got me nowhere. Worse than nowhere. He still got trapped in his own self-destructive web, tearing apart our family in the process and putting a black mark on our lives that we'll never get rid of. Maybe Tobias is the same.

He probably thinks I'm caught up in his wave of chaos and ruin, but I think he's caught up in mine. Because everyone I let myself truly care about turns out this way, and the harder I fight to save them, the worse it gets.

I'm distantly trying to buck against these ideas—because I didn't spend all that money on therapy for nothing—before they completely shift my thinking, when the footage changes. They're done smashing everything I own. I'm expecting them to leave, but instead, Eamon pulls Tobias over to him. Once I realize what's happening, it's so, so, so much worse than anything that's come before.

Nothing I've experienced in my life has prepared me for the kind of impotent rage that I feel as the footage continues. Watching Eamon hurt and violate anyone, but especially someone I would tear apart the world for...

Eamon holds eye contact with the camera the entire time. He knows exactly what he's doing, and his message is received. The sight of his hands on the skin that I've worshiped makes my stomach churn, but I hold it back.

Tears are useless here. So is cursing or anger or anything else.

I want him fucking dead. I want to find him and destroy his life worse than he's ever destroyed anyone else's. I want him to think of all the pain and suffering he inflicted on Tobias as a gentle dream compared to what he's about to suffer.

Of course, the rational part of me is never truly silent. It reminds me that I am not Liam Neeson, and this is not a revenge movie. The reality of me finding Eamon, subduing him, stringing him up so I can torture him to death, and then escaping any legal consequences for it is less than zero.

I'm not that guy. And more importantly, if I ever can get Tobias away from him, Tobias needs me a lot more than he needs the shredded remains of Eamon's corpse in exchange for me spending the rest of my life in prison.

At least, I think he needs me. I hope he does. I'll be here for him as long as he wants me, at the very least.

It's not as impressive as severed fingers in a jar, but it's what I've got, I guess. I just need to bring him *home*.

Still bristling with disgust, I make a snap decision and delete the footage. Then I get up, ignore the slight sway to my movements from all that gin, and destroy the camera. I'll tell the cops whoever broke in did it. I'm not letting Tobias take the fall for shit, obviously.

If I have to listen to one more cop condescend to me about Tobias being an adult and how unlikely it is that another man could be forcing him to do anything he didn't want to, I really will turn into some kind of violent, avenging angel. It's fucking repugnant.

With shaking, hate-fueled fingers, I dial 911. I mentally prepare myself to deal with the insurance claim as well, and all the garbage that will entail. I tell myself over and over that this is for Tobias.

Driving around the city won't save him. Fantasizing about eviscerating Eamon won't save him, even if I do keep going back and forth on whether that needs to happen.

Right now, *I can't save him.*

It tears me apart to admit it, but I can't. All I can do is make sure I'm here and kind of, mostly standing for when he manages to save himself. Again.

Chapter Nineteen

TOBIAS

I expected to feel like a zombie the whole way back from the Feral Possum. Normally, the worse Eamon is on a particular day, the more my mind checks out. It's easier that way. But for some reason, the part of my brain that lets me detach—that unhooks itself from the dock and allows my consciousness to drift away until I can passively observe from a safe distance instead of participate—seems to be broken.

Instead, I feel shivery and intense. My prey-senses are dialed up to their maximum level, and I'm hyper-aware of every flicker of movement or sound or scent that I can perceive.

Eamon is continuing to be extra as fuck. Tapping his fingers, snorting more of whatever meth or coke he's been pounding, chain-smoking like it's the eighties, rambling about his glorious victory over Gunnar, who he clearly perceives to be some kind of competition.

Which doesn't make any sense. Even he should know that. Competition implies there's a choice, and I have no choice here. Unless he thinks I also don't have a choice with Gunnar, because that's just how relationships work to him, so he's competing with Gunnar for who can keep me chained in a tower the most tightly?

Fuck if I know. I want to go back to being exhausted and stressed out. This wired, alert, close-to-panic-but-not-quite version of myself is something I'm not used to and don't fucking care for.

When he finally pulls the car in and throws it into park, I look around.

"We're not going home?"

His home, obviously. Not mine. All of my homes have been razed to the ground by his existence.

We're in the parking lot of a motel. The whole place is long and low and flat, including the building, and we're within both eye and earshot of the freeway. It's not a chain, and looks like it's on its last legs before it gets bought out by one, which makes me think we're here for the discretion rather than the decor.

"Fuck that," Eamon says before sniffing loudly. A brief image of him having such a colossal nosebleed that he hemorrhages to death right here in the parking lot flashes in my mind, but it doesn't happen. "I'm sick of people meddling. Everybody wants to meddle. Everybody has an opinion. You should thank me, too. If your boyfriend comes looking for us, I'll fucking kill him. At least here, we're off the grid until everyone comes to their senses. I just need a few days until Patrick cools down and accepts that I am the one who should be taking over the Banna. And you're going to keep me company."

Jesus, he really has gone full *Wolf of Wall Street*. I can taste the unhinged from here, and it's difficult not to sigh. This issue is one of his greatest hits. Patrick is his shitty boss—my shitty boss too, I guess, although I'm sure he also wants me dead by now. Eamon has been rambling about becoming his 'successor' as long as I've known him. As if any hick-ass backwoods mafia is going to want their leader to be someone like him.

Maybe they could get over the fact that he fucks men. Maybe they all buy into his Spartan bullshit about real men exerting their dominance over others *blah blah blah*. But whoever he fucks, he's still a mess. I'm sure he hasn't impressed them by spending all this time chasing me around town because I bruised his ego by running away. He must be neglecting whatever it is he does for them when he's not coked-out and paranoid.

Resigned, I follow him toward the very outer edge of the one-story building. I'm still wired, but I have it under control. The motel is split into several arms, all jutting out from the main entrance, with rooms on either side of the arm and each room directly accessible from the parking lot.

We're at the very end of one of the arms. Private, just the way he likes it. I wouldn't be surprised if he bought out the rooms around us and paid or threatened whatever passes for maid service in this place to stay away.

In all my time with him, I've experienced a lot. But there's been at least a veneer of civility over it. No matter how much brutality he exerted, there was always the facsimile of some kind of relationship, and he bothered to make excuses or at least convince me that whatever he did was my fault.

He was teaching me. Correcting me. Punishing me. Whatever he thought sold his dominance and my subservience.

I feel like this time, all that's about to go out the window. I'm graduating from constant, insidious terror combined with brief moments of violence to being chained to a radiator until someone eventually finds my corpse. I can see the whole thing playing out in my mind's eye.

I don't want to die chained to a radiator.

It's a weird thought. "I don't want to die," should be a complete sentence. And it is. Sort of.

But in all the possible futures my subconscious has laid out for me, each with their own levels of humiliation and debasement, none have been quite so fucking dry as to starve to death after Eamon's heart explodes from doing cheap blow that's probably laced with fentanyl. Or he gets executed by his boss and doesn't come back to unlock me. Or whatever else.

I don't know why I latch on to the thought, but once I do, I can't let go. I made my peace with the idea of dying young since before I even fully understood it. Since long before Eamon. It just seemed like the future for people like me.

But the dreary, depressing, slow-motion concept of wasting away in this godawful motel room makes me want to grab the world and fucking shake it until ridiculous shit like this stops happening to people.

It's dumb. It's all a waste. There's no purpose to any of this, but still, here I am.

Maybe I am detaching myself from reality again, because this train of thought is weird, even for me. For whatever reason, this specific hypothetical has got its claws in me. I feel more motivated to escape my radiator-fate than anything else Eamon may or have in store for me.

Or maybe it's the lingering shadow of Gunnar's face at the periphery of my vision, telling me I deserve better than this. I don't know that I deserve a lot. I constantly scramble back and forth between how many of Eamon's punishments I really did earn by my own weaknesses and failings, and how much of it is just him vomiting his aggression on the world. Some days, I think it's all him. Sometimes it feels like it's all me. It depends.

Right now, I know with more certainty than I've ever known anything that I do not deserve this.

I want to go home. To whatever's left of it.

Fuck it. I'd rather die trying than slowly rot here, anyway.

All these thoughts distract me while Eamon hustles us both inside. He's looking around the desolate parking lot, as if anyone here gives a fuck what we're doing. He could bend me over in the parking lot and the only response we might get is someone jacking off as they watch.

Inside, he keeps the lights off. The blinds are drawn, and the whole room is messy, like he's been here for a while. There's a half-drunk bottle of rye on the small Formica table next to the bed, although it doesn't smell as bad as I would expect it to if he's truly been on a bender. It's possible he was holding it together until the past couple of days. If he'd been fucked up this whole time, there's no way it would be this clean.

Eamon throws down his keys and phone. He kicks off his shoes and pants immediately, collapsing on the bed to settle in for the night, although his gun gets placed on the nightstand next to him like always.

He watches his gun, but not that closely. He knows I wouldn't. And I really won't. He can still overpower me, and it's too easy for the fucking thing to go off in the middle of the struggle. If I'm escaping anything, it's not by shooting him with his own gun, as satisfying as that sounds.

It's also not by smothering him with a pillow, or anything else as dramatic. I hate to admit it to myself, but now that I finally feel the spark of actually wanting to leave, of wanting to live, I have to seize it. Before it flickers and is extinguished by more pain.

The only weapons I have to use against him are speed and seduction. And in a space this small, speed isn't going to happen.

Pieces of a plan are fragmented in my mind, but I do my best to pull them into something useable. I look around, desperate to find anything to work to my advantage, but there's nothing. Nothing except his own inherent weaknesses.

There's a small mini fridge in the corner that looks like it's about to cause an electrical fire. I walk over to it and pull out one of the beers I assumed would be inside, bringing it to him with a meek expression. Then I kick off my own shoes and crawl into bed. I lie next to him, like I'm waiting for permission.

When he looks at me with his eyebrows raised, I tap into every swirling piece of rage and sadness I can access, and I let the tears fall.

"I'm so sorry," I say, babbling while I sob as cinematically as possible. "I didn't mean to run. I'm sorry. I'll make it up to you."

He looks a little surprised, but that quickly smooths out into a preening, self-satisfied smirk. When you truly believe you're this deserving of something, it's easy to be convinced that you're finally getting it.

Eamon lets me cling to his side, although the stiffness and unyielding discomfort of his body against mine would be noticeable even if I didn't fucking despise him.

Gunnar has never felt like that. Everywhere Eamon is sharp and hard, Gunnar is soft. He's just as strong, but his body is thicker and more substantial. He has this way of not just feeling physically soft, but also melting into even the slightest touch from me. Like he's a fucking Tempur-Pedic pillow that's designed to conform to my shape.

Eamon is designed to disrupt every plane and surface he comes into contact with. He's nothing but sharp angles and brittle, cold textures.

I pretend anyway, though. I don't want to taint my memories of Gunnar, but it's what I need in this moment. Letting myself remember how he felt under me allows me to throw myself at Eamon like the world's most apologetic puppy, weeping and hiccupping and begging him to forgive me.

As soon as his hand finds the back of my head, I know he's taken the bait.

For a second, I think about trying to bite his fucking dick off. I saw a movie once where a girl bit the dude's dick and rubbed something painful in his eyes to escape. I've always held that scene in a special, tender place in my heart.

It would be satisfying, at least. Well, it would be until he shot me. With all the junk he's shoved up his nose, I don't know how much he's feeling of anything and he would definitely be able to let rage and drugs fuel him through my brutal dismemberment before he bled to death.

No, thank you.

Once again, I remind myself that all I have is the long game. It feels pathetic and disgusting, but it's safe.

It's the only thing that might get me home. I want to go fucking home.

So, I force myself to cry even more, knowing how much he enjoys it, and I let him fucking push me. Enjoy it while you can, asshole. If this is what it takes to lull you into trusting me again, fine. It's not like I have any dignity left to protect.

I just want to leave in one piece. I can take a little more punishment. If I have to.

I thought it would be enough. As soon as he fell asleep, I could go. But no, he doesn't trust me that much, apparently. No matter how much I pretend and debase myself in the process.

He locks the door at night with an extra padlock and keeps the key around his neck. We don't leave during the day. I don't know where the Banna think he is, or if they finally want him dead as well. I don't know what his endgame is, except I think he probably doesn't have one. He's getting fucked up enough to stay mean, but not enough to get stupid and vulnerable.

I'm hanging in the balance, and nothing seems to shift one way or the other.

The only plus is that he hasn't literally chained me to the radiator yet, but I can feel it coming.

On the third day, we run out of beer and food.

"Go," he says, pointing at the front door with the muzzle of his gun while I stand there, slack-jawed. "Go to the store. You can walk."

I squint. Either he's getting paranoid or he's genuinely in danger now, if he's not even willing to leave the room anymore. But that still doesn't make sense that he would let me leave. He doesn't really believe I'm coming back.

Slowly, not making any sudden movements or appearing too excited, I pull on my shoes. I stand up, trying not to wince as my body protests any kind of movement after the punishment it's been taking. My jaw trembles at the sudden pain, but I think I hide it well enough.

Eamon doesn't like signs of weakness unless they're specifically for his entertainment, and I don't want to risk pissing him off before I get the chance to leave. I head to the door, maintaining the same slow and careful pace.

I can almost feel the sunshine on my face. He tosses me the key to the extra lock, and I manage to catch it with shaking hands. When it clicks and releases the latch, every cell in my body seems to sigh in relief.

My hand is on the door handle when he finally speaks again, and the sound of his voice makes me freeze.

"If you're not back in thirty minutes, your boyfriend dies." Ah. That's it. There's the catch. "I don't mean I'll go get him and kill him. I mean there's someone waiting, and all it will take is one phone call. The second that minute flips over, and he's fucking dead. Do you hear me? Same thing goes if you think you can rat to the cops. Or if anything happens to me. If you step out of line one teeny tiny bit... He dies. Think about that while you're walking."

My stomach sinks. He must be bluffing. Or is he? Is that too much to risk?

He's not some evil mastermind with a space laser pointed at Gunnar's head. He doesn't have any allies left. He assumes I'm too weak and scared to question it. He's bluffing.

Right?

Either way, I slip out of the room without looking back. My stomach clenches, acid sloshing inside me with each step I take. The farther I get from the room, the faster I move, until I'm practically jogging.

I'm still headed toward the store. Is that my subconscious telling me I should believe Eamon and not risk Gunnar's life? It's one thing to cost my own life with this stupidity, but I can't let him pay the price for any of it.

I can't run fast enough to make it to Gunnar within half an hour. I don't even really know where we are, although I'm sure I could figure it out after a while.

Both options are a gamble. Either I obey Eamon and nothing changes, except I get one more sunset closer to the end. Or I run, and Gunnar could be dead by the time I get to him.

If I had good judgment, I wouldn't be in this fucking situation in the first place. Overthinking is the only form of thinking I have, and rationality doesn't play a big role in that.

Fuck.

He must be bluffing.

He has to be.

Unless he's not.

Chapter Twenty

GUNNAR

There's a loud *clink* as Kasia slaps a glass of water down in front of me, jerking me out of my malaise.

Or maybe it wasn't really a malaise, because I wasn't thinking about anything. Just staring into space. My overwhelming affect for the past three days has been the 'embodiment of human misery' according to her, and she seems to be getting sick of it. I think I'm justified, considering no one's any closer to finding Tobias and the chances of him coming home alive shrink every minute. She insists it's not helping anyone for me to wallow until he's actually dead or we know what's happening.

What I know is that the cops have made it clear they consider this a personal matter among criminals, and therefore not their problem. Some of them have come from a more compassionate angle. They say the law is not built for this situation, so their hands are tied. Others have barely concealed their contempt, and implied everyone here is getting what they deserve. I should have known better than to get involved with a troubled kid, the kid should learn to stand up for himself or leave, and anyone who's too stupid to know Eamon is bad news is not someone worth saving.

Those aren't the words that come out of their mouths per se, but they're underlying every snide comment and disgusted look that I've received so far.

Personally, I've fantasized about garroting every single police officer in Possum Hollow over the past 72 hours. It hasn't helped, though. It's helped more than they have, but that's not saying much.

Anyone who looks at this situation and sees anything other than the most textbook case of abuse is an idiot or an abuser themselves. Or both.

But we're talking about cops, so the statistics speak for themselves.

"Are you helping or moping?" she asks. "Because Sav's missing—again—and I feel like I'm doing all the work to clean up *your* bar."

She's right. I had to call in professionals to repair the lines that were cut, as well as hire some industrial fans to dry the floor, but the rest of the cleaning and repairs are doable ourselves. And since I'm almost completely out of money after neglecting my business in general, then having to close for a week for repairs, that's all I've got.

It's possible the constant hum from the fans is making me feel even more cracked than the situation is.

"I'm sorry," I say, making a point of looking her in the eye for once. "You're right. You should go home."

She huffs. "That's not what I meant. I'm here to work and I'll go home when I need to. Although you are paying me for all this eventually, obviously. I'm saying I need you here as well. You're not helping him by sitting there, staring into the middle distance all day. When he does come back, he'd probably like you to not be bankrupt and homeless."

I'm too tired to fight. I haven't been sleeping, for obvious reasons. I spend all night bouncing between working on the bar ineffectively and texting everyone I know for updates that are always meaningless. Especially since Sav, my best contact in the criminal side of things, has been almost entirely absent and quiet ever since Tobias disappeared.

I hope it means he's doing something wildly illegal to help and doesn't want to implicate me in it; not that he's also in trouble with the Banna for something.

At least once a night, I go out and drive around. As if I might find him wandering by the side of the road. It's pointless, and it doesn't make me feel any better, but I don't have any other options.

"Thank you, Kas," I say, pushing off the stool to look around for something productive I should be doing.

Eventually, my sluggish brain kicks into gear and I start washing all the new glasses that arrived today.

We work together in silence for a long time, but it's a heavy kind of silence. I can't figure out if she has something she wants to say, but is hesitating, or if she's trying to figure out what she's supposed to say.

Once I'm up and moving, I feel a frenetic, chaotic burst of energy take over. This has been happening as well, and I don't know if it's better or worse than staring blankly at the wall.

I don't recognize either of these versions of myself. At least with this one I'm getting things done, but I'm moving so fast my hands are shaking. My breath is practically rattling in my chest, and I'm constantly knocking into things or swearing as I drop shit because of my sudden clumsiness. I'm fueled by anger.

Not a focused rage, or any powerful urge for violence. It's this helpless, desperate, impotent feeling that screams inside me, making my fingers numb and my heart race. My muscles are so tense I could snap like charred, brittle old sheet metal, and every single obstacle I face tightens my chest even more like there's a noose around it.

By the time I feel a migraine forming, it's too late to stop it. There's a spot over my left forehead that has turned into stone—stiff and unrelentingly heavy, weighing down on my brain enough it might liquify and start dripping out of my nose. My neck is even more tense than the rest of me, nausea grips my stomach which is squeezing emptiness in time to my chaotic heartbeat, and the world is too fucking bright.

And no matter what I do, all those fucking memories of the shit I went through with my family seventeen years ago. Waiting. Because as soon as I drop my guard, they want in on the party, no matter how worthless the act of dwelling on old shit is.

I need everything to stop. Every single thing. I don't control a goddamn piece of it though, so all I can do is let my rage and frustration mount.

"Gunnar!" Kasia shouts, breaking through the fog in my brain.

I pivot sharply on my back foot to look at her, too many glasses in my hand, but a wave of dizziness comes out of nowhere and smacks me so hard I almost faint.

Spots of bright light dance in front of me as I sway on my feet and try to take a single deep breath.

Nothing about this is fucking fair.

Where is he? Why isn't he here?

The urge to rage and scream and blame the world gets stronger every day. I feel too much like the version of myself I thought I'd left behind. I was supposed to move past all that, and instead it only took a brand new tragedy to bring it all crawling back to the surface.

"What?" I ask, trying and failing to keep the snappiness out of my tone.

"What the fuck is wrong with you? Can you sit down, please? You look like you're about to pass out."

Kasia's eyes are wide, and she looks more emotional than I've seen her in a long time. I've disturbed the most unflappable person I know, apparently.

"I'm fine," I say, swallowing hard again to choke back the bile that's climbing up the back of my throat.

"Please stop doing this. Whatever this is—" she gestures at me, "—it isn't you. You're freaking me out. You're supposed to be the normal one."

I blow out a breath, the dual urges to accept my rage and scream at her or sit down and have a conversation warring for dominance inside me.

I must not be physically equipped to house that kind of conflict today, because instead, I start fucking crying. Again. It's one choked sob that rips out of the deepest part of my body, like it had to claw its way to the surface.

I bring my hand to my face, covering my eyes as I try to swallow it back. And I do, but the tears have already formed at the corner of my eyes and my shoulders are trembling at the effort of restraining myself. I can't tell if it's grief crying or rage crying or both, but it wants out.

I'm the one who's desperate to keep it inside. Like this is the only thing I've decided I can control. I take a long, shuddering breath and swallow, even though my tongue feels like it's too thick for my mouth.

"Jesus," Kasia whispers, before I hear footsteps moving toward me.

She pats my back, because she's one of the least touchy-feely people I know, and this is awkward as hell for her. When I feel her step closer, like she's thinking about hugging me, I take a half step back and shrug her off. My hand is still over my eyes, so I can't see her. I'm concentrating on breathing slowly, quashing all the sudden bright and staggering emotions trying to overtake my body.

Kasia doesn't hug me, but she doesn't move away, either. She keeps awkwardly patting my shoulder while I stand there and breathe.

"I'm sorry, boss. I'm sorry."

It's all she says, thank fuck. I think I would start to rage again if she tried to give me mindless platitudes, but that's not really her style.

Time stretches out until it becomes intangible. I breathe while Kasia stands there, and no one moves until I hear the door scrape open. Immediately, I find the will to focus, because maybe it's Sav and he has news. My hand falls away from my face as I look for whoever just walked in.

Someone gasps, but I don't know if it's Kasia or me. My mind is sluggish, so she might have processed what we're both looking at more quickly.

Tobias. Standing in the doorway, looking like he's frozen in time. He's paler than normal, bruises peppering the skin I can see, and his hands are shaking while his body sways.

The sheer fragility of the movement snaps me out of my own imminent collapse. Because I might be tired and way too emotional, but Tobias looks like he's about to collapse. He's staring at me, one hand still resting on the door behind him, his eyes dark and unfocused, even though they're pointed at me, his lips parted as he takes quick, shallow breaths.

I cross the room in a split second, holding out my arms. Normally, I'd be more careful not to move suddenly and startle him, because I learned that lesson the first time. But not when he looks this close to hitting the ground. There's a moment where it seems like his body tries to flinch but doesn't quite manage it. Then I get my hands on him.

My arms encircle his waist, and his gaze finally focuses on my face. His head tips back, and he grabs at the front of my shirt with weak hands. It's so close to what he did the first night he came to me, I almost cry all over again.

Then his knees buckle. Once I have his weight, the last bit of his energy gives out, and I pick him up before he hits the ground. His arms come up to rest on my shoulders and his legs wrap around my waist, like he has just enough energy to hang on but not enough to hold himself up.

"Gunnar," he says, his voice cracking with exhaustion.

He must have walked here. Or run. The bar is so far from anywhere if you're on foot. Fuck, I should have been out driving and looking for him, instead of tending to my own pathetic meltdowns.

"I'm here, baby boy. I'm here. You're safe."

I keep crooning any soothing nonsense I can think of as I walk him back into the bar. There's nowhere comfortable for him to lie down, so Kasia clears a space, and I set him on the bar itself until we've all gotten our bearings.

"Did he hurt you?" Tobias asks, still panting.

Kasia passes him the glass of water that she practically hurled at me before, and I help him hold it while he takes a sip because his hand is shaking.

"Me? Nobody hurt me, baby, what do you mean? How injured are you?"

It's hard to keep my voice quiet when I'm still raging with a thousand different emotions, but I know I have to. Flying off the handle right now is the last thing he needs.

From what I can tell, he looks better than the last time he came. He has bruises, but they're smaller, at different stages of healing from the past few days and none of them indicating significant damage. He seems exhausted from however far he had to walk, but not like he's favoring any limbs. And most importantly, he's here in one living, breathing piece.

Which is more than I can say for Eamon if I ever fucking see him again.

"He said he would kill you," Tobias says, still breathless. "If I didn't come back, he said someone was waiting here to kill you. That was hours ago. I didn't know if you'd be dead by the time I got here, but I had to try. I hoped he was bluffing. I couldn't just... stay. Not anymore."

His jaw shakes, the way it would if he were too cold. I think it's his body trying to cry but being too dehydrated and frozen to do anything about it.

I rub his arms for a second, in case he really is cold. His skin is too hot to the touch from all the exercise, but that'll change quickly now that he's stopped moving. It might not be the depths of winter yet and the sun is shining outside, but it's definitely not warm out there and he's only wearing a sweatshirt and jeans. The same ones he was wearing when Eamon took him.

Realizing I'm reacting too slowly, I whip off my hoodie and tug it over his head. It's bulky to get it over the sweatshirt, but he closes his eyes and relaxes as soon as it's on him. Then I wrap him up in my arms again and pull him into my chest.

"I'm okay, Tobias. Nothing happened. No one's here. He must have lied."

Kasia meets my eyes over Tobias's shoulder, where she's standing at the other side of the bar.

"I'm calling the cops," she says, pulling out her phone.

"No!" Tobias's voice is muffled where he's buried in my shirt, but we can both hear him.

Kasia bites her lip, looking conflicted for a second. Then she makes a face at me, because this sucks, but we both know it has to happen, and walks away from the bar to make the call.

I lean back just enough to look him in the eye. His skin is blotchy, and dark circles almost seem to weigh his eyes down, but he's just as beautiful as ever. The same delicate features covering the sharpest, scrappiest person I've ever met.

"We don't have a choice, baby. I've been trying to file report you as a missing person for three days, but they wouldn't let me. Now that you're back, you have to tell them what he did. I hate them too, but we can't pretend like nothing happened, or it's easier for him to do it again. Please. Even if it's a waste of time, can you humor me?"

He doesn't answer. Instead, he buries his face right back in my shirt and clings to me more tightly than before.

"Call Sav and Micah. They can help," he says eventually.

Kasia is already wandering back over, her phone still in her hand.

"I tried. Sav's phone is still turned off and Micah isn't answering. I called 911, though."

Tobias's shoulders heave at that, but he doesn't make a sound.

"They're coming," she continues. "I'm sorry, Tobias. I know how it feels. It sucks, but sometimes it's the best worst option."

The gravity in her voice reminds me, and probably Tobias as well, that she really does know how he feels. When she reaches out and slowly, gently strokes the hair on the back of his head, he actually relaxes into it.

We stand together like that for a long time, letting our collective sadness fill the room until there's no space for any more words.

Chapter Twenty-One

TOBIAS

By the time the cops arrive, the race for which feeling wants to take over my body has ended in a photo finish, and I have equal parts hangover, utter exhaustion, and lingering terror behind the wheel.

The fact that Gunnar is still alive, and no one has shown up to hurt him yet, even hours after I left Eamon... it's promising. But it doesn't mean anything. Maybe Eamon fell asleep and doesn't know I'm gone yet. Or maybe he had to spend time bailing on the motel in case I sent the cops after him, but he'll come back to finish us both off later.

We're never actually going to be free of him. No one can keep us safe.

At least the walk across town and halfway up Route 20—ducking into the bushes to stay out of sight of every car that passed—wore my body out so much that the fear can't get much of a foothold. I can feel it clicking inside me like an engine trying to turn over, but it never catches. It's just there. Waiting.

The hangover is bothering me more than the rest of it. Eamon kept me as liquored up as he was for the last three days, if not more, because that's what he always does. He also had me snorting his mystery drug. There was no sleep, just endless abuse and listening to his paranoia. My body is brittle and dry, my stomach is churning because I can't remember when I last ate something, and the inside of my mouth tastes like a tar pit.

At least my insides match my outsides, for once. I should really ask Gunnar for food or something, but I can't bring myself to. I'm too comfortable. After the initial shock of everything wore off, we were just waiting for the cops. He brought me over to a booth in the far corner.

I didn't want to sit here at first, because I've sat exactly here with Eamon too many times. But then Gunnar slid into the corner, propped both legs up on the long bench seat and invited me to lie between them.

That felt good. That felt like a tiny fractured piece of relief from everything else. There's a glass of water on the table that Kasia refilled before she had to go home to her kids, which Gunnar keeps bringing to my mouth to make me take sips of. I do it to humor him, even though I'd rather not.

I just want to sleep.

Instead, I'm lying here, propped on his chest and cocooned in his arms, when the cops finally burst in. They're loud and everything they do and say seems too sharp. Almost immediately, I close my eyes and quietly pray for them to go away.

I don't care if it makes me weak or pathetic. Right now, I'm allowing myself to be weak. I don't give a shit anymore. I don't want to talk to cops, who I find about a hair's breadth more tolerable than the Banna but significantly more disruptive, and I don't want to make decisions about anything for myself.

Just for today, I want to let someone else be in charge. If that makes me a victim or a shitty person or whatever, then fuck it. What else is new?

"Tobias?" Gunnar whispers in my ear, but I squeeze my eyes shut even tighter in response and turn my face into his chest, like a child.

He doesn't push. He strokes my hair with one big, warm hand and continues to hold me tightly with the other. I can hear him talking to the cops in a low voice over my head, but I make the conscious effort not to hear what they're saying.

It doesn't last for long, though.

"Baby, can you wake up for a second, please?"

Ugh, how can I keep ignoring him if he's going to be this sweet? Disgusting.

I peel apart my gummy eyelids, even though it takes the strength of ten fucking men, and let the world come into focus around me.

Two men in uniform are standing in front of me, their faces a mixture of pity, discomfort, and boredom. Fantastic.

"Can you tell us what happened?" the one with darker hair and a slightly more sympathetic expression says. Although he's still shuffling his weight from side to side like he'd rather be anywhere but here, while his partner drifts into full boredom and looks out the window, his fingers tucked into his body armor.

Jesus Christ, why is experiencing it legitimately almost easier than talking about it?

With as blank of a face and tone as I can manage—because I'll be goddamned if I let these two chucklefucks see inside my head along with everyone else who gets to peek in there—I answer them.

"Eamon showed up at the hospital. He took me to a motel, padlocked the door from the inside, and kept me there for three days. He drugged me, fucked me, and told me if I tried to leave, he'd kill me."

Gunnar stiffens beneath me but doesn't say anything. None of this is news to him, but I guess it's different when I'm talking about it, instead of it being some abstract concept.

Distantly, I wonder if he watched the security footage from the night I trashed the bar. I look around, memories of that night and everything I did suddenly superimposed on top of how it looks now. Then I picture myself bent over the bar while Eamon grins up at the fucking camera and how wonder disgusted Gunnar must have been to see it happen.

I've very carefully blocked all those thoughts out of my mind since the moment it was over, but as soon as the trickle begins, it turns into a flood.

"Fuck," I say, as my mouth floods with bitter saliva and my body feels suddenly weightless.

I launch myself off Gunnar's lap, pulling out of his grip and pushing past the two startled cops until I hit the floor on my hands and knees. Then my stomach heaves, over and over and over. All the water I've drunk comes up, but that's not enough. I cough, drool trailing from my mouth and tears streaming from my eyes, even though I probably can't afford to lose more liquid.

My stomach cramps, then heaves again, like a desperate, dying thing giving a last-ditch shove against some immovable obstacle. Something clenches inside me, and a thin liquid fills my throat before spilling onto the floor.

It's bright yellow and looks more like snot than vomit. I've experienced a lot of disgusting things in my life, but this might be one of the worst. As soon as it's out, I don't feel better, but I do feel vacant. The cramping continues, but it eases off enough that I can try to catch my breath.

The world was coming in and out of focus for a minute there, so I'm too late when I start processing information again. One of the officers is already talking into his radio, requesting an ambulance and having it confirmed by dispatch. Gunnar is hovering over me with his hand on my back. When I manage to turn enough to look at him, though, he looks more freaked out than I expected.

"What?" I ask, my voice so fucking raspy I can barely push the word out.

"You don't look good, Tobias. Maybe we should go to the hospital."

His hand keeps rubbing my back as he says it, but it doesn't do anything to tamp down the fear that jolts through me at the thought.

"No!" I jerk away from him, fighting back another wave of nausea.

I know, realistically, that the hospital is just as dangerous as everywhere else. Eamon could be anywhere. But they can't take me back there when it feels like I just got out.

Gunnar sighs, and I know he's putting two and two together about why I don't want to go. Not to mention how little interest I have in being touched by anyone other than him, let alone stripped down and prodded in the name of medicine.

I'm still crouching on the floor, trying to avoid all the vomit, even though it's mostly water, while also leaning as far away from the cops as I can without having to actually get up and move.

"Oh, you're going to the hospital, kid," Bored Officer says. "I'm not being blamed if you suddenly die. Plus, you need a what's-it-called. A rape kit. If you want to press charges for the sexual assault you were talking about." He looks at the other officer, and in a lower voice, but still not quiet enough for me not to hear, he asks, "They do rape kits for men, right?"

"Get out. Fuck off. Both of you."

My eyes snap open and I look at Gunnar. He's seething, grinding his teeth and barely able to hold back his own rage. I've never seen him like this. He looks like he's ten feet tall, even though he's crouching on the ground next to me and my puke.

Even the cops are taken aback.

"We need a statement, sir," Sympathetic Cop says, exhaustion evident in his voice.

"Then you can talk to him respectfully. He doesn't have to go to the hospital if he doesn't want to, he doesn't have to have a rape kit, and the two of you standing over him, bossing him around and asking rude questions isn't fucking helpful."

He spits the words out one at a time, like he'd rather be chewing fire than explaining this to them. It warms me a little, even more than the hoodie he put on me when I arrived that I'm still swimming in.

They have a stare down for longer than I think is necessary, but I guess I've never thought of myself as an 'alpha male', so this isn't exactly shit I participate in.

Eventually, the cops seem to relent. Gunnar helps pull me back up on the bench seat, while I work on walling off all the thoughts that made me dive off to puke my guts out in the first place. The cops shuffle awkwardly to the side, and everyone seems content to leave my stomach lining on the floor for the foreseeable future.

After that, the cops ask their questions in a dull monotone, and I answer them in as few words as possible. I think I float off somewhere, because I don't absorb most of the things I'm saying. I can feel the leatherette of the seat underneath me, especially the cracked part where it tucks into the wood, because the cracks are sharp and itchy and digging into my thigh. I can feel Gunnar's hands on me, weighing me down, because we're back in the same position as before. And I'm almost overwhelmed by the scent of liquor and commercial cleaner that makes the bar seem similar but also different.

That's it. That's all my senses feel like taking in. Everything else is a haze. I think I give the cops a more detailed timeline, as well as a description of the motel. I tell them about how I was able to leave and the threat he made against Gunnar. I tell them how many weapons he has. I tell them I don't know where he would go, because he's so fucked up right now and on the outs with the Banna, he could be anywhere.

They make their notes, punctuating the conversation with unnecessary sighs but not saying the words 'rape kit' anymore. Eamon is never going to get caught, and if he is arrested, there's about a million things he'll get charged for before anyone gives a good goddamn about whether I technically gave or possibly implied consent before he used me.

It's irrelevant. I'm not talking about it ever again.

I let them take pictures of the worst of my bruises, lifting up my shirt and tilting my face into the light for them, but only to get it over with as quickly as possible. At least no one has to touch me for pictures.

They'd sent someone else to the motel as soon as I gave them the description, so before we're even done with the questioning, we have news that Eamon isn't there and the room has been cleaned. Immaculately cleaned. I don't know what that means, and my brain is too fuzzy to speculate.

The ambulance shows up without sirens, thank god, because for whatever reason I feel like that might have been the thing to throw my last vibrating nerve into a catatonic state. They park by the door and turn on a few blue lights, then pile into the bar.

I unclench a little when I recognize Tristan. The pool of EMT staff in this area is small, and I know almost all of them from how often I've had to call an ambulance for Lola, by this point. Tristan has something about him that's comforting, though. I don't know what, because his bedside manner is non-existent, and he always looks like he both can and possibly will bench-press me.

Maybe it's because of the way he seems to dote on her. They're always whispering to each other like they're fucking friends, and she needs as many of those as she can get. Distantly, I hope he's been checking on her in the hospital while I couldn't, but examining that feeling too closely also opens up the door to more shame than I'm prepared to process right now, so I lock it shut.

And behind Tristan is... Cade. Fuck. Who I barely know but tried to choke me out the last time I saw him.

I deserved it, to be fair. His boyfriend got stabbed, and I was part of the robbery-gone-wrong that caused it. But none of it was ever supposed to go down like that. It was another one of Eamon's brilliant plans that inevitably ended in everyone but him getting fucked over.

They walk in and immediately scan the scene with sharp eyes. I expect Cade to glower at me, but his face is as neutral as Tristan. They're both the picture of professionalism.

Which I kind of hate. I don't want more professionals clomping around and making snide fucking comments. That's the petulant child in me talking, though.

"Boys," Tristan says as a greeting, his arms crossed over his chest as he gives both us and the cops a once over. "Everyone having a good day, I take it?"

"He needs to go the hospital," the dark-haired cop says, tossing his head in my direction.

You wouldn't notice it if you weren't acutely attuned to watching men for the small warnings in their body language, but I can see the way Tristan bristles at the command.

"We'll see. You have everything you need from him?"

The cops both nod.

"Good. You can go."

Bored Cop looks taken aback, like he's about to argue, but the other one makes eye contact with him and shrugs. They don't want to be here any more than I want them here. Take your get out of jail free card and go, assholes.

Tristan and Cade both muscle forward, not-so-subtly occupying the space where the cops were and encouraging them to move away. As soon as they're standing in front of me like a wall, I feel like I can breathe. Even though I don't know if I can trust them, I know for sure I can't trust the men behind them.

They relent. Cop One and Cop Two promise to be in touch, a statement they make with negative enthusiasm, then wander out of the building and back to their cruiser like they have no place better to be.

I take a deep, full breath and let my ribcage expand.

Tristan smiles as he looks me up and down. It's a sad smile, but more empathetic than pity-filled, so I'll take it.

"You scared us, kid. We've been looking for you. I'm glad you found your way back."

I nod, because I'm suddenly feeling choked up and words are beyond me. The idea that it was more than just Gunnar trying to find me isn't something I can swallow right now, even if it's true.

Tristan crouches down in front of me, the softness in his body language a complete one-eighty from how he was with the cops. Behind him, Cade is fishing medical equipment out of a giant bag, but also has a softer expression than before. He's not looking at me like he wants me dead, at least.

"Where are you hurt?" Tristan asks.

"I'm fine."

They're the only words I manage to squeeze out, and I swear the entire room collectively rolls their eyes.

"He doesn't want to go to the hospital," Gunnar says, as if I'm not there.

The sudden surge of anger that hits me stands in total contradiction to how much I was mentally whining about wanting him to take care of everything a few minutes ago. Before I even realize it, I feel like I'm about to crash out, and my mouth is spitting venom.

"I can speak for myself," I snap.

Gunnar tenses, then relaxes slowly underneath me.

"I know," he whispers directly in my ear, before placing a kiss against my temple. I realize suddenly that I probably smell disgusting, and I have to fight not to crawl off him all over again. "I'm sorry."

Tristan and Cade are both watching us with careful, calculating expressions. After a few seconds, Tristan drags over a stool and pats the seat.

"Okay, are you able to hop up here for me?" he asks, before taking a big step back out of my space to let me do it.

I feel stiff and slow, but I gradually unfold myself from the booth and do as he says, leaning on Gunnar a little for support.

Once I'm up, Tristan sits on a similar stool, so he's looking at me from almost the same height instead of leaning over me.

"Okay, kid. Do you want to avoid going to the hospital if you can?"

I bite my lip and look at the ground, the sudden wave of boldness from before abandoning me. I feel naked without Gunnar behind me.

"Gotcha. How about we check you out and do what we can for you here to begin with. I'm probably going to officially recommend going to the hospital after, because you look like you've been through the wars. But you're always within your right to refuse unless something really fucking serious is happening. Deal? I won't do anything without your permission, and I'm not going to force you or trick you into doing something you don't want."

I let out a long breath. I kind of knew all this already, and I trust Tristan. As much as I trust anyone, really. But knowing it and hearing him say it straight up are two different things.

"Okay."

"Perfect." He nods. "Do you want Gunnar to stay, or wait upstairs?"

My eyes flick up, and panic grips my chest.

"Stay," I say, already looking around for him, even though he's right here.

"No problem." Tristan puts his hands out to placate me, while Gunnar perches on the table so he's more in my eyeline. "Cade's going to take your vitals, and I'll ask you some questions. Remember, you don't have to answer, but it'll help me if you do. And all of this stays between us. If you change your mind and want Gunnar to step out for a second, we can do that too. You're in charge here, and we're not in a rush."

I'm nodding, but this is rapidly turning into too much information to absorb. I just want it to be over, and if it can't be over, I want them to tell me what to do. Anything that doesn't involve going to the hospital or taking my clothes off.

Cade approaches me, warning me he's going to put a blood pressure cuff on me and letting me nod before he starts. He gets to work once he has permission, taking my blood pressure and putting a clip on my finger to measure something, then listening to my chest with a stethoscope.

He asks me each time before he touches me, and moves around me carefully, but without that hangdog pity look I was expecting. And without bringing up any of the anger I know he still has for me. He just works through it one thing at a time, giving me soft smiles and speaking in a quiet voice. It's almost soothing, except I'm so nervous that I'm the one who finally flips and says something.

"I'm sorry," I blurt out at random.

He frowns, pulling the stethoscope out of his ears.

"Why?"

"About Silas. I'm sorry. I didn't want to be there. I never wanted to be there. It was all... I made a lot of shitty choices. I'm sorry your boyfriend got stabbed. That sucks."

Cade's eyebrows raise, and I feel like an utter moron. *That sucks?* Yes, Tobias. Getting stabbed sucks. How articulate.

After a few seconds, Cade's face smoothes out and he smiles at me. A real one, not a soft, patient smile like before.

"I think we can call that water under the bridge at this point," he says.

"How is he?"

I'm mostly asking about his stab wound, but the way Cade's face clouds over at the words, I can see there's something more at play there.

"He's..." The words trail off, and Cade swallows hard while not looking at me and fussing with the equipment. "He's Silas. Y'know. Life is hard sometimes."

There's a little twinge in my heart at the words, because even without knowing the context, I'm very familiar with the feeling.

"Yeah," I say. "You guys are good, though?"

As much as I don't know them, I feel a desperate need for them to stay together. Like how people get with celebrities. Like the continued existence of their love, despite both of them being fuck ups, makes the potential for my future happiness more real.

When Cade thinks about his answer, his expression shifts from worried to a broad, genuine smile, and this time he really does look me in the eye.

"Yeah. I love him. Nothing's changing that." He tilts his head, like he's taking me in for the first time. "Now come on, let's get you fixed up. I think we both have enough other shit to worry about than holding grudges. Deal?"

He holds out his fist, which I bump, and he bops away back to his work looking genuinely content.

It's the most surreal interaction I've had with someone in a while, and I vomited on a cop's shoes like half an hour ago.

After that, things go more smoothly. Tristan asks me questions about what happened, but he manages to not phrase things like I'm the scum of the earth, which is nice. They tell me I'm dehydrated, which isn't shocking, so they hook me up to some fluids. Someone—I think Gunnar—finally cleans up the puke. Tristan goes through the pros and cons of going to the hospital for a rape kit, which I stare blankly at the wall for, even if he phrases it all as respectfully as possible. When I refuse again, everyone drops it.

Tristan reminds me about STD testing, and I remember Micah organized that for me last time. Something in the mail.

God, no one would ever think the aftermath of something so dramatic is this mind-numbingly tedious.

By the end of it, I've been filled with fluids, given a painkiller which helps me drift even more, signed the iPad to refuse transport to the hospital, and watched Tristan hand Gunnar a piece of paper with a bunch of names of services he recommends, because I'm too tired to concentrate on anything now.

They pack up their shit, and Tristan comes back to lean toward me, now that I'm back in Gunnar's arms because I was slipping off the stool.

"If anything gets worse, you call me, kid. Even if it's off the books. We don't leave people behind."

I'm obviously too hydrated now, because my eyes are trying to fill with tears and I feel like a dumbass for it.

"Thanks," I say, even though it sounds pathetic.

Gunnar thanks them both as well, and they let themselves out.

"I think it's time for you to sleep, little one." Gunnar looks down at me. "How does that sound? We can deal with the rest of the bullshit tomorrow."

"Mmm."

I push my face further into his chest for the millionth time so far today. I can't truly wrap my head around the fact that this morning I was still in the motel, and now I'm here.

"Shower later. Sleep first," I say, mumbling.

"Okay."

Gunnar stands up, scooping me into his arms as he goes. I'm too tired. I can't care about how bad I must smell or how disgusting I am. I don't even care if I still have Eamon's sweat on my skin.

I just want to sleep.

"You'll watch while I sleep?"

"Of course I will, baby."

I'm out before we even get upstairs.

Chapter Twenty-Two

GUNNAR

As I watch Tobias finally rest, I want to feel peaceful. I should feel peaceful. He's here and safe. He's not nearly as injured as he could be. I deposited him on the couch, because I know how comfortable he feels there, and put on one of his favorite gore-filled movies on in the background before covering him with more blankets than I probably needed to.

Now I'm sitting, watching him and keeping him safe, and he believes in that enough to let himself really rest.

Everything is fine. Or it's going to be fine.

So why do I feel like I'm so full of rage that I'm choking on it?

All the images are playing on repeat in my head while I sit. Everything I can imagine Eamon doing to him, interspersed with what I saw on that goddamn security footage. I try to distract myself by making a list of everything Tobias needs to do when he's feeling up to it.

Micah gave us a little care package with PrEP and DoxyPEP before, so he's mostly covered on that front. Not 100%, but better than nothing. Tobias told me he was on PrEP regularly before this all went down, so he's only had some inconsistencies in being able to take it, instead of being completely unprotected.

I find the website Tristan recommended anyway and order another home STD screening panel. The fact that I have to get this makes me feel nauseous, but I'd rather face the truth than ignore it and have him get sick.

There's other stuff, as well. More legal stuff than just the police report. Seeing if he'll be willing to try for a protective order, although I can already see him saying no. I look up support groups he probably won't go to—spoiler alert: they're fucking thin on the ground out here if you're not into Jesus—and make notes about therapists he definitely won't let me pay for him to see. If I could even afford them, anyway.

It doesn't help. I'm trying to be proactive, but instead that angry, impotent feeling is coming back even stronger than before.

The only thing that doesn't make me useless is something so unrealistic that it's laughable. I picture killing Eamon in a thousand different ways. I plan out how I could hunt him down. How I might find him holed up in another sleazy hotel and surprise him.

I'm a little bigger than him, but he fights for a living, so I'd have to be prepared. I could shoot him before he even knows I'm there. Or I could do something to immobilize him, like a stun gun or a tranquilizer, before tying him up and telling him how much he deserved it as I tortured him to death.

Maybe it's the grotesque movie playing in the background. I hate violence. Even when I was angry all the time, it never gave me this specific kind of bloodlust. But it's the only thing I can think of that doesn't make me feel like I'm about to vibrate out of my skin with how useless I am.

It goes on for hours until I feel utterly consumed by it. I have nothing else to do but think these sick, soothing thoughts and wait for Tobias to wake up again.

He doesn't wake up with a gasp, like I was expecting him to. I can tell he's awake because of the way his body suddenly stiffens, but he doesn't move, and his eyes stay closed. I don't move either, giving him the chance to work through whatever he's thinking about.

When his eyes do eventually open, he looks around the dark room for a while before focusing on me.

"Good morning," I whisper. "Or good night, technically."

It's 3am, and he's been asleep for about nine hours. Thank god, because he needed it. I'm eternally grateful to Tristan for whatever painkiller he gave him. Even if he said it was a non-narcotic, it clearly helped.

"You stayed awake this whole time?" he asks, sitting up against the arm of the couch.

"I promised."

I try to smile at him, but it doesn't feel right. I shouldn't be able to smile when I've done nothing but simmer in my worthless anger all this time.

He brings up a hand to scrub at his eyes and makes a face at me.

"I'm sorry, I didn't mean—"

"Yeah, you did," I say, cutting him off. "It's fine. I wanted to. I'm glad you slept."

I move forward until I'm perching on the couch with him. He sways, like he's inexorably leaning into my orbit, and it makes my heart squeeze uncontrollably.

"I should shower," he says, still sleepy.

"Yeah." I push one dark curl out of his eyes, but it immediately tumbles back. "Do you want me in there with you or to go alone?"

His whole posture changes, shrinking in on himself.

"Alone, please," he says in a small voice that I fucking hate.

"No, baby, of course. I didn't mean you can't. And I didn't mean it in a weird way. Just in case you felt weak, or anything. I'll be out here, okay? I won't come in unless you yell for me."

Tobias looks at me. He looks at me hard, like he's looking inside me, and I have to resist the sudden urge to squirm.

"Gunnar, I don't..." His voice trails off, but then he takes a deep breath and tries again. "I don't know how I can thank you for all of this."

Like always, I have the lingering fear that he'll think he owes me something in return. It's weaker now, though.

I trust him. I don't know if I trust myself to help him in all the ways he needs, no matter how much I want to. But I trust him to tell me when I screw it up.

"You never need to thank me, Tobias." I don't let myself touch him as I say it, but I try to get all the meaning I can into it. "I'd do my small part a thousand more times for nothing in return. All I need is for you to be safe."

It's clear from his expression that he doesn't believe me, but he doesn't fight me on it. I lean back, giving him as much space as possible to get up and head to the bathroom. He gives me another lingering look as he goes, walking slowly, still obviously hurting. I look away, though.

At first, I was worried about poisoning him with my anger. Now I'm trying to remind myself not to get too lost in my own handwringing that I lose sight of what's important.

And no one is here to tell me what to do.

~

Unfortunately, I have to work. After a mostly sleepless week and one entirely sleepless night, it's the last thing I want to do, but it's my bar and no one else is going to do it for me. Today we're supposed to be reopening, now that the repairs are mostly finished, and I badly need some money coming into the register to start plugging the hole that Eamon put in this place.

Who knows how long the insurance claim will take to come through, if it does at all? I deleted the security footage, but this whole situation still stinks of impropriety. I wouldn't be surprised if they found a reason to deny the claim or even accuse me of being in on it.

Insurance fraud charges are the last thing I need, so I'm trying not to think about it. I almost didn't file the claim. It's not fraud. It was a crime that I had nothing to do with, and Tobias had no control over. But I get how it could be difficult to see it that way if you're not on the inside.

Hopefully, the company takes it all at face value that someone just broke in and trashed the place, and doesn't consider my many, many police reports about Eamon and Tobias to be connected.

These are all the thoughts racing through my head as I get the bar ready to open. I asked Tobias if he wanted to hang out with me down here, but he refused. I hate it. I'd feel so much better if he was in my line of sight. It's not like Eamon doesn't know where he is, and at least if I can see him, I can see exactly what's going on with him.

He put his foot down, though. I think my irritation must have been obvious to him, because after he told me he wasn't coming downstairs, he'd practically given me the silent treatment. Something about him is different this time. He's more closed off.

I get these moments where he looks at me with intense vulnerability or gratitude, but then a wall comes down. I have no idea if it's something I've done, or just something going on inside his head.

Like everything else the past few days, it seems to make me angry. Not at Tobias, but at the situation. Or maybe at myself for not being able to fix it.

Which is why I'm currently angrily cleaning things that have already been cleaned, like a housewife in an old mafia movie, when Sav comes in.

He looks around the place, giving a low whistle. I'm aware that it's not completely back to normal, but he doesn't need to point it out. At least it's up to code.

"Where the fuck have you been?" I can't control the snappiness in my tone.

Sav doesn't say anything. He looks at me, his eyes wider than usual, but the same inscrutable expression as always on his face.

I huff, but my irritation is still riding shotgun, and it refuses to let me back down yet, so I ignore him and get back to cleaning. Sav continues to walk inside, doing a slow inspection of the place before joining me behind the bar.

"You don't look good," he says.

I stop what I'm doing and practically throw my rag across the bar when I look at him.

"Yeah, well I've had a lot on my mind. Tobias is back and alive, in case you didn't know. If you care."

Sav's expression darkens, and when he leans in toward me, I get the barest glimpse into the kind of man he used to be before he changed. The violence that simmers underneath his normally tranquil surface.

I'm not very easily intimidated, but it's enough to make my breath catch.

He seems to realize it though and backs off after only a few seconds.

"I did know. I'm glad," he says, sounding carefully neutral. "Now you can both move on with your lives."

I frown, but my head is so full of angry static, I feel like I'm only hearing half the words he says. "Sure, until Eamon comes back, and we do this all over again."

Because that. That's the thing that's driving me insane. Living in limbo like this; never able to truly settle. Will Eamon come back? Will Tobias move on from the trauma? Will Tobias move on from me, or am I just a stopgap?

It's all too much to juggle emotionally, so I settle for a blanket of seething rage instead and picture Eamon's head exploding like a water balloon.

"I should have killed that motherfucker," I mutter to myself.

I'm pretty sure Sav hears me, but apart from arching an eyebrow, he doesn't say anything.

After that, things are quiet. I seethe. Sav helps prep. Kasia shows up and eventually we open to the same steady stream of locals that we normally serve at this time of day.

Time stretches on and on, and I do my best to put on the mask of the affable, mentally stable bar owner and not obsess about what Tobias might be doing upstairs.

By the end of the night, I'm so exhausted I can barely see straight. We're still not technically closed, but Kasia kicks me out, calling me a 'little bitch' because my brooding is giving her anxiety. I'm glad for the reprieve from having to talk to people, even though talking to people is normally one of my favorite parts of the job.

I think I just need to see for myself that Tobias is okay, and then get some sleep.

Of course, I haven't even made it up the stairs before my phone rings. I jump to answer it, in case it's the police with news or the insurance company with an update, even though only my sleep-addled brain would think any of that would happen this late at night.

No. It's my mother. Which immediately makes me heave out a giant sigh, then flood with guilt for that being my first reaction.

I haven't gone to visit her since everything started. Normally, I see her once a week. Which means I haven't missed that much, because Tobias has only been staying with me for…

Wow. It's incredible to think how much my life has changed in a couple of weeks. I can't go back to being the person I was before, though, pretending I didn't care about him as much as I do. It would be futile.

"Hi, Mom," I say when I finally get the balls to slide my thumb over and accept the call.

"There you are. I was beginning to think you were dead. I haven't heard from you in weeks."

She sounds more irked than concerned, but I ignore it.

"I'm sorry. I've been helping a friend with some legal issues, and it's been distracting. I should have called."

She's silent. There's a lot said in that silence that I don't want to hear, and I find myself rubbing at my temples as I stare at the peeling paint next to the staircase. I want to finish getting upstairs and be done with the day, not go fourteen rounds on what is and isn't an appropriate way to spend my life.

"I hope you're staying out of trouble." The terseness is unmistakable.

"Of course. I'm just trying to help someone out who's in trouble."

She doesn't say anything but makes a huffing noise that's so familiar I can picture the exact face she must be making right now. Like she's sucking on a lemon.

"Meddling does more harm than good. I thought you'd learned your lesson by now."

The white-hot rage that swells up in me is so entirely disproportionate to what she says, I'm a little shocked by it. It's yet another sign that I'm quickly spiraling out of control. Gritting my teeth, I decide I have no patience left for platitudes.

"Look, it's late. You should be in bed and I'm exhausted. I'll come visit soon. I can't talk right now."

I don't bother to say 'goodbye' before hanging up the phone, because I don't think my mouth will form the shape.

It's like there's a wellspring of old hurt inside me that has a thin piece of plyboard slapped over it. Most of the time it's fine, but when she touches it from just the right angle, even with the lightest brush of her fingers, it cracks, and old, bubbling venom pours out to fill my veins as if it never left.

With a deep, shuddering breath, I square my shoulders and finish making my way up to the apartment. The least I can do is not take out this attitude on Tobias. Hopefully, he at least got some rest today while I was working. Maybe he's feeling better and I can convince him to come sleep in the bed tonight.

The apartment is quiet when I knock and then let myself in, but that's what I expected. It's dark, apart from the flicker of the TV. On the screen is a movie I now recognize; Tobias has watched it enough times since he's stayed with me, and I turn away before I'm forced to watch a particularly gruesome murder sequence for the fourth or fifth time in my life.

He's on the couch, like I expected. I move closer to see if he's sleeping, but as soon as I do, the smell hits me.

Alcohol. A wall of fucking alcohol. Stronger than I probably smell of it, and I've been serving it all night.

On the ground next to the couch is a mostly empty bottle of vodka that was mostly full when I left for work before, and Tobias is turning to look at me with bleary eyes.

Even in the low light, I can see that his cheeks are burning red, which always happens when he drinks and would give him away even if the rest of it didn't. But he's got the whole drunk package going for him: his movements are slow and sloppy when he turns to look at me, his eyes are slightly unfocused, his hair is a mess, as if he's been pulling at it, and he has to blink owlishly at me several times before he seems to process if he's going to speak or not.

"Hey," is all he says in the end.

I can't contain my urge to sigh. "Hey."

"How was work?" he asks, with an unmistakable slur to his words.

"It was fine. How are you?"

The fact that he's pretending everything is normal and we're having this banal conversation is cranking up my anger even more, for some reason. This is why I didn't want to leave him alone. This is just one more way that he's in danger, and if I can't watch him, how can I keep him safe?

"Drunk," he says, letting his body collapse back onto the arm of the couch after leaning forward to greet me. "But I'm much more relaxed, so I guess it did the trick."

He holds his hands up as he says it, moving them through the air in a nonsensical pattern which I guess is meant to reflect how relaxed he feels. He studies his own hands as they move, all his gestures syrup-slow, then eventually turns his gaze back to me.

"You look angry."

It's a statement, not a question. And while he doesn't quite shrink in on himself as he says it, there's a hint of uncertainty in his posture.

I try to dispel my anger. My irrational, lingering anger that has been mounting day by day, hour by hour since the moment he was taken.

Hurling it at him would be not only useless, but just about the cruelest thing I could do. He's been the brunt of enough anger for one lifetime. But no matter how much I try to breathe through it and suppress the feelings, they stay right at the surface, roiling and chaotic, begging to be let out.

I'm standing there taking one deep breath after another, my legs spread wide, and my fists clenched. I can only imagine what I look like. All the images of Tobias and Eamon and my fucking dead father are rolling into one and plastering themselves on the inside of my eyeballs until I feel like my brain is about to melt out of my face like hot lava.

"I'm going to take a shower." It's the only thing I can think of to say that gets me a little distance until I can pull my head out of my ass.

Tobias sits up again, though, looking alarmed. "What's wrong?"

"Nothing, I just… I need to shower. I'll be back. Don't fucking drink anymore."

I turn toward the bathroom, but a noise behind me draws my attention back to him. Tobias is up and off the couch, scrambling to get to me on clumsy feet.

"*Nonono*," he says all in one breath. "Don't be mad. I'm sorry. I'll be good. I didn't mean to. I just couldn't breathe. It was so fucking exhausting, and I wanted everything to be quiet. I'll stop, I promise. Please don't be mad."

The words are an assault on my senses, rapid-fire attempts to placate me like my unspoken anger has tripped some kind of warning system in his brain that's pushing him to appease me at any costs. Guilt churns inside me, and I can't even look at him when he grabs for my shirt to pull me to him.

"I'm sorry," he says again, desperate, before pulling me harder.

I don't want to look at him. I don't want to exist in the toxic dynamic that we've somehow managed to create in the last minute and a half, because I don't know how to crawl my way out of it. But he yanks me hard, too drunk to be cautious, and it ends with me whipping my whole body to face him.

Whatever look is on my face, I don't want to know. It makes him shrink back in instinctive, protective fear. He lets go of my shirt immediately and takes a step back, his gaze dropping to the floor, and I feel like the scum of the fucking earth.

None of what's happening here is right, but I'm still standing here, not stopping it.

"I'm sorry," he says again, this time a whisper. The flush on his cheeks is even darker than before, and there's a sway to his body that he's trying and failing to hide.

My hands shake as I try to grasp onto something rational inside myself—anything—and feel like the old me. The calm, collected version of myself who always knows what to say instead. Because repressing my emotions is clearly not enough for him to not be affected by them, and ignoring this irrational anger isn't making it go away.

An idea hits me out of nowhere. It's the best I've got, so I do it.

I sit. I sit down on the floor, crossing my legs and looking up at Tobias. Now he's the one looming over me, at least, and I can stop feeling like I'm halfway to becoming a monster who haunts his dreams.

"No, I'm sorry," I say. "I'm upset and I shouldn't have let it scare you like that. I'm not angry at you. I'm angry, but not at you. I didn't mean to scare you."

I hold my hands out to him as I say it. He slowly takes in a deep breath, and I can see the fear leech out of him.

I can also see the moment that embarrassment tries to crawl in to replace it as Tobias starts shuffling his feet and looking away from me, but I don't let it.

"Hey," I say softly. "Don't be embarrassed. I'm the asshole right now, okay?" He nods. Reaching up, I hold out one hand to see if he'll take it.

Tobias slips his warm fingers between mine and then follows as I tug him down to the floor, sitting opposite me in the same position, mirrored so our knees are touching.

"I'm sorry," I repeat. "I was pissed about something else before I even came in here, and then I saw the vodka and I started to get scared, which I guess turned into more pissed, and then I scared you. Which scared me back. I'm sorry."

Tobias nods, ducking his head and his gaze at the same time. "It's not your fault I'm a mess."

"No, but it's my fault I'm a mess. I shouldn't be falling apart right now. That's your job."

I'm trying to make him smile, but it doesn't land. He's not smiling, and neither am I. There's an unspoken tension between us, I think, because neither of us knows what the fuck we're doing from here.

"Actually," I rub my forehead with one hand, trying to relieve the pressure lingering there but not succeeding. "I've been kind of a disaster the past few days. Even more of a disaster than you would expect, given the circumstances. And it probably has to do with some childhood shit that I try not to think about, so instead I'm just walking around, acting like an asshole all the time for no reason. Well, for no obvious reason."

Tobias finally lifts his face so he can look me in the eye. He's still alcohol-hazy, but his focus is entirely on me, which makes this a little harder.

I hate talking about this. I only went to therapy to talk about it when it became obvious that if I didn't, the messy anger I was carrying was going to boil over and potentially kill me, and now I feel like I'm right back where I was seventeen years ago. Except this time, Tobias is in the sights of my unregulated emotions.

Which isn't something I'm willing to risk.

"So, it sounds worse than it is. Well, it is awful. But it sounds so bad when you say it. Which is why I never talk about it to anyone, but I guess you deserve to know. Just listen to the whole story before you make any judgments. Okay?"

He nods.

I take a deep breath and try to wall off the part of my brain that produces mental images, like I always do when I think about this. Eventually, when I'm still nowhere close to ready, I speak.

"When I was nineteen years old, my brother killed my father."

Tobias looks at me with wide eyes. "What the fuck?"

"Yeah, I know. Just let me tell you the whole thing."

Chapter Twenty-Three

TOBIAS

I don't know if it's the alcohol, the adrenaline, or just my brain finally giving up on active participation in the world, but I swear the words he says don't penetrate my consciousness.

His brother... *killed his father?* It sounds like a Telenovela.

Gunnar squeezes my hand where it's still held in his, and the warmth and familiar strength of his grip brings me back to reality.

I think he's about to keep telling the story, and I know I'm supposed to listen, but the words tumble out, anyway.

"But I thought you were normal?"

Gunnar stares at me for a second, then makes a huffing noise that's on the cusp of being laughter.

"Is anyone really normal?" he asks, already looking a thousand times more like himself than he did a few minutes ago when he walked in.

I swear, nothing has scared me quite like the sight of him standing there, bristling with unvoiced anger as he looked down at me like the broken mess that I am. At first, my instinct told me I was in danger.

Then my higher thought processes had engaged, and I knew that I wasn't. It was a weird feeling. It's not like I made a logical argument with myself that Gunnar would never hurt me. It was more like the alarm was ringing, but when I looked at the threat, my body refused to believe it was real. Gunnar wouldn't hurt me. Not like that.

But that didn't mean I wasn't still panicking. Because although even my most paranoid, alcohol-saturated brain still trusts Gunnar not to hurt me physically, I felt even more afraid at the idea that he might be getting sick of my bullshit.

Him leaving me is a very real fear. Because he should. I don't do anything but drag him down, and there's no sign of me getting better anytime soon. That was the fear that had me scrambling to my feet to stop him from walking away from me.

If I'd been afraid of *him*, I would have kept cowering on the couch. Instead, I ran to him, practically begging him not to leave me because I'm so much of a mess I can't make it through a day by myself without drowning the silence in alcohol and fictional violence.

Gunnar looks to the side, his eyes unfocused as he thinks about whatever story he's trying to force himself to tell me. I want to let him know he doesn't have to share if he doesn't want to, but the truth is that I'm dying to know. He can't start something so bonkers and then just drop it. So, I hold my tongue.

"I guess my family was normal," he starts. "I had a mom and a dad, my brother was two years younger than me. It was all very nuclear family, white picket fence. Or a slightly rough-around-the-edges version of it. My dad owned a pawnshop that did pretty well. You know how it is around here. There was always food on the table and bills always got paid. They owned their own home. That kind of thing."

I'm watching him, but he pauses to chew on some intangible thought for a few minutes before he continues.

"I was kind of difficult as a kid. My parents weren't exactly the warmest people, if you know what I mean, and I struggled a lot. This isn't a fun place to be closeted, especially back then, and I was still figuring a lot of stuff out. I wasn't a disaster, but I was just stressed out all the time, and I think my parents gradually realized that having children was a lot more work than they wanted it to be. It caused a lot of friction in the house, and my brother—Lukas—got lost in the shuffle sometimes.

"I partied a lot in high school. Drank a lot, did a lot of drugs. I came out of it pretty unscathed, thankfully, but Lukas followed in my footsteps, of course. He didn't just stick to partying, though. He started dealing a little, then dealing more, and before I even noticed anything was happening, he was in way too deep with some local guys who did a lot of the stuff that the Banna does now."

He gets quiet again, but this time I see the emotion brimming in his eyes. It's a stark contrast to all that anger that he was holding earlier. That he's been holding since I got back, I guess, now that I let myself think about it. Without pausing to second-guess myself, I move forward, crawling into his lap until my back is pressed against his chest and his arms are resting over my shoulders, wrapped around me where they belong.

Gunnar freezes at first, before taking in a deep breath and letting it out, with so much of the tension in his body going with it. He tangles his fingers in mine again, playing with them absently while he keeps talking.

"Anyway. It all happened so fast. By the time I pulled my head out of my own ass long enough to realize what was going on... I don't know. I tried to fix it, but I underestimated how serious it was. I've thought a lot about what I wish I'd done differently, and I don't have a good answer. I'm sure this is all sounding familiar to you right now."

I nod, letting him feel the movement against his chest because I'm not sure I'm capable of vocalizing anything right now. Yeah, this does all feel very familiar.

"I still don't know the details of exactly what happened. I think he owed money, and thought the easiest way to get it would be to rob our dad's pawnshop. It's a cash-heavy business, and he knew the ins and outs of it, so he thought he could get away clean. He came in with a friend all dressed up, expecting to scare the shit out of my dad, I guess. They were high at the time, and it probably seemed smart. Dad wasn't taking it, though. He fought them, because he had a short fucking temper, especially for shit like that. I honestly don't know what Lukas was thinking. As if it was Dad's first time getting rolled in a town like this?"

His voice trails off as he loses track of what he's saying. I burrow in deeper to the protective shell of his chest, trying to let the warmth of him chase off the chill from all my own memories that are crowding around me right now.

"Anyway. There was a struggle, a gun went off. You know. Dad died. Lukas went down for it, and he made it about a year and a half into his prison sentence before he got killed in a brawl. He was collateral damage, I think. Just in the wrong place, wrong time. Like every other aspect of his life."

Gunnar leans down and presses his forehead against my shoulder. His next words are muffled, but I can still hear them, and the feeling of his hot breath on me as he speaks is like an anchor.

"It was all a total waste. That's the worst part. It was completely pointless. Gangs work so hard to look glamorous and cool, but everyone ends up like this. These clusterfuck endings where nothing but sadness comes out of it. My mom's life was ruined. She and my dad had their faults, but they were fucking in love and she never got over it. She just mopes around the house and lives off his life insurance. I spent years being a wreck and feeling like it was all my fault until I decided to pull myself together and try to at least help other people. Something to make up for how selfish I was as a kid. But they're still dead. My family still barely exists, and the gangs are still just as powerful and ruining as many lives as they were before."

That's it. I can feel the end of his story without him needing to announce it, as well as I can feel all the unspoken implications of it—seeing his bar destroyed, seeing me get pulled back into Eamon's shit—it was probably more than just a rational amount of upsetting. Because it was all a shadow of the shit that he already lived through once and failed to prevent.

I get it. I always feel like I'm stuck reliving the same shitty consequences of my actions over and over again, and it makes me so angry I want to scream until I puke.

It makes sense now why he's been so much more on edge than I expected.

We sit in silence for a long time, burying ourselves deeper in the comfort of each other's presence, even though we're also the source of each other's pain. I trace the edges of Gunnar's fingers, feeling where the skin is callused and where it's soft, and he continues to breathe in the scent of my neck.

"I'm sorry, Gunnar." It's the only thing I can think of to say.

He squeezes me a little tighter.

"It's not your fault. You didn't do anything wrong. You were caught up in a bunch of bullshit, just like Lukas was."

"Yeah, but you didn't do anything wrong, either," I say. His silence tells me he doesn't totally agree, and I know better than anyone how difficult a point that is to argue, so I let it lie. Eventually, I ask the question that's burning a hole in my chest. "Where do we go from here?"

Gunnar lifts his head, nosing along the side of my face and placing a kiss there before he speaks.

"Why don't we go to bed for now, and talk about this later. Sober. And less… in our heads."

I make a small, affirmative noise, because the liquor is starting to hit me harder than I'd like. All the peace it gave me before is being replaced by the itching, crawling anxiety that I knew would show up eventually. Alcohol is always a trade-off—deaden the immediate screaming anxiety, but in exchange you get this insidious, residual version showing up later.

Sometimes it's worth it, sometimes it's not. I've never been accused of having the best judgement, so who knows if I made the right choice this time?

I just need more of him. More than I have. As much as he'll give me. For every bit of peace that I'm able to carve out of the world with vodka or anything else, it's nothing compared to the peace I get from him.

I see the way he looks at me, though. Like I'm damaged or dangerous or something. Like we're right back to where we started, and he's worried about me imprinting on him and preparing to offer up sex in exchange for rescue services rendered.

If there's a way to get it through his thick skull how much I fucking want him, I'm all ears. Because the feeling of all this bullshit is burning inside me, and I *know* that he's the best thing to get it out of me. He's the only thing that's ever made me feel like a real person who deserves good things. Clinging to that isn't some kind of misplaced gratitude. It's my desperation to keep feeling that way.

"Gunnar," I say, my voice lowering into the sultry range as I turn and press my lips to his.

I'm still too drunk not to be sloppy, but I'm full of enthusiasm. Genuine enthusiasm, too, which isn't something I've felt very often in my life. I don't know if that makes me sick or a pervert. Maybe I should want to wall myself off in a cave and never want to have sex again after what I've been through.

It feels like they're two different things in my mind, though. The Eamon shit and the Gunnar shit. The Eamon shit is a poison, still trapped inside me and leeching my blood, bit by bit. While the Gunnar shit is a bright spark of something I actually *want* to do other than lie on the couch all day.

Just thinking about it gets me hard. I feel frantic with the need to do something about it.

Please don't take this feeling away from me.

Of course, Gunnar pulls away from the kiss almost as quickly as it began. He doesn't move far, but far enough that I can't taste him anymore. There's an awkward silence while he stares at me, but then his face softens, and he pushes my tangled, couch-matted hair out of my eyes.

"Come on, baby," he says. "Let's talk more in the morning. I'm tired, you're drunk and tired. Showering and then water and then bed. Actual bed, not couch bed. We can piece together the rusted pieces of our lives in the daylight, okay? I'll still love you just as much tomorrow."

I blink. Then Gunnar blinks, while my brain is slowly, arduously backtracking to go over all the words that just came out of his mouth.

Did he just say...?

The tension around his mouth and the fact that I can see the whites of his eyes so clearly tells me that yes, he did say it, and no, he did not mean to.

My brain feels more fuzzy and alcohol-sodden than ever. Maybe he's right. Dealing with all these complicated issues tomorrow sounds like a great idea.

I stand up first, swaying on my feet enough that Gunnar shoots up immediately to steady me. The air around us still reeks of awkward silence, but I think we're both pushing past it.

"Can I shower first?" I ask.

Before, I was thinking about asking to shower together. Now that the alcohol has unlocked this desperate, loudly horny part of me that wants to join in the party of drowning out emotion with external sensations, I was all in on trying to convince Gunnar to check his ethics at the door. The thought of his hands on me, his lips on me, his hard cock pressed against me; all while the water fell down around us and the noise drowned out my thoughts, it makes me practically giddy.

I notice that my brain carefully ducks the issue of whether we're actually fucking in this hypothetical, but I figure I'll cross that bridge when I come to it.

Now, though, the awkwardness between us is like a landmine and I need a little space before I detonate it.

"Of course, baby. Did you eat?"

I shrug as I walk away, pulling up my shirt and discarding it somewhere I can't see.

"I'll take that as a no," he calls out after me, before heading to the kitchen.

The fact that he's making me food keeps me warm and focused all the way through my shower. He not only cares enough to make it for me, but he noticed I needed it when I couldn't have identified any of my needs with a fucking guide dog.

No, I refuse to give this up. It's too good. He can have whatever doubts he wants about my motives. If he thinks I'm grateful or desperate, I don't care. As long as he still wants me, I'm staying right fucking here. And I'm going to show him exactly how much he means to me.

Chapter Twenty-Four

GUNNAR

I wake up to the sound of Tobias whimpering and the bed shaking with the force of his movement. As soon as I open my eyes, the fog of sleep clears away so I can see what's happening.

It's not like he wasn't having nightmares before. It's possible he always will, although I'm not exactly an expert on the subject. I know still have nightmares about shit that wasn't anywhere near as visceral as the trauma he's carrying.

I watch him in the low light for a few minutes, running my fingers gently down the side of his face. It's so dark, all I can see of him is shades of gray, but it's more than enough to make out his anguish. He's curled on his side, with small, raw noises coming from his mouth while his fingers flex in front of his chest. Part of me thinks he's reaching for me in his sleep, while another part dismisses that as part of my savior complex.

It's impossible to know when to trust my own judgement where Tobias is concerned. After all the work we did to sew that particular bag of issues shut, it's been ripped wide open again. I'm right back where I started, weighing each thought and decision to see if it's genuinely in his best interest, or if I'm really motivated by my own wants.

It's terrifying. Utterly, bone-chillingly terrifying. If there's one thing that makes me want to retch, it's the thought that I could let my worst impulses get the better of me. Even if my impulses aren't garbage ones like wanting to fuck him... I don't care if he never wants to have sex again. That's not the point. I'm more concerned about the deep-seated desire to center myself as the hero of his story.

The thought twists in my head until I'm scared to move or breathe or even touch him sometimes, which doesn't help him either.

He came to me. He wants me. Denying him the comfort that he wants isn't any better and is just as much of a *fuck you* to his autonomy as the rest of it.

I have to walk the line. To be the man he deserves without letting it feed my own ego, or all this falls apart.

I'm still stroking his skin as I think this through. I'm not supposed to wake him. I read it online when I was deep diving into trauma recovery. It's not like this is a brand-new subject for me, but I've never been this closely involved before. Normally, I limit myself to offering a place to stay, maybe a job, and the occasional shoulder to cry on.

I work very hard not to get invested. With Tobias, I'm lying here, wide awake and more invested than I've been in my life.

Tobias opens his eyes, although he stares at me like he's not seeing anything for a long time. Then he takes in a small, sharp breath, and the world seems to come into focus.

"Gunnar?"

"Yeah, baby," I say, keeping my voice soft and low as I take his face in my hands. "It's me. You had a nightmare."

He shivers, working his body closer to mine under the covers before finally fisting my shirt in his hands the way he was trying to in his sleep.

"Okay." The word comes out muffled, because he's already sinking lower and pressing his face against my chest.

I can see light creeping in around the curtains, so at least we made it through most of the night before he woke up. Between the time I spent before bed making him eat, shower, and hydrate, then a decent amount of sleep, he'll at least have been able to metabolize all that fucking vodka.

I assume he's trying to fall back asleep, so I shift until my arms are wrapped around him and hold him tight. But his breathing doesn't even out again. It stays fast while he keeps squeezing me to him, and for a second, I wonder if he's having a panic attack.

Just when I'm about to lean back and look at him, though, I feel his teeth scrape across my chest through the fabric of my shirt. At the same time, his deft fingers dig into my ribs, and he drags his hips against mine in a way that can only be described as seductive.

It's so fucking unexpected, I freeze. He keeps going for a few more seconds, teasing my nipple through my shirt and making arousal shoot through me when I wasn't prepared for it. I gasp, before palming the back of his head and tugging him up where I can look him in the eye.

"Baby, what are you doing?"

His voice is quiet, still sleep-soft and thick with his own arousal.

"Fuck me, Gunnar," he murmurs, grinding against me again for emphasis.

My brain goes entirely blank at the thought; I'm so caught off-guard.

What do I do? My body is already on board, lighting up at the barest touch from him, like always. So much of me wants to be that close to him, like it'll cement the connection between us in a way that no one can rip apart.

But I never expected him to want it so soon.

"Maybe we should talk about it first," I say, still holding him close because the last thing I want is for him to feel like I'm rejecting him.

"There's nothing to talk about," he says before kissing me, plunging his tongue into my mouth while he continues to grind against me, his hands sliding down to squeeze the flesh of my ass. "I want you—*mmph*—inside me." Now his cock is half-hard, and he drags it slowly against me before wrapping his legs around my hips as well as he can in this position.

I kiss him back, letting my hands roam up the expanse of his back while he squeezes me tight.

"Fuck, I want you too, baby," I whisper in between kisses.

I can already picture it. He would look so beautiful beneath me, flushed with arousal and begging for more.

But that mental image triggers another one—the memory of how he froze up when I accidentally put too much of my weight on top of him. I still ache from the guilt of making him feel that way. How much worse would it be if we got halfway through sex and he started to panic?

The memory would be tainted forever for both of us. It could set him even further back in his recovery. It could make him frightened of me.

Or even worse, he could start to panic and not tell me, pretending everything was fine. Because he's strong and I know how much he wants to feel 'normal' again.

Fuck.

I want this more than anything, but I don't want it to be a disaster we can never recover from.

He's still kissing me, slowly but deeply enough to make my head swim a little. We don't break apart until he starts tugging my t-shirt over my head. It gets thrown somewhere on the floor. Then his hands are all over my chest, palming my pecs and teasing my nipples, quickly being joined by his eager little mouth. We're side to side, but he's hooked his leg over my hip until he's almost entirely wrapped around me, and it already feels like we're a few thin layers of fabric away from this new kind of intimacy.

When he reaches down to shuck his sleep pants, I snap out of it. The arousal and apprehension are neck and neck for control of my emotions.

"Tobias, wait. I wanna talk about this first."

He freezes, looking at me. Not upset, per se, but with something cracking in his expression. When he kisses me again, it's more fevered. More desperate. He keeps talking, but only in breaks between having his lips on my lips and his tongue in my mouth, with his hands clutching every part of me as close as it can get.

"No," he says. "Please, I need this." He grinds his hips against me again, his heels digging into my ass now, like he's trying to roll my weight on top of him, although now I can feel him trembling. "I need you. Fuck it out of me, please. I want it out. I want it all out."

His voice gets more ragged and breathless in the worst possible way the longer he talks. His movements are sloppy and desperate, and everything starts to feel off.

Eventually, I pull his hands away from me as gently as I can and hold them between us. He's shaking obviously now, his breath coming rapidly in the panicked way, not like he's turned on, even though he keeps trying to grind against me and his cock is still hard.

"I want this too, baby, but we should slow down. You don't look—"

"What?" He interrupts me, a sudden sharpness to his tone that I'm already intimately familiar with from the many, many other times I've underestimated him and pissed him off. "I don't look okay? I don't look normal? I'm not fucking okay. I'm not normal. I'm shit, and I feel like shit, and I'm asking you to help me feel better. So, unless you secretly like it when I feel like shit, or you're now so fucking repulsed by me that you don't want to touch me at all—"

"Hey," I snap, because it's my turn to cut him off. "Stop. Don't put words in my mouth. None of that is true. But you're shaking and you just woke up from a nightmare because you walked your ass back here from a three-day, all-expense-paid vacation to sexual assault land! I don't think it's particularly radical for me to suggest that this isn't the best time for me to bend you over and get my rocks off."

I regret everything I say the second I say it. The words feel like poison on my tongue. Not just what I'm saying, but the anger as I say it. Because it sounds angry to him and any other rational person, but only I know that I'm not really angry, I'm fucking terrified.

I'm terrified all the time. Like I'll breathe wrong or touch him wrong or make yet another shitty choice, and he'll be hurt because of it.

Bottling up all that fear was a terrible choice, because he looks well and truly hurt, and it's all my fault. I can see the pain in his face for a few seconds as I reach for him, already trying to apologize, but he immediately tries to cover it with anger. He rolls over like he's about to get out of bed, and my heart pounds with more guilt and fear.

"Wait, Tobias," I say, forcing myself to sound calmer than I feel. "I'm so sorry. That was shitty, and I didn't mean any of it to come out like that. Please don't go."

He freezes, half-off the bed already. Slowly, though, he lets his weight drop back down and turns to face me. He's not touching me anymore. Instead, he's sitting cross-legged on the mattress, pulling a pillow into his lap to hold. It's better than running away, though.

"I'm scared," I tell him, going for naked honesty. "I want you so much, and I want to feel that close to you. But I'm scared to hurt you or frighten you or make things worse between us. I know that's selfish, but it's true."

"I thought after we talked last night, we were good. I thought things were normal between us. I want to go back to normal."

I frown. "We are good. But we're not normal. I don't feel fucking normal either. You're not the only one. And I don't want you to force yourself to do something uncomfortable because you think I want it."

Tobias avoids eye contact at all costs, tension obvious in every muscle of his body.

Finally, after a long silence, he mumbles his words to the comforter.

"What if *I* want it?"

I reach out, placing my fingers beneath his chin to tilt his face up so I can see him. "What?"

"I'm not always doing things just to appease you. What if I asked because I want it?" he asks, more sure of himself now. "Does that make me some kind of pervert? Like I'm sick for not wanting to spend all my time crying in a corner?"

He sounds angry, but I can't tell if he's angry with me, himself, or just the universe.

"Am I, Gunnar? Am I a freak?"

"Oh, honey," I sigh, reaching out to pull him toward me. "You're not a freak. I don't think there's a right or wrong way to feel after going through a bunch of fucked-up trauma. I just want to give you what you need—what we both need, probably—without triggering you or fucking everything up."

After a few more moments of silence, I realize what's been staring me in the face this whole time.

"What if you fucked me?" I ask.

Tobias leans back, looking at me with bloodshot eyes.

"What?"

"You said you're ready to have sex and you want to feel something different. Why don't you fuck me? Then you're in control, but it's still bringing us as close as it would the other way around."

Tobias is still staring at me like I've grown a second head, and I'm not sure if he hates the idea or is just confused.

"You'd let me?" he finally asks.

Oh, my sweet baby gay. Sometimes I forget how inexperienced he is.

"Of course," I say, taking his face in my hands and sweeping my thumbs over both cheeks. "People like different things. I know I like to top a lot of the time because I kind of have a thing about control, but it's not like a rule. I've had a great time bottoming before, and even if I'd never tried it, I'd damn well be ready to do it for you, if it was what you needed."

Tobias still looks uncertain, chewing on his bottom lip, which I didn't totally expect.

"Unless you don't want to," I add. "Have you ever topped before?"

"Uh, a girl, once. In high school. Or maybe girls don't count. It was awful, anyway."

He blushes, and I fight to keep a straight face because it's fucking adorable, but I don't want him to think I'm laughing at him.

Instead, I pull him into a kiss. I tease his mouth open with my tongue, getting him to open up to me slowly, until we're both distracted from all the awkwardness I just brought crashing down on us.

By the time we break apart again, he's panting and I can see his erection tenting his sleep pants, convincing me even more that this is what he wants.

"Please, Gunnar," he says. "I want more."

We go slow. I focus on keeping him close to me, holding his gaze and making sure he's not checking out the way he's done before. But he's present the entire time. The more of my attention I give him, the more worked up he gets until he's grinding shamelessly against me, humping his leaking erection against my bare thigh, fingering me open while I whisper gentle praise in his ear.

Once I'm ready, I grab a condom that I fished out of the nightstand from next to the lube and watch him put it on. He looks nervous, but not scared. And the overwhelming aura of desire in the room is choking the life out of any other emotion that tries to butt its way in right now.

I arrange myself on my front so he has easy access and spread myself open for him, enjoying the feeling of his slender body weighing me down.

"That's it, baby," I say as he finally pushes inside me.

His fingers are kneading the flesh of my sides like a nervous tic, but I love it. Just another reminder that he's here with me, and nowhere else.

"You're okay?" There's a quiver to his voice when he speaks.

"I'm okay." I turn around, looking at him over my shoulder. He looks phenomenal. Arching his back while a flush crawls over the pale, sand-toned skin of his chest. The muscles in his arms defined by how hard he's holding on to me, and his abs tensing and relaxing over and over as he tries to hold himself in place. His mouth is open just enough for him to pant and for me to catch a glimpse of that pink, wet tongue that I wish was in my mouth right now, and his eyes are at half-mast. "You can move, Tobias. Please."

The first thrust he gives is tentative, but it still feels good. I wasn't lying when I said it had been a long time since I've bottomed, but I had missed it. Pleasure is already unfurling deep in my gut, and my hips are loosening as I rock back into him.

"That's it, baby boy. Don't hold back. Fuck, you feel good inside me."

The words end on a moan. He picks up the pace, his movements becoming more confident the longer I encourage him with my words and all the noises he's pulling out of me.

"Fuck yes. Right there," I moan as he starts hitting me at a different angle.

Tobias drapes his body over mine, so we're skin to skin. I can feel his hot breath puffing on my ear, and I want to turn around and kiss him, but I feel like he might be lost in the moment. He's squeezing the skin on my sides so tightly it's going to bruise, but I don't care.

His lips find the back of my neck, but he can't seem to concentrate enough to kiss me, instead mouthing at the skin as he breathes heavily. He pistons his hips, pumping into me quickly now, matching his puffs of breath and making little grunting noises that would be adorable if I weren't too distracted by how fucking good this feels.

"That's it, baby. Are you gonna make me come?" My cock is hard and heavy, pointing down at the mattress and drooling precum, so I find his hand blindly with mine and guide it to wrap around my length. "You feel so good. Be a good boy and make me come, then give me everything you've got. I want every drop in those tight little balls deep inside me, got it?"

Tobias makes a noise that might have been *uh-huh* but might have just been an exhale. He gets to work jerking me, tossing my body back and forth between the two points of pleasure until I'm moaning loudly and rolling my hips into every thrust he gives me.

"Oh fuck, perfect, Tobias." I barely manage to spit the words out before I'm spraying cum over the sheets, every muscle in my body tightening.

I can hear Tobias gasp as I unconsciously squeeze his cock, and his thrusts pick up pace even more until he's fucking me with a kind of messy desperation that I find impossibly sexy.

"Can I?" he asks in a cracking voice. "Please."

"Go on, baby. Fill me up. Give it all to me, like a good boy." I milk his cock with my ass as I say it, joy filtering through me as his pace stutters and he thrusts as deep inside me as he can.

He's so quiet, I wouldn't know he was coming if I couldn't feel it. Not that I can feel the cum itself with the condom in the way, but I can feel the throb and twitch of him unloading inside me, as well as the stiffness of his whole body as he squeezes me impossibly tight.

He doesn't even take a breath until he's done. Then he takes in one long, heaving inhale, followed by another. I can't tell if it's a good thing or not without looking at him, so I gingerly pull myself forward until he slips out of me, before turning over to face him.

It isn't panic on his face. It's not quite pleasure, either. It feels like it could go either way, though, so I do my best to nudge it in the right direction.

"Come here, baby," I murmur, holding out my arms to him.

He collapses on me immediately. His body is in between my legs, the condom an unpleasant tactile sensation where his softening erection is pressed against me that I choose to ignore. His arms wrap around me the same way mine wrap around his, then he's nosing his way into the spot between my chin and shoulder. The spot that he always seems to seek out and fit into so perfectly.

"You did so well, baby."

I run my hand up and down the long line of his back while he continues to breathe. I murmur more soothing nonsense in his ear the whole time, telling him what a good boy he is and how good he made me feel. I tell him we can do that as many times as he wants, or we don't have to do it again if he doesn't want to.

Slowly, he sags. The tension leaves his body and his breathing evens out.

I finally chance a look at him, craning my neck.

"Are you okay?"

He nods, his face serious but his eyes clear.

"I'm okay. Thanks, Gunnar. That was good. That was a good idea." Tobias blows out a long breath and his mouth tilts up at the end like he's almost trying to smile, but he looks too exhausted to get very far. "I feel a little better now."

"Do you wanna get cleaned up?"

Tobias moans. "No, but I think we have to."

He pushes off me, groaning some more with the movement. I snag his wrist gently first though, pulling him into a kiss.

"What was that for?" he asks when I break away.

"I think you're pretty fucking awesome," I say, because it's true, and it's the only clear thought in my head right now. There are other words—words that spilled out of me by mistake last night and we both ignored—but I manage to keep them in for now.

He blushes. This boy has the audacity to blush right after he just fucked me like his life depended on it, and it's adorable as sin.

"Yeah, well. You're one to talk."

I can't help but smile at him. I'm aware that he's only really good with words when he's telling me to go fuck myself. Then, he's shockingly loquacious.

You're one to talk is still one of the sweetest things he's said to me, and I'll carry it around in my heart forever with all the others.

Chapter Twenty-Five

TOBIAS

After I shot every last bit of brain matter out of my cock, Gunnar and I both went back to sleep until much, much later in the day. When we wake up again, things feel less awkward between us. Not *not* awkward, but better.

On the upside, after all Gunnar's mandatory food, water, rest in a bed and subsequent orgasms, I only have the barest hint of a hangover. Even though I was a dumbass and inhaled more vodka than my body knew what to do with yesterday. Gunnar gives me shit about this, of course, and asks to trade metabolisms.

He makes a lot of self-deprecating jokes about how old he is, which I low-key kind of hate. He's not old. He's probably felt old his entire life, after what he went through with his family. I know exactly how that feels. I don't think I've ever thought of myself as young or innocent. At least not since I was literally a toddler.

That kind of emotional burden wears on you. It's another reason I think he and I belong together, because we both get it. But sometimes I worry he's one penny drop away from having some insane crisis of conscience and breaking it off entirely.

These are the thoughts consuming me as we both move quietly around the apartment and get ready for the day. They're so distracting that it isn't until I'm standing there—dressed in Gunnar's oldest and smallest gym clothes and looking ridiculous; but clean and about as presentable as I get—that I realize I have nowhere to fucking go.

It hits me like a gunshot.

I'm just... here? I just exist?

What the fuck am I supposed to do now? Even though Eamon is still out there, he knows where I am now, so I don't have to put energy into hiding like I did before. I should focus on how to stay safe from him, but that still feels impossible, so I push it to the side for now.

I think technically this is supposed to be my 'happily ever after' or whatever. Or as close as I'm going to get to one. But all I feel is all-consuming stress and fear with no solutions, and no ability to focus long enough to find solutions. I'd give anything for someone to point me in any fucking direction other than standing here like I'm waiting to be snatched again.

TV did not prepare me for this part. This gaping, empty vastness stretching out in front of me where I'm somehow supposed to build a new life from nothing. If I had the tools to do that, I would never have ended up with Eamon in the first place.

"Tobias?"

Gunnar's voice cuts through the fog in my head like always, deep and mellifluous, anchoring me to reality.

"Yeah?"

"What's wrong? You've been staring into space for minutes."

He moves to stand in front of me, tilting his head down, his eyes dark except for that one bright blue segment, but concern etched on every inch of his face. As per usual, when I'm around.

I try to dig deep and find the words to express what suddenly stopped me in my tracks.

"I uh, I realized I don't have anywhere to go, I guess. Maybe ever? Does that make sense? Like... what the fuck do I do now? Am I hiding up here for the rest of my life in case Eamon comes back? Am I trusting the fuckwit cops to find him? Am I trying to get a job, or what? Who tells me what to do now?"

Gunnar scrunches his face up in a way that would have made me look like a little kid, but he still manages to make dignified. Elegant, beardy asshole.

"I think you take it one step at a time. No one can tell you what to do, so you just figure it out, little by little, and let the people around you help. There's nothing else you can do." He takes both my hands in his, enveloping me in his warmth. "If you want my vote, though, I don't think hiding up here forever is a good idea. I want to keep you safe in case Eamon comes back more than anyone, but I'm worried about you sitting up here in the dark all day. Why don't you at least come hang out with me downstairs today, and we'll take it from there?"

I turn the concept over in my mind, and in the end, I nod. I'm chewing on my lip, because the idea of being out in the open, even inside the Feral Possum, still makes me nervous. But the thought of spending another day trapped up here with nothing but my own thoughts for company makes me even more nervous.

More than anything, I want to see Lola. Gunnar has been keeping tabs on her via Tristan, and she's okay but still in the hospital. I need to see her. I miss her more than I realized I was capable of missing another human. But no matter how much bravado I'm trying to throw down in front of Gunnar, just imagining walking into that hospital right now makes me break out in a cold sweat.

Maybe sitting in the bar all day is a compromise. Like a step in the right direction.

"Okay," I say, before a thought suddenly occurs to me. "But if you spend the whole time babysitting me and trying to snatch alcohol out of my hands, I'm going to scream."

Gunnar's face twists. "Tobias..."

"No," I interrupt. I don't even know if I want a drink right now, but I can already picture him neglecting his job to obsessively monitor me, and it makes me itch. "I can't do the whole controlling thing again. I know you're trying to look out for me instead of trying to make me submit to you, or whatever, but I still can't do it. If I have to spend the rest of my life walking on eggshells, wondering if what I'm doing is pissing you off or if I'm about to have a drink yanked out of my hand, I think I'll genuinely fucking lose it. Not with you. Please don't turn this into that."

This time, Gunnar looks like I slapped him. His face is pale and his eyes are wide, while he's loosened his grip on my hands so much they would drop away from his touch if I didn't hold them there.

He opens his mouth a few times like he's about to speak, but no words come out. Finally, once he's churned through his thoughts for a while, he answers me.

"I'm sorry. I never want you to feel afraid of me. Even if it's just afraid of disappointing me. I want to take care of you so fucking much, I forget sometimes how far it pushes me. I can't... I'll stop. I promise."

I snort. "Don't make promises you can't keep. Just try. I have to make my own choices, for better or worse, remember? Otherwise, I'm just trading a shitty cage for a nicer one. I'm sorry. I'm not trying to be a dick, but this is important to me."

My voice wavers a little, because I realize as the words are exiting my mouth how important it actually is to me. And just how insane it is that I went from thinking it to vocalizing it all at once, and he's actually fucking listening to me.

I'll never get used to this, I think.

"I'll try," he says in the end, still looking unconvinced. "I'm worried about you, though. I don't like the drinking."

At least we're being honest now.

"I don't have a drinking problem!" The words are out of my mouth on instinct, something I've thought a thousand times before. "I have a life problem.

And a personality problem. And an Eamon problem. Sometimes it gets too much, and booze helps quiet it, is all."

He sighs, like my individual words have weighed down his chest, one by one.

"That's how it starts for a lot of people, Tobias. I see it every day at the bar, and I almost became it myself, after my dad died. I know how easy it is to let everything get fuzzy until you're relying on the easiest, most convenient crutches instead of fixing your problems." I must be making a face, because Gunnar studies me for a second and then pulls me into a hug, kissing the top of my head before he continues. "I saw how you drank before, sometimes. Remember? I'm just worried. And you said your dad was an alcoholic, which makes me more worried, because there's a genetic factor to these things."

I pull back. "No, I said he was a drunk and a piece of shit, just like his dad. Oh, and a racist. I don't think we really have a lot in common."

I didn't mean to get defensive, but something about Gunnar's words is hitting too close to parts of me that are too raw, and I want this conversation to be over.

"True," he says, bringing his hands to my face and sweeping his thumbs over my cheekbones, the way he always does when he seems to think I'm about to disappear. "You're nothing like him. And I'm not saying you have to seal yourself away in a box and never look at alcohol again. I stopped drinking too much when I dealt with my issues instead of hiding from them. For some people, that works. For others, there's never going to be an option other than all or nothing. You can only figure that out if you admit there's something to be concerned about and tackle it."

He takes in a deep breath, studying me while he picks his next words carefully.

"How about this? We agree that I'm never going to stop worrying about you, because it's futile. And I'll tell you when I'm worried. But I will never try to take away your choices. Even if you're making bad ones." He pauses for a second, looking pensive. "Unless it's life or death. I'm not making any promises, then.

But generally speaking, I won't interfere with your choices, as long as you let me be here for you when things go sideways."

"I feel like you're getting the raw end of that deal," I mutter, because it's true.

Gunnar smiles at me, utterly beatific and looking like all his cares are about to melt away. "Yeah, but I get you. Any deal is worth that, in the end."

I can only hold eye contact with him for a few seconds, because the intensity of whatever feelings are crawling and swelling inside me is too much to bear. I look down, gathering my thoughts before I look back up.

"You're my choice, you know," I say in a quiet voice. "Don't forget that. I might make some shitty choices, but I'm choosing you. Not because you're convenient or because I feel like I owe you. You could offer me a thousand and one other options, and I'd choose you every time. I think you might be the only good choice I've ever made."

Gunnar's smile turns into a grin before he leans in to kiss me. I open myself up to him, going soft in his grip as he lazily tongue-fucks me until we both forget what we were fighting about.

Downstairs, I do my best to quell my nerves, but it's not easy. Even before the doors open and the customers come in, I'm on edge. My senses are hard-wired for the maximum amount of alertness that my body is capable of. Not that it's ever stopped a threat, but it leaves me better prepared if I know what's coming.

Now I'm jumping at every noise that stands out against the general din, as well as constantly subconsciously searching for sounds and smells that would tip me off if Eamon were here.

I think I see his face in the shadows about a dozen times before I finally call it and get a drink. I don't care that Gunnar is frowning at me from across the room. He should be proud of the restraint I'm showing by asking Kasia to pour me a beer and then sitting on my stool to drink it like any other customer—albeit not a paying one—instead of crawling behind the bar, folding myself into the smallest possible space I can find and chugging warm vodka from the bottle.

No one tries to talk to me, at least. I'm sure there's been more than a little gossip about me floating around, but my association with the Banna—however theoretical, at this point—makes most people steer clear. Which I'm grateful for, but it reminds me that I have yet another hole to dig myself out of that I hadn't considered yet.

Have the Banna even noticed I'm gone? I know Patrick thought I was a degenerate from day one, and mostly seemed to keep me around as some kind of distraction or reward for Eamon. At the time, I told myself it didn't matter if they respected me. It's not like I was trying to make a career in the mafia or something. I just needed the money.

I never had a plan beyond that. If someone had asked me at the time, I would have said I'll deal with the future when it happens. In retrospect, I think there wasn't any part of me that believed I would live long enough for it to matter. I was racing against the clock. All I wanted was to make enough money to keep Lola alive before someone—anyone—finally rubbed me out of existence.

Now this impossible, ineffable future that I never thought I'd have is here. Kind of. Assuming Eamon doesn't come back to rip it all away again.

And I have no fucking clue if I'm supposed to be making new plans, or still waiting around for the inevitable.

These thoughts lead me to a second beer, and then a third. After that though, I switch to water. Because while the alcohol has produced a glorious fuzziness that's dulling the sharp edges of all my issues, there's something else that is even more appealing to me right now.

Gunnar. I know he won't want to fool around if he thinks I'm drunk, but there's still hours before close and I'll sacrifice having a panic attack in the bathroom if it means I can spend the rest of the night losing myself in him upstairs.

I don't want to think about the future. He's the only part of my future that seems real, and I want to hang on to it.

Fucking him last night was weird. It's not something I even thought I'd do, and it felt a little discordant with what my body wanted to do. But I was so overwhelmed by the need to touch and be touched, I would have taken it in any form.

I just need to get all that old shit off me. It's invisible, I know. It's not even real, it's more of a mental layer of stickiness that I perceive all over my skin. But no matter how unreal it is, I can still feel it. Every time Gunnar and I touch each other, a little more of that toxic substance burns away. I think I can sweat it all off if I try hard enough.

I don't want to think or heal or make healthy choices or whatever else Gunnar is contemplating with those big sad eyes of his. I want to fuck until I can't remember my own name, let alone anyone who ever touched me before him or what they might have done.

The logical part of my mind knows this won't really work. All that shit will still be there. But I'm not in the mood to listen to logic right now, and the three beers have given me warm cheeks, a twitchy energy, and just enough confidence to tell logical-me to go fuck himself.

I'm on my third glass of water—which makes me neutral or something in terms of alcohol, surely—when Sav wanders over. I've barely seen him since I've been back, and Gunnar says he's been MIA without explanation for a lot of the week, but he's been too distracted to ask. He's sporting a lot of fresh and newly fading bruises that I don't ask about out of politeness.

We come from the same world. He's just much higher up the food chain. Or he was, or something. I'm still not totally clear about what he's doing working here instead of there, and I don't want to ask.

"Tobias," he says, nodding his head.

He's a man of few words. It makes him seem mysterious, mostly because he's ripped and covered head to toe in tattoos, but the more I get to know him, the more I suspect he's legitimately just shy.

"Sav," I say, for lack of any other words coming into my head.

"You doing okay?"

He stares me down, and I can't tell if he's asking me if I need another drink or if I've recovered from my violent vacation. Or maybe both.

"I'm fine. Are you okay?" I eye the bruises.

Sav shrugs. "You seem jumpy. Are you worried fuck-face is going to come in? Or is this about my father?"

I freeze, and I swear my whole-ass jaw drops.

"What? Patrick is your *father?*"

I haven't had the opportunity to spend a lot of my life gossiping in my life, but this must be what it feels like. I swear it's like a curtain got pulled. They kind of look similar, I guess. Although most of the Banna look like generic, mean, tattooed, white guys. They all run together, after a point.

"How the fuck did I not know this?"

Sav winces, then shrugs, although he looks a little embarrassed. "You've been busy."

I whip my head from side to side, trying to process the greater implications of this information while checking no one's actively eavesdropping on us. I catch sight of Gunnar pretending not to be watching me and doing a terrible job of it, and when I wink at him to let him know he's been caught, he at least has the decency to blush.

Watching a man that's all that... *man* go all pink-cheeked and embarrassed when I wink at him is swiftly rising to the top of my 'hottest things in the universe' chart.

Then I turn my attention back to Sav.

"So, if Patrick—lord high dipshit of the Banna—" dear *god* it feels good to talk shit about him, even if it could still get me killed, I'm so very fucking past caring, "—is your father, then why aren't you sitting on a gilded throne or some shit? Shouldn't you be supervising all the high-end deals and, I don't know, snorting coke off the biker bunnies' tits? That's what those assholes are all gunning for, as far as I can tell. Every one of them I've had more than a ten-second conversation with seems to fully embrace the cliché."

Sav is staring at me like I've lost it, but I'm buzzing with adrenaline now. My nerves from before have burned away for some reason, and I feel like I'm ten feet tall.

Fuck these guys. If the crown prince of the redneck mafia can be over here washing dishes for a living, doesn't that mean one lowly little thief that they never even liked can slip off into the night?

Or maybe I'm so burned out on being afraid of everything I just hit max capacity like a brick wall, and now my brain is swinging wildly in the other direction.

Fuck everything. Maybe I'll just be happy from now on. Who cares if they kill me?

Sav clears his throat before he speaks, because my thoughts have obviously drifted again.

"I didn't want to do it anymore," he says. "It's not supposed to be something you can leave, but some things are worth trying, at least."

His somber tone ratchets down my high a little bit. I feel stupid for getting so worked up over nothing, and that little adrenaline buzz, along with the brief, artificial euphoria it brought with it, flees my body and leaves a black hole of nothing behind it.

I nod, because I'm not sure what I'm supposed to say.

Sav turns to go back to work, but I stop him.

"Do you think he'll come for me? Your father? Or will he let me go, because he never wanted someone like me there in the first place?"

The look he gives me in return is so confusing, I couldn't begin to guess what he means by it. He looks pained. Almost guilty. But also like he has something to say that he's not saying.

I sit there quietly, waiting for the words to come, but he doesn't answer my question. He looks at me for a few more seconds before turning away, leaving me with more questions than I had in the first place.

Whatever that means for my future, it can't be good. Sav has to know something he's not telling me. Otherwise, there would be no reason for him to stay quiet.

My brain gets sluggish at the thought. I've vacillated between some form of scared, angry, and over-excited too many times today, and I already feel worn-out. All I want to do is count down the minutes until the shift is over and I can replace all these feelings with Gunnar.

Chapter Twenty-Six

GUNNAR

I wasn't lying when I told Tobias I enjoy bottoming sometimes, even if I generally prefer to top. And I definitely enjoy it with him, because watching him come alive—taking control of himself and what he wants—is absolutely exhilarating.

I am surprised by the way he's seemed to grab hold of it with both hands and refuse to let go since that first time. Metaphorically and literally, I suppose. It feels like the more sex we have, the more he wants it. Like he's burying himself in it.

Of course, I have no idea if it's a healthy way to cope, or if it's even my place to make that judgement. For now, I'm going along with it. He's telling me straight up what he needs, and it's something I can give him.

That doesn't mean I'm not keeping an eye on him, though. He's treading water. Anyone can see that. He's still drinking every day, but choosing when and how much very carefully. I think that's mostly to appease me, even if I haven't said anything out loud since we first spoke about it.

He comes down to the bar with me. Every time he looks just as on edge as the last. It never fades, and neither of us ever forgets the looming threat that's keeping him from settling, whether it's real or not. The cops have absolutely nothing to help us, except their blind conviction that Eamon skipped town.

I want to talk to Sav about it just so I can get anyone's fucking opinion that isn't my own, because there comes a point where you're so deep in a situation the words don't even make sense anymore. He's called out so many times in the past couple of days, though. I haven't seen him apart from the first night I brought Tobias downstairs, when he was covered in bruises and even more taciturn than usual.

I can't get Tobias to feel less uneasy when he's outside the apartment. I can't get any actual information from people on either side of the law. And no matter what my fantasies are telling me, I'm probably not capable of tracking Eamon down wherever he's hiding and strangling him to death so Tobias can finally know some peace.

The only thing that seems to make him feel calm is sex. It feels counterintuitive. Like sex should be the last thing he wants, and especially the kind of visceral, heart-pounding sex we've moved on to since the first time. But after we're done, once we've cleaned up, and he curls into my chest to finally fall asleep, is the only time I see him look truly tranquil.

This morning, he's anything but tranquil. From the second he wakes up, there's a deep groove etched in his forehead and mountains of worry behind those honey-brown eyes. He rests on my chest, his head rising and falling steadily as I breathe, letting me card my fingers through his hair. But I can feel the disquiet seeping through him like a toxin.

I can't push him. If I push him, he gets even more withdrawn. Instead, I try to keep myself as steady as possible. I'm not sure if he's even aware of it, but I've finally figured out that whenever I'm physically the most predictable—calm, still, breathing slowly and doing nothing or some kind of repetitive, mundane activity—those are the times he finds it easiest to open up to me about things.

It makes sense when I think about it. I kind of feel stupid for taking so long to get to this point. Conveniently, I'm generally a calm person whenever the world isn't burning down around me, so Tobias can hopefully take some comfort in my natural state.

"Can we go see my lola today?" he asks, shattering the silence.

I frown down at the top of his head, even though he can't see me from this angle, but I don't stop running my fingers through his hair.

"Of course. We have plenty of time before the bar opens. Is that what's bothering you?"

Silence. I can practically feel all the guilt and anxiety churning in his brain, but none of it comes out in the form of words, no matter how much time I give him, so I keep talking.

"Tristan's been taking care of her, like I told you. He's buddy-buddy with all the nurses there and he goes to visit her literally every day. I know she's worried about you, but she knows you're not there for a good reason, and she's not all alone. Everyone understands why it's been hard to go back."

Tobias keeps silent for a little while longer, before turning over to prop up his chin on his hands, still on my chest but able to look me in the eye now.

"I appreciate it. I really do. I know that she and Tristan are weirdly close for a random old lady and her paramedic." I huff a laugh, because it's true. But Tristan is that kind of person. He doesn't make a lot of friends, but whenever he does, they're the most unlikely kind and he seems to latch on and not let go. "But it's my job. I'm supposed to be there. I don't even know when she's getting released or what care she needs. Taking care of her is probably the only thing I've ever done right in my life, and now I've let it all fall apart, to what? Lie around here all day? So what if the hospital fucking terrifies me? I'm fucking terrified here, too. At this point, I'm pretty sure you could bring me Eamon's head in a cardboard box and I would still be terrified, even though there's nothing to be scared of. It's like it's baked into me."

He shivers as he says the last part, and I pull the blankets up around his bare shoulders before hugging him to my chest as hard as I dare.

"It'll get better, honey. I promise. Everything gets better eventually."

Tobias turns his face into my skin again so he's not looking at me, and his words are muffled when he speaks. "Or maybe I'll just get so used to it, it'll seem normal. I don't really care anymore. Let's just go, so I can do one productive thing with my life."

It takes all I have not to sigh, because this is starting to feel like a conversation we're going to have ad nauseam.

He needs to talk to someone about all this guilt before it weighs him down so much he can't breathe.

Tentatively, I broach the subject.

"Baby, I know there's a lot going on right now, but can we please talk about therapy? I think it might help. I went for a long time after everything with my dad and Lukas, and I honestly think it's the reason I'm here right now as a functional human being."

Tobias snorts, still not looking up at me, his breath hot and damp against my skin.

"Sure. With all the money I have lying around. And all my legal, marketable skills."

"I'm sure we can find the money," I say, already knowing I'm edging into dangerous territory.

Now his head does pop up, and there's fire in his eyes.

"No, there's no 'we' here. I'm not letting you take care of me all day and drain your bank account at the same time. It's just me. *I* need money to live, and money to pay Lola's medical bills. *I* need to find a job and some way of sustaining myself that doesn't involve organized crime. The last thing *I* need is to start throwing money away, talking about things in the past that I can't change. I might as well put cash on the lawn and set fire to it for all the good it's going to do me."

He ramps up in intensity as he speaks, even though he's not pulling away from me. I can see the fear simmering just below the surface of all this anger, though. Not just the anxious, residual fear of his trauma, but his fear of an unknown future. Which bugs the shit out of me, because that's the part I can help with, if he'd just let me.

I can keep him from getting too in his head about it, I guess. We can revisit the other stuff later.

"Tobias," I say, smiling even though he's scowling at me like a drenched kitten right now. Or maybe an angry porcupine. "We don't have a lawn."

His eyes narrow. Okay, it wasn't that funny, but it was better than nothing. Eventually, he makes a huffing noise that's in the vicinity of laughter, but at least the tension of the conversation is cut off at the knees.

Crawling off my body, he starts looking around for something to wear.

"Why don't we stop by your grandmother's place on the way and get some of your stuff. Then you won't constantly be drowning in my old clothes. We can get you a new phone, too, while we're at it. Pick up your bike and bring it here. All the things."

Tobias freezes, a long-sleeved henley in his hands that he's been wearing for the past two days. As much as I love him in my clothes and haven't pushed him on this because I know he finds it comforting, we have to step out of this post-crisis bubble, eventually.

If only so I can stop doing laundry every day.

"Tobias? Does that sound okay?"

"Yeah. Does that mean—" He cuts himself off, swallowing hard before turning around to look me in the eye. "Does that mean I'm staying?"

His expression is hard as he says it. Like he's challenging me, or daring me to say no. I don't know if I'll ever get used to the pendulum swings of Tobias's personality. He has so much strength, including this kind of feral intensity whenever something really pushes his buttons to make him angry. But life and circumstances have also taught him how to wilt and fade into the background.

It's a dichotomy he never seems to have a firm grasp on, jumping from one to the other without realizing it.

I'm fucking here for it. He can swing from one extreme to the other to his heart's content. I just love getting to witness any moment that seems like it's the real him shining through, instead of what he was conditioned to be.

"Yeah, baby," I say, keeping my voice quiet and my expression gentle as I reach for him. "You're staying. As long as you want to."

He lets me pull him into a hug, but stays stiff and unyielding in my arms.

"And if I want to leave?" he asks.

"You can always leave. I'll help you, if that's what you want. You can go home to your lola, and I'll still help you find a job and all the rest of it. You're not obligated to stay." Even if the thought of him not being here every day breaks my fucking heart. "But baby?" Tobias leans back to look up at me. "Please stay," I continue. "I'm asking you, not telling you. Please, please stay. If you want to. I want you to."

It's not the most elegant way to ask someone to officially move in with you, but the emotion brimming in Tobias's eyes tells me it resonated with something inside him.

He opens his mouth, like he's about to speak. Honestly, for all my begging, it had never occurred to me that he might say no. I thought this was a done deal. I thought we were in love, even if we weren't quite saying it yet.

Then a shadow passes over his face and he tears his gaze away from mine.

"We should go, before it gets too late," he says.

That's it. Conversation closed. I have no idea what I said wrong, and even less of an idea when he's going to be willing to talk about it again.

The drive to the hospital is quiet. Tobias seems pensive, and I'm trying—no matter how fucking unbearable it is—to give him the space to work through his thoughts.

Initially, I was going to stop by his grandmother's place on the way to grab some of his stuff, but I decide to leave that for the time being. I don't want to spark something he's not ready to deal with after the awkward turn the conversation took before we left the house.

Maybe he just needs to see Anika. That might make him feel better. Tristan told me she's doing much better, and seeing her looking well might make Tobias ease up on some of the self-flagellation.

As soon as we get there, I can feel the tension mounting in him. It looks a lot different in the day than at night. It's a big regional hospital, so there's lots of hustle and bustle. The parking lot is full and everywhere you look there are nurses, doctors, patients, family and whoever else coming and going. The lights are bright, so there are no dark corners, and the security presence is much more visible now than it was when he was taken.

Still, I can feel him practically vibrating with nerves. His eyes dart around constantly, like he's assessing for threats, although he seems to be consciously keeping his body still and smooth as we walk through the building. The guilt that's coursing through me at not being able to help him is almost overwhelming. Every second is like a cheese grater on my skin, with all my nerve-endings screaming at me to *do something*.

But I can't. This is something we both have to face.

I do thread my fingers through his hand, though. It makes him jump, but then he settles and squeezes my palm, even though he's not looking at me.

It's a long walk up to her floor. There are a lot of elevators and winding hallways to go through, and with the thick layer of stress sitting over us, the whole journey seems to take forever. I'm worried he's going to snap.

Then, just as we're approaching the unit she's on, something does seem to shift inside him. Not in a good way, but not in the panicked or destructive way that I was worried about, either.

He just... shuts down. He's still walking and holding my hand, but his eyes are suddenly far away instead of examining the world around us for threats, and he's loose-limbed as he moves, like a marionette with unattended strings.

Nothing has changed by the time we reach her room, and he's so silent I'm only certain he's breathing because he's still conscious. He reaches for the door handle, but I gently take his hand to turn him toward me for a second.

"Tobias? Are you alright? We can come back another time if you need to."

He listens to me, then nods slowly, like the question took some time to process.

"I'm fine. I want to see her. Let's go in."

"Okay. But I'm here if you need me."

I make sure to trail behind when he finally opens the door and steps inside. I'm here for him, but I don't want to intrude on their moment. I probably should have asked him if he wanted me to wait outside, but it's too late for that now.

Plus, he's not the only one with irrational-hospital-kidnapping anxiety. I'll go if he wants me to, but I'd much rather keep him where I can see him until we get the hell out of here.

As soon as Tobias and Anika see each other, things get emotional. I almost tear up as well, like I'm watching one of those YouTube videos of dogs being reunited with person after years of being apart.

They hug and huddle close, whispering to each other in intense tones, with voices too low for me to hear. I don't want to intrude, so I try to look away as well. I think Anika is speaking to him mostly in Tagalog, while Tobias is answering her in English, but even if I can't make out the words, the choked-up emotion in their voices is unmistakable.

I'm pretty sure I head Tobias whisper, "I'm sorry," over and over, and it breaks my fucking heart. Part of me wants to tell his grandmother everything that happened to him. She deserves to know how much of a fighter he is, and how much he survived just to come back here for her. I know it would hurt her too much to know the truth, though.

After a few minutes, Tobias looks up at me. His eyes are bloodshot and bright with tears, but I'd take this any day over the shut-down version of him I saw just a few minutes ago. He's sitting, perched on the edge of her bed with her soft-looking hand held in his, and gestures to me to come closer.

I can't repress the small smile that takes over my face as I move toward them.

"Lola, you remember Gunnar. He came with me when I visited before," he says, before chewing at his bottom lip as we both think of all the unsaid things that followed that visit.

Anika nods. "I remember. Hello, Gunnar. Are you the one who's been keeping my apo so busy all this time?"

I wince. "Yes and no, ma'am. It's been a difficult couple of weeks. I've been trying to help."

"None of that," she says, shaking her head at me. "No 'ma'am'. It makes me feel old." She looks me up and down, not bothering to hide the evaluation in her gaze, but not unkind with it either. "How old are you?"

"Thirty-six," I say, barely swallowing the 'ma'am' that almost came out at the end. I feel too much like a teenager right now, showing up to pick up my date for the prom. I haven't been nervous like this to meet someone's family in ten years. It's unsettling, and it's making my brain get all its wires crossed.

She seems to consider this, and I worry for a second she's about to tell Tobias to stay the fuck away from me because I'm too old for him. I wouldn't judge her. But I'm way, way too deep in this to let go that easily now, so for everyone's sake, I hope she doesn't. I'm not sure what exactly Tobias told her we are, but it's clear that she knows I'm more than just a random friend who gave him a ride to the hospital, and she's evaluating me accordingly.

"That's good," she says in the end, letting me release the breath I was holding. She squeezes Tobias's hand before reaching out with her other hand, trailing an IV line, to chuck him under the chin. "He looks like a grownup with a good job. I like it. You deserve someone to take care of you. There's more to life than taking care of me all the time."

Tobias frowns, stealing a glance at me before leaning in closer to her. "I'm still taking care of you, Lola. Nothing's changed."

She smiles, but doesn't answer him directly. Instead, she turns to me again.

"You can call me 'auntie'."

I nod. I'm not sure what this means, but I feel like I've been accepted. At least in a probationary way.

"Auntie," I say, before Tobias interrupts to get her attention.

"I told you, nothing's changing. You'll get better and then I'll come home with you."

A knock at the door interrupts the conversation, but no one says anything before it opens and someone steps inside.

A doctor, I'm guessing based on the white coat, stethoscope, and iPad. She's in her fifties, with pale skin and the lost look of the chronically overworked, but there's an inherent friendliness to her expression that offsets my sudden anxiety at seeing a stranger in the room.

"Mrs. Tanikon, how are you feeling today?" she asks.

"Better, doctor. My grandson is here to visit." Anika points at Tobias.

The doctor freezes for a second before smoothing out the shock on her face.

"The famous Mr. Tanikon. We've been trying to get ahold of you. But your paramedic friend said that you were temporarily unavailable."

Tobias grimaces, his gaze darting to the floor before he looks at the doctor again. Clearly, the connection between the police report I filed at this very hospital a week ago and his mysterious absences hasn't been made. While I'm sure he's glad not everyone knows his business, it's probably also humiliating to seem like an absentee grandson.

"I'm sorry. It was an emergency," he says, tripping over his words a little. "I'm here now. I'm back. I just don't have a phone yet. I'll get one, though."

"Alright," she says, that professional, plastic smile not moving an inch. "We should talk about your grandmother's care after she's discharged, though." The doctor turns to me before saying, "And you are?"

"He can stay," Anika interrupts. "Everyone can stay. I don't care what you need to talk about. Just tell them whatever it is so we can deal with it and I can finally get out of this hospital bed."

She smiles through the brusque interruption, but it's clear who's in charge of this room, and it's not the doctor.

It doesn't seem to matter. I'm sure she has other patients to get to and just wants to get on with her day. As soon as she opens her mouth, an incomprehensible torrent of information spills out. Tobias looks shell-shocked, and like he's barely taking any of it in, so I try to pay attention. Anika looks unfazed, so I'm guessing this isn't the first time she's heard this.

Words like 'necrotic wound' and 'almost amputated' seem to put a chill in Tobias, as well as 'chronic atrial fibrillation'. But I think what rocks him the most is when the doctor recommends in no uncertain terms that Anika doesn't go home, but instead transfers to a skilled nursing facility for wound management and rehabilitation. The doctor implies that she could recover enough mobility and independence to eventually go back home, but there's not a lot of optimism in her voice as she says it.

It's a lot of information. There are pamphlets and some generic reassurances before the doctors whisks out of the room again. I can see Tobias winding right back up with guilt, but so can his grandmother. Before he gets the chance to talk to her about any of it, she tells him very kindly that she's tired. She suggests we go home to talk about it, and come back to visit her again tomorrow.

And thank you, Anika. I need a minute to breathe. Because the amount of care she's going to need is intense if Tobias refuses to let her go to a facility. I've been trying to figure out how to get him to take care of himself, and if he's throwing all his energy into doing something that sounds unmanageable for any one person, let alone someone in his position who is supposed to be recovering from their own shit...

I don't know. I'll think of something.

We say our goodbyes, and the ride home is just as silent as the ride there was. At least Tobias does ask to stop at the trailer for some clothes, although he won't let me come in. I'm not sure if it's because he's embarrassed by it, even though there's nothing to be embarrassed by. I live above a bar, and even from the outside I can tell that it's a nice, well-kept little home the two of them have.

His bike is still here. It looks just as rundown and crappy as I remember from watching him pull up to the bar on it a million times, and I quietly hope that I have longer before having to watch him ride around on that death trap again.

I add 'find money for a safe car' to my mental Tobias list, along with everything else. If he's okay with it.

While I'm waiting for him, I order a new phone for him to be delivered and realize I'm an idiot for not doing it sooner. It's not like we haven't been distracted, though.

We barely exchange any words until we're in the parking lot of the Feral Possum. He has an old duffel bag on his lap and an exhausted expression on his face. I turn toward him with no idea of what to say to make it better, but still filled with the desperate need to try.

"Tobias—"

"Can we just go inside first?" he asks, cutting me off. "I think I need a minute before I can deal with this."

I pause, then push through anyway. "I was going to say I love you. I know you're scared, because this is a lot, but don't forget that, okay?" I take a deep breath in, because even though this isn't technically the first time I've said it to him, it still feels like a landmark moment for us, and I don't know how I'll survive if he turns away from it. "I love you. We're in this together. No matter how fucked up you feel sometimes. I'm fucked up too, remember? It's still a team effort."

Tobias looks at me, tears welling in his eyes for what isn't even the second or third time today. God, no wonder he looks so exhausted. He doesn't say anything, but he does lean across the center console to press his lips to mine.

It's not a passionate kiss, but I can taste the desperation in it. I can feel how much he wants to say it back. He pushes his tongue in my mouth instead, and I answer in kind, because I know exactly what he means by it.

Like always, I can be patient. I'll stay quiet and still, and when he's ready, he'll come to me.

We break apart, Tobias still silent but nodding at me. His Adam's apple bobs as he swallows, and I brush away the tears that are starting to leak out of his eyes.

With a few deep breaths, he seems to shake himself out of it, and we both get out of the car. We walk into the bar instead of using the outside stairs, because I want to check and see if Sav actually showed up for morning prep like he said he would.

He's here. He's here, and as soon as we walk in, he turns to look at us. Both of his fists are resting on the bar as he leans his weight into it, and the expression on his face is enough to make me stop in my tracks.

"What's wrong? Is he here?" I ask, suddenly on red alert.

"Nothing's wrong." Sav gestures to both of us, ushering us inside. "It's just..." he trails off, staring off to the side before snapping his attention back to us. "We should talk. I think it's time that I tell you Eamon's not coming back."

I raise my eyebrows at him, hoping he means what I think he means, but not willing to jump the gun.

Sav looks at me like he doesn't want to spell it out, but I keep staring at him.

"Okay, fine, you want to hear the words? He's dead. Eamon's dead. You're fucking welcome."

Chapter Twenty-Seven

TOBIAS

"What?"

I hear my own voice as the word comes out, but it seems echoey and distant, like I didn't really say it. I repeat myself, just to check, but it sounds the same. I might repeat myself a couple of times, I'm not sure.

The way Sav and Gunnar are both looking at me like a lost little lamb is a strong hint that I might not be taking this news very well.

"Maybe we should talk about this upstairs." Gunnar looks nervous, his gaze flicking between me and Sav.

"No." I try to mentally shake myself out of my stupor. It doesn't totally work, so I physically shake my head, and that wakes me up a little. Reality sinks in and I feel like my mind is at least attempting to wrap itself around what Sav just said. "Let's just get it over with. I'm sure there isn't much to say, right?"

Sav nods once, tight-lipped. I don't even want to speculate what he knows. I don't really care.

"He's dead?" I ask, to quiet the anxiety spiking in my mind.

He nods again. "Dead. All the way dead, not 'set you up for a jump scare later', horror-movie mostly dead. *Dead* dead."

I appreciate his candor. I think I needed the long version of the sentence for it to sink in.

Gunnar opens his mouth silently for a second, searching for the right words. "And you... You know this for sure? It's not just hearsay?"

Sav looks at him now, his mouth set in a straight line and his knuckles whitening where his fists rest on the bar.

"Like I said. Dead."

"Okay." Gunnar nods, looking a little shell-shocked as well. "Okay. That's good. Okay."

"You're babbling, sweetie." I don't know why I find it hilarious that he's coming unglued when I am as well, but it's almost surreal enough to make me laugh.

Gunnar snaps his head to the side, his eyes wide as he takes me in and his mouth halfway open to protest. Then he thinks about it for a second, and a nervous exhale-chuckle sound slips out of him.

"Yeah, well, you started it," he says, half of his mouth curling up in a small smile as he looks at me.

"I'm a helpless victim. I'm supposed to be in shock, remember? You're supposed to be the calm, rational one. If you start babbling and getting hysterical as well, who's going to carry me to the fainting couch while I recover from this terrible ordeal?"

The whole thing comes out in this completely flat, deadpan voice, but my eyes are bright and I can feel a hint of a smile playing around my face as well.

It's enough to make Gunnar crack. He laughs then, deeply. It's pure relief, I think. The kind of crash that comes after being strung together by nothing but adrenaline and anxiety for too many days to keep track of.

"You're okay?" he asks as he reaches out, pulling me into his side for a half-hug. Before I can even answer, he kisses the top of my head in that way he does sometimes, and I can feel a blush threatening to paint my cheeks at the raw affection. I duck my face into his neck to hide it, but it's still there.

"I'm okay," I mumble directly into his skin, before breathing in the scent of him to help fix myself in this moment.

We're interrupted by the sound of Sav clearing his throat, and we both turn our attention back to him. He's staring at us, his face blank, but obviously not nearly as amused by the situation as we are.

Not that we're legitimately amused. More hysterically relieved.

"You guys are weird," he says. "I guess you match that way. Anyway, I just wanted to let you know. And you don't want to know the details, but there have been some changes in the Banna hierarchy. Some people have shuffled around. Long story short, no one expects you back. You are being granted a walking pass as a one-time exception for services rendered."

My eyebrows raise, because as elated as I am to not be hunted down by a bunch of mafia thugs, I want to know exactly what he's implying.

"By 'shuffled around', do you mean Patrick? Is someone else taking charge?" I stare at him for a second before the pieces click into place. "Are you taking charge?"

Sav snorts, and it's the most emotion I've seen from him so far in this murder-adjacent conversation. "Fuck no. I hate those dumbcunts. I'm not leading shit. I'm staying right here, with you guys. And Micah."

His voice catches a little when he says 'Micah', but I don't call him out on it. I still don't understand the nature of their relationship, but I'm getting a strong impression that it's less brotherly and more something else. He'll tell us when he's ready.

"So that's it?" Gunnar asks, looking between the two of us. "It's all just over? I didn't have to sell the soul of my firstborn in a dark alley or something? This seems kind of anticlimactic, I'm not going to lie."

Another snort from Sav. "Trust me. It was very climactic, you just weren't there for it. Again: you're welcome."

That's when it kind of hits home just what he means. He really fixed everything for me. This guy who I barely even know—probably because he's grateful to Gunnar, like the rest of us—risked god-knows-what and blotted all my mafia and Eamon-related problems out of existence.

I still have what feels like a thousand other problems, but that's a big fucking head start.

I'm walking before I can think about it too much. It only takes a few seconds to duck around to the other side of the bar, stand up on my tiptoes because Sav's too tall for his own good, and wrap my arms around him.

He's stiff as a fucking board. I imagine Patrick was not a 'hugging' kind of father. Mine wasn't either, to be honest. You can't hug thin air. And I've never been known for my laid-back, affectionate approach to friendships. Or for my friendships, really.

But he deserves it. I hold him until he softens up just enough to hug me back, patting me on the back awkwardly for a second before I finally let him go.

"Thanks, bro." I step back, inclining my head one more time to show him I'm serious. "I owe you a lot."

He huffs and looks away from me before responding. "You don't owe me anything, Tobias. I owe a lot more than this. We're square."

There's so much sadness in him when he says it, I can practically taste the emotion dripping off his words. I don't push it, though. I know what that kind of guilt feels like, and there's not a lot anyone else can say to make it better.

"Okay," Gunnar says yet again. "We're gonna go upstairs and get ready for work. We'll be back around open. You good, Sav?"

The man nods, turning away from us and picking up a rag to indicate the time for sharing and caring is now over.

When Gunnar turns to me, I feel utterly drained. It's barely noon, and I already feel like I've lived a quarter of my lifespan just today.

I should have known the relief was too good to last. I move through the apartment in a daze, showering and finally changing into clothes that fit me correctly. Even if it immediately causes a pang of emptiness to not smell like Gunnar and feel the fabric of his clothes on my skin.

We rest and clean up a little, all of it in relative silence. I think we're both processing. It's almost time to go downstairs, and I know I should bite my tongue, but the silence is starting to eat at me.

I can't stop thinking about the conversation we had at the hospital this morning, and I know if we don't talk about it now, it'll eat at me for the next ten hours.

"I'm not putting her in a home," I say, fracturing our fragile peace.

Gunnar freezes, halfway through making some sandwiches. He seems to consider the words for a minute before putting down the knife and putting the lid back on the mayonnaise, abandoning lunch for now.

"I don't think the doctor was talking about a home, like a nursing home. It's a rehab facility, so she can receive medical care."

"She's not even seventy yet!" The anger that hits me is sudden and unexpected, but it immediately decides it wants to steer the course of the conversation. "I'm not farming her out. I can't do that. We don't do that."

Gunnar stays very still, and it fucking irritates me how even and quiet his voice comes out. Even though I know he's doing it to be considerate to me, because he doesn't want to accidentally scare me, or something.

"It's not farming her out, Tobias. She needs complex medical care. It doesn't even have to be forever, but it definitely has to be for a while. The doctor said if the wound gets worse, they might have to amputate her foot. She can't even walk right now, plus all the heart stuff that I didn't even understand. I don't think any one person would be capable of taking care of her, even if you were with her 24/7. She needs more care than you can give her."

His gentle, soothing tone irritates me. The truth of his words irritates me. All my own inadequacies fucking stack up to irritate me.

I dig my heels in. I don't know why. Crossing my arms over my chest, I look him square in the eye and say, "I'm not farming her out. Especially not here. What if the nurses are racist? What if they treat her like shit? She needs me."

"Tobias, I'm not trying to tell you what to do. You can live in the trailer if you want. But I think you should listen to the doctors when it comes to this. I know it's another money stress, but let me help you figure it out."

"I can't do it. We don't do that."

He stares at me for a minute, like I'm a fortress and he's making his plan of logical attack to get to me. When he moves closer, I pull back, because I don't want him to touch me right now, but all he does is take a seat on the couch. I don't sit, because I need to pace, but he looks up at me expectantly while I move.

"We who? Explain to me what's going on in your head right now to get you this worked up. I want to understand."

I bite my lip for a minute, not looking at him and taking a few steps back and forth. Partially because I don't really know how to articulate what's upsetting me, and partially because I don't want to tell him. It feels so fucking vulnerable, and he's already seen me stripped raw in ways no one else ever will.

He keeps looking at me though, with that steady, patient gaze. I remind myself of what I told him the other night: I chose him. I *choose* him. Dragging my busted ass to his doorstep that night was probably the best thing I ever did for myself, and if I don't fuck it all up, I think I could actually have a 'rest of my life' just because he's in it.

Because I love him. And I should love myself first, or whatever. But right now, loving him feels easier. More stable. Especially when he keeps sitting there like he could wait out a million fucking temper tantrums and never bat an eye about it.

"Look, I'm a terrible Filipino person. I'm not white, I just have my gross, neo-Nazi father's genetic donation, but I'm also fucking awful at being not-white. I don't have fucking culture. I can count on one hand the amount of Filipino people I've met who I'm not blood related to. I kind of speak Tagalog, but mostly not."

I take a deep breath before I continue. I don't think this is the road Gunnar expected me to take when I started talking, based on his 'oh-shit' expression, but he's still listening.

"Remember I told you my dad sucked? He left right after I was born, or maybe before. I don't really know. But *his* dad was still in Mishicot, and that man basically drove us the fuck out of town. Racist fucking prick. He hated my mom and whatever 'shame' she had supposedly brought on his family. My mom won't even talk about it anymore. I barely remember the details, but they weren't good. We left when I was still in elementary school.

"I think it hit her hard. She was young, you know. And Lola couldn't come with her because my grandfather was sick at the time. It was a whole thing. Anyway, when she met my stepdad, she threw herself so hard into her new life there was never a chance of looking back. Her kids may be half-native, but they're raised 100% in his culture. Even she picked up a rez accent. Half the people there just assume she's from Alaska or something. She peaced the fuck out of every other part of her life to make a new one, and it didn't matter that I didn't fit in there at all.

"So, I'm barely fucking Asian, except when I got shipped back to stay with Lola over the summers to keep me out of the way. I'm not fucking white, because racists still look at me and don't like what they see. And I'm 0% native, unlike the rest of the people I grew up with. Basically, I don't belong anywhere. I'm not shit.

"But if there's any single part of being Filipino that got hammered into me, it's that you take care of your fucking family. Especially your elders. I came here for her. She loves me. She needs me. I can't give that up because she's become inconvenient, or I'd be even more of a disappointment to my family than I am already."

My breath is heaving by the time I finish speaking. It was a long speech, mostly coming out in run-on sentences while I waved my hands in the air and hoped I was making some kind of sense.

I'm expecting Gunnar to look at me with apprehension. Or second-hand embarrassment, because I just childhood-trauma vomited all over him. Instead, he's giving me the same look he gave me before, downstairs.

The 'poor Tobias' look. The one that I mostly hate, but also sometimes kind of not, because it tends to come right before he gets all knight-in-shining-armor and fixes shit for me.

Which I'm probably supposed to hate even more, but I'm way too tired to pretend to have any pride left.

"What?" I ask, because he's not saying anything.

He hesitates, like he doesn't want to piss me off, but then his shoulders drop and he looks at me.

"She'll still love you, even if you don't physically take care of her every day. You don't have to earn her love. I don't know her well, but I'm confident about that. You take care of her by being around and being her grandson. The other stuff is just window dressing."

Now it's my turn for my shoulders to slump. That wasn't what I was trying to say with any of that. The way he says it makes it seem like it was maybe what I was thinking, though.

I sit down on the couch next to him, because all my anger and hyperbole just ran straight down the drain. Gunnar picks up my hand, impossibly gentle as always, even though he should be too big to feel so delicate.

"I don't know how it feels to go through the shit you just described. But I do know how it feels to be lost. And to feel cut off from your family, or your community. It sucks. Everything gets harder. I know you say that taking care of your grandmother is important, but when people say 'take care of your elders', they mean as part of a community. As part of a family unit. Not as one single person, trying to do it all by themselves with no support. Why is this burden on you but not your mom?"

"Dude, she has other kids. She deserves a chance at a real life after everything she went through to have me. It wasn't her fault her baby daddy's father was a psychopath."

"I know. That's my point: everyone has different circumstances. She does deserve a fresh start. But so do you. It wasn't your fault you were born. Or any of the other stuff that came after. I wish you would stop trying to take on the burden of everything that happens as if it was caused by your personal, primordial sin."

A wave of exhaustion hits me. He's right. I know he's right, and I'm too tired to fight him on it anymore. Knowing he's right doesn't make me feel any less guilty, but it makes me less interested in arguing about it.

Feeling a little pathetic, I lie down with my head in his lap. When his fingers push into my hair, like always, the tension starts to melt from my body, bit by bit.

"What do I do, then?"

"Talk to your grandmother. Ask her what she wants to do. Don't worry about the money yet. Let's figure the first part out and then we'll deal with that." He pauses. "Thank you for telling me, though. I kind of expected you to hang on to this for days."

I almost smile, but not quite.

"Yeah, well, all the brooding was getting kind of tiring. You make things easier to deal with when I talk to you. I don't know why."

I hear Gunnar snort overhead.

"That's what happens when you're in a relationship. A healthy one, at least. I know it's weird. I'm not exactly used to it either."

I'm still lying in his lap, staring across the room instead of at him when I say the next words. It's the only way I think I can do it, though. It'll be easier next time.

"I love you, Gunnar."

His breath catches, but he only freezes for a moment before he goes back to playing with my hair.

"Well, you better. You're stuck with me."

His soft laugh breaks the tension enough that I sit up, faking a glare before I also start to laugh. Gunnar grabs me, rearranging all my limbs until I'm straddling his lap, and pulls me into a kiss that goes from affectionate to devouring each other in roughly four seconds.

My hands grab at him everywhere I can reach—every inch of his flesh is solid but soft, and I can't stop touching him, like I need a reminder of the reality of his presence.

I don't care about the conversation we just had right now. I don't care that we're supposed to be going downstairs in a minute. I just need him. More of him.

I need to remind myself how real this all is.

"I know you wanted to wait," I say as I break off the kiss, already breathless from his proximity and the feel of those big, warm hands everywhere they're touching me. "But I want you. I like what we've been doing, but I still want you to fuck me. I think I need it. I'm not trying to push you. I get that it's weird, after seeing... what you saw."

I can't help the way I instinctively turn away as I bring up the thing we both don't want to talk about. Everything on the security tape that I know he must have watched after seeing me destroying his home at Eamon's direction. Shame does its best to pulse to the surface, no matter how hard I fight it.

It's not my fault. Everything that happened isn't my fault. He keeps saying it and I keep saying it and sometimes I even kind of mean it, but it doesn't make it any easier to *feel* the words on the inside.

The repulsion that I imagine Gunnar must have felt when he actually saw me with Eamon, instead of just hearing about it, is a constant weight on my mind. I know he says he wasn't repulsed by me, but still. It's all tangled up in a knot that's so tight I think it'll never be undone, and we'll keep circling around this issue for the rest of our lives.

I want him inside me. There's no explanation for how I know, but I'm confident that the feeling of it will make another shackle of memory fall away and I'll be lighter afterward. But I can't use him like my own personal sex toy or force him to push through his own discomfort, either.

Gunnar doesn't sigh, exactly. He huffs, his lips in a tight line as he looks me up and down. He keeps holding me close, more of our skin pressed together than not, and the air around us already feels hot with anticipation.

"I'm scared," he says, in a soft voice.

It's the last thing I expected.

When I frown at him, he pulls me closer for a quick kiss. Like a reassurance before he continues.

"I'm scared to hurt you. I know that's selfish, and I should be focused on what you need, but it's true. I think about you getting scared, and then about how shitty I would feel, and then about how much worse it would be the next time, and the whole thing spirals into an endless catastrophic train of thought in my head. Which is completely unlike me. I'm always rational, for fuck's sake." He smiles at me. There's tension around his eyes but it's a real smile, because it's honestly a relief that we're finally talking about how fucked up we both feel. "I think you bring out the most irrational side of me, Tobias."

Words fail me. He brings out all the irrationality in me, too. He makes me feel crazy enough that I ran to him again and again, even when all my protective instincts told me it was too dangerous.

Instead of speaking, I nuzzle into his neck, enjoying the soft scrape of his beard against my cheek and dragging my teeth along any open skin I can find.

"I know what you mean," I finally say. "I'm terrified I'm going to fuck this up."

When I finally pull away and look him in the eye again, lust has overtaken the nervousness in his eyes, and I feel like we're thinking the same thing.

"Let's do it anyway."

Gunnar nods slowly, his eyes transfixed on my mouth for some reason. My lips sting a little, like they might be puffy already from the beard burn.

Before I kiss him again, I stand up. First, I run into the bedroom to grab condoms and lube, then I pull off my clothes as quickly as I can before any residual nerves can set in. Gunnar does the same, but more slowly. He unfastens the top few buttons on his shirt, then reaches behind his head to pull it off and cast it aside. He's just as deliberate with his pants, unzipping them and shucking them, boxers included, while holding eye contact with me the entire time.

As soon as we're both naked, I climb back onto his lap. He gathers me into him, making me feel small and contained. It's an alien sensation, but one I have more and more when we're together.

We kiss for a long time. Lazily, like we're going to do it forever. Neither of us bother to bring up the places we're supposed to be. This feels more important.

Our erections graze against each other, and I'm already simmering with an embarrassing amount of eagerness. I'm nervous as well, but the nerves flitter around me, never quite finding a solid place to settle. While the arousal and intensity that I see mirrored in Gunnar's eyes feels rooted; right down through the couch and into the earth below. It's immoveable.

Gunnar starts with slow movements. He wraps his hand around both our cocks, stroking us steadily until I'm whining and begging for more. Then he lets go, reaching for my hole and stroking me there, too. Not pushing in, but exploring me with tender passes of the pads of his fingers.

I shudder, because his touch is lighting up nerve endings I didn't even know I had.

"Are you okay?"

With my forehead pressed against his, I nod.

"I'm here. Nowhere else. I'm okay."

I don't know if I'm reassuring him, myself, or both of us, but I mean it.

There's some fumbling and rustling as he grabs around for the lube, but once his fingers are wet, they find their place again. Still, he doesn't push in. He just strokes me, and the teasing feels impossible. Like I'm going to explode.

His reticence is a physical presence in the room. I grab his face with both hands, rolling my hips slowly until I'm grinding down onto his fingers, and look him in the eye.

"I'm nervous, too, Gunnar. But I trust you. Even if I freak out, I think we'll both feel better once we've pushed through it. It's just one time. I promise, we're going to do it a thousand more times after this, if I get my way. Who cares if some of them suck? Law of large numbers, baby."

I give him a shaky grin, hoping I'm selling the bravado thing. I do mean it, though. If there's anyone in the world I can trust, it's Gunnar. I'm not giving up on something I know I want, even if it takes a couple tries to get it right.

"Okay. Okay." He mumbles the words to himself like a mantra. "Just tell me if you want me to stop. Promise?"

"I promise," I say, breathless with anticipation.

My cock is straining toward him, already desperate to come and with absolutely no regard for my mind's reservations on what we're about to do.

Gunnar pushes into me excruciatingly slowly. He starts with one finger but quickly makes it two, teasing my entrance with shallow motions like he's got all the time in the world. He works his way in, letting my body open up to him, and the whole time I'm stuck writhing and whimpering like a wanton thing, desperate for every bit of touch that he gives me.

"More," I say, panting into his mouth before kissing him.

"Someone's greedy." I feel him smile against my mouth as he kisses me back, then breaks off again to look at me. "Look at you. Doing so well. Riding my fingers, desperate to come and asking me so nicely for more. What a good boy."

I shiver, and Gunnar lets out a low chuckle that doesn't help matters in the I-need-to-come department.

My hips grind down onto his hand as he pushes deeper, stroking inside me, while his thumb presses against me from the outside. The second he finds my prostate, an embarrassingly high-pitched whine is pulled out of me.

"Please, please, please," I chant, practically bouncing on his hand like I'm already getting fucked.

His fingers stroke me inside again, and I can feel the precum trickling from the head of my cock. I'm so close, I just need a little more.

"So needy," he whispers, although this time it sounds like it's to himself, almost like he's in awe.

He moves inside me, stroking and putting constant pressure in exactly the right spot to make the world blur and my thighs shake. I'm so close, but I need more. I need him to touch my cock. I need him inside me.

I need him to tell me I can come.

"Do you want to come now, or with my cock inside you?" he asks, gently finger-fucking me at the same time, like a fucking sadist.

"*Hng*." I wrap my arms around his shoulders and pull him closer, still bouncing my hips like I can force his fingers deeper. "More. Fuck. Inside, please. I want you inside."

"What a good boy," he whispers, before kissing the side of my face with a gentleness that doesn't fit with the savage tear of pleasure that his hand is causing me right now. "Good boys always get what they ask for."

I almost choke, clenching around his hand as my body tries to come, but can't quite get there. My cock is flexing in mid-air, desperate for contact, and he's still teasing me like he's enjoying my frustration.

I whine again when he pulls his fingers out, leaving me empty and gaping. But then he rips open the condom package and slips it on one-handed, exuding the same simple confidence he does with most things, and I feel myself settle.

This is right. This is good.

I want this.

Once he's positioned at my hole with one hand on the base of his cock, he uses his other hand to cup my cheek for a second.

"Are you still okay?"

"Yes. I promise." I swallow, then watch the way his bearded throat bobs as he echoes the motion. "I trust you."

For some reason, it feels even more monumental saying those words than it would have to tell him I love him again. It felt like I needed to repeat them out loud.

He holds my gaze as he pushes into me. The movement is slow and steady but unwavering, just like him. He gives me time to adjust, but no matter how long I wait for the panic to hit, it doesn't.

Once he's fully seated, I nod, wiggling my hips a little to make him gasp.

"Good. It's good."

I'm not exactly writing poetry over here, but I think he knows what I mean. It's enough to make him smile, anyway. A slow, syrupy smile, just like the rest of this. With one hand on the back of my head, he urges me into a kiss.

His thrusts are slow and steady, as well. We share a constant, sloppy kiss, and let the rhythm build a little at a time, until I'm riding him as hard as my body wants me to and we're both too breathless to do anything more than graze our lips together.

"Good?" he asks.

"Good." I nod, then bring his hand to my cock. "More, please."

He strokes me in time with his thrusts, and I feel myself approach the precipice of the orgasm that's been teasing me for so long.

"As much as you want, baby. As much as you want. Now come for me."

Finally, his words push me over the edge. I stiffen, my body tightening around his cock as I spill ropes of hot cum over his fingers.

Gunnar's watching me so closely, I can almost see the way his eyes light up as I ride out my orgasm in front of me. He holds me close, fucking into me a few more times, still not too hard, but with more desperation than he let himself before. Then I get to watch him unravel as well, while I feel his cock pulse inside me.

The moment seems to go on forever, but I think that's a trick of my mind. Like I'm trying to savor it.

I know this doesn't mean we won't have any sex-trauma disasters in the future, but I'm okay with that. This time was perfect. Other times will be perfect, too.

I have Gunnar. That's the only thing I care about. Like he said, the rest of it is window dressing.

When he finally takes in a full, gasping breath, the first thing he does is touch my face again and look me in the eye.

"Good?" he asks. It feels like code, now. We've said it so many times.

"Good."

My forehead thunks to his again, and we both breathe in each other's air.

Gunnar sighs, all the unspoken fear he was holding back going with it, before he replies with a smile.

"Good. Fucking perfect."

Epilogue

TOBIAS

Three Months Later

"I think they're teaching her to cheat," I say to Gunnar as we walk to the car.

"She's not cheating, you just suck at mahjong."

He's laughing at me. His face isn't, but he is on the inside. I can always tell.

"That's racist. You're all being racist." I point at him over the car when we both move to our respective sides. "Them for forcing the old Asian lady to play a Chinese game, even though she's not Chinese, and you for making fun of me for losing."

I hold a straight face the entire time we're getting inside and sitting down, but the second the doors close, Gunnar bursts out laughing. It's too infectious to hold out, and when he pulls me in toward him and kisses my cheek, still laughing through it, I can't help but smile as well.

"Sure, baby. You're right. The whole world is against you."

"Prick," I mutter under my breath, pulling away from him even though I'm still smiling.

I can't let him think he's right about everything, even though he almost always is. It'll go to his head.

He was right about the stupid nursing facility, and that still pisses me off. I didn't think she'd want to go, but as soon as I had asked her, she told me there was no question about it. She was going.

I can't watch you kill yourself to take care of me anymore, Apo. Your mother let us both down. I'm not letting you down, too.

She sold her car, plus the trailer and the land she owned, in the end. I never thought she'd part with it. She'd lived there since before I was born. She didn't want to hang on to something previous only to watch me rot inside it, she said.

It all felt wrong. But Gunnar was right. It was her choice. Between that, her social security, and some leftover insurance money from the bar that I still feel cripplingly guilty for accepting, we had enough to make it work.

I was still worried about the nurses being racist or shitty, because I know what this town is like. That wasn't a joke. But we did a bunch of research, and of course Tristan got way too involved in the process, and it turned out that one of the best places in the area is actually in Possum Hollow. So, she's not far.

It's barely fifteen minutes to go see her if I take my Ninja, or twenty-five if I go in the car with Gunnar's old man driving.

She likes it there. The nurses are all her new besties, because they're excited to have a patient so young, sharp-minded, and relatively mobile. They hang out with her on their breaks and keep her entertained when I'm not around. It worked out as well as it could have, I suppose.

I still hope she'll be able to come home eventually. We'll see what happens. We'd have to have a bigger home for her to come to, and right now I'm struggling to save up enough money to get this fucking snake tattoo on my neck covered up.

I was going to get it removed, but then I found out how much more expensive that is and decided against it. Now Gunnar keeps telling me I need to get it replaced with a giant possum, in honor of the bar.

I'll keep thinking about it.

"I don't think we've found a single game that you're good at, baby. Maybe this is a sign you should spend less time with your emotional support horror films, and more time socializing with human beings."

Gunnar is staring at the road as he drives, but he's not bothering to hide his smile as he makes fun of me. I punch him in the arm anyway, driving or not.

"I had a neglectful childhood! Isn't that what got you all hot and bothered in the first place? If I was good at normal things, I wouldn't trigger your broken-toy kink and then where would we be?"

Gunnar looks at me out of the corner of his eye, half-bemused, half-scowling. This probably counts as 'negative self-talk', which I know drives him fucking nuts.

But fuck, come on. At least all the trauma made me funny.

"I'm kidding, I'm kidding." I hold up my hands for emphasis.

Gunnar's eyes are on the road, while I scroll mindlessly through social media on my phone. It's not something I ever really did before. Digital footprints don't mesh well with a criminal lifestyle, and I was also so stressed all the time, I didn't have the capacity to care about something that trivial.

Now, it's kind of nice. Like another veneer of normality over my life I never thought I'd have.

I'm thumbing through videos on TikTok when the algorithm seems to keep showing me different versions of the same thing one after the other, so I finally stop to look.

It's a mashup of clips of a male gymnast. The shots are mostly from phone cameras instead of professional ones, and nothing about this is screaming Olympics-level-famous. I'm searching my brain to see if I've been thirsting over male gymnast videos or something to make this fall into my feed, but I can't remember anything relevant.

Then I see why—every fucking person I know in Possum Hollow and the surrounding area has liked and shared these videos. The caption tells me that it's about a local athlete getting chosen for 'nationals', which is apparently a big deal.

I thought we were more of a football area, but I've never been known for my love of sports, so who the fuck knows? Either way, everyone's apparently salivating over the idea of this guy representing our shitty little neighborhood on a national platform. And also salivating over him, because in addition to all the jumping and twisting bullshit, he seems to be an expert at posting thirst traps.

Something about it nags at me. *He* nags at me. Then I read his name, and all the pieces fall into place.

Finch Lewandowski, from Mishicot, population 196. *Lewandowski*. A last name I can't even pronounce, but would have been mine if my mother hadn't insisted on changing my birth certificate at the last minute.

So that's what my half-brother looks like. I've seen one shitty old picture of my sperm donor, and the resemblance between them is on point. I'm surprised I didn't notice it sooner, but I guess I wasn't expecting a long-lost relative to reach out of my phone and slap me in the brain.

For a second, I consider telling Gunnar. I know how much he wants me to confront my childhood, or whatever. He told me it's never too late to reach out to this guy if I want the chance at more family.

I think Gunnar and my lola are all the family I need.

I'll tell him about it later. Once I've processed it a little. Maybe I'll talk to the guys about it tonight, actually. They normally understand my reticence to get involved with new people, in a way no one else seems to. Which reminds me to remind Gunnar.

"I'll be back later than usual tonight. I only have a half shift, but then I have the thing after."

Gunnar's gaze flicks to me again, but he quickly corrects himself and looks back at the road.

'*The thing*' is not to be discussed in detail. I don't like mentioning it, let alone really talking about it. Because of this, he treats everything to do with it like Venetian glass. Like it's something precious, and if he breathes the wrong way, it'll splinter into pieces.

He's probably right. I refused his offer of bankrolling me going to therapy so many times; we agreed to disagree so we could just stop arguing about it. Even though I know there's a fucking pin in that subject in his brain, and we're coming back to it one day.

What he did convince me to do, as a compromise, is start going to this stupid support group. I don't even like the words 'support group'. I like 'survivor group' a lot less though, so it remains '*the thing*' whenever it's mentioned.

It's virtual, so I could technically do it at home. I get too antsy, though. The apartment feels too big, and I spend the entire time looking over my shoulder. It's easier if I'm in the car by myself, and I can sit in some distant corner of a parking lot, lock the doors, and join the Zoom on my phone. It feels more private than the apartment, whether anyone else is there or not.

Gunnar found it for me, of course. I assumed it was going to be me and a bunch of women, but of course he went out in the big, wide internet and found one specifically for members of the alphabet mafia. Which means I'm always saying stupid shit, because it turns out taking dick all my life isn't the same as actually knowing other gay people. Half the time it feels like they're speaking a whole other language that I'll never be able to learn.

They're chill, though. They don't get pissy if I say something dumb. I don't talk a lot, anyway. Mostly it's just nice to sit and listen to the others, and not feel like the only person on the planet who has the same stupid set of problems. It's better than drinking myself to sleep every night, anyway, a habit Gunnar seemed terrified I was about to launch myself into that I've managed to avoid. With a little effort.

So, Gunnar helped me sort out everything with my lola. Then he helped me find a bar job in Mission Flats and wrote me an entirely fabricated recommendation before teaching me how to bartend on the fly, so they'd hire me. Then he found me this *whatever* group and lends me his car so I can drive to work and join the Zoom after.

Fuck, it's like a life starter pack. He should trademark it and package it to other wayward youths. Except not any of the parts that include his dick, because that's mine.

We pull into the parking lot of the Feral Possum, but instead of getting out of the car, Gunnar looks at me with an unreadable expression.

"Are you good, baby?" he asks at last.

I frown, because I don't know where this sudden concern has come from. Sometimes it's easy to forget that he can feel insecure, too. He seems so put together. I spend a lot of time swimming around in my own head, I have to make a point to come out and remind him that he's the reason I'm as good as I am.

So, I smile at him. A real one, not like I was teasing him earlier.

"Yeah, Gunnar. I'm perfect." Then I realize what I said and scrunch up my nose. "Well, as perfect as I get."

He laughs, but it's enough to break the tension.

"I'll always think you're perfect, baby."

When he leans over, I don't hesitate to let him kiss me. Because yeah, I'm still fucked up. Probably beyond repair. But also, I really am perfect.

Two things can be true at the same time. It's a hell of a lot closer to perfect than I ever thought I'd get.

Which is why I tell him I love him, kiss him one more time, then race him inside. Because I might suck at mahjong, but I'll always be faster than him.

He loves to chase me, anyway. It's a win-win.

XXX THE END XXX

Up Next

Possum Hollow Book 4
Available for Preorder, Out March 26th, 2025
The second half of Silas & Cade's love story

✗

Possum Hollow Book 4.5
Release TBD
Rebecca & Wish Novella

✗

Savage, Sins of the Banna Book 1
Available now as a serial on REAM along with other subscriber benefits and Possum Hollow bonus content
Micah & Savage

Available for Preorder, Out on Amazon February 26th, 2025

X

And more standalone novels coming soon, set in the Possum Hollow world.

Acknowledgements

There is not enough rambling babble in the world to say how much I appreciate my alpha and beta readers: Amy, Ash, Cara, George, Lauri. I would never have finished this without you, and if I had it would have made a lot less sense. Just 300 pages of Tobias and Gunnar snarking at each other from opposite sides of the couch.

About the Author

Erin Russell is a queer author living in Los Angeles. They love to write hurt/comfort romance about neurodiverse characters. They hate writing author bios, but are extremely candid on social media.

Oh, and they love possums.

χ

Connect with Erin:

Made in the USA
Monee, IL
10 January 2025